Something Beautiful Happened

PAMELA TCHIDA

Acknowledgements

Dedicated to all of my wonderfully crazy and kind family and friends.

To my strong and wise father Don and my sweet and gentle mother Maryrose - I am me because of both of you, and I embrace this every day.

To my ghost readers Ginger, Linda, Maryrose, Marilyn, Jean, Annie, Shelley and Bernadette - and my editors Annie and Don - you made me work, think and drink too many cups of coffee as I poured over this manuscript and your suggestions and changes. I will be forever thankful for your encouragements for me to finish, publish and take the chance! To my many angels after the 2013 flash flood in my home town of Calgary, Alberta. Don, Ginger and Aiden and Jean - you helped me peace and solace in the truest and most genuine of forms. Mom, Dad, Tim, Michael, and of course Jayda, my other angels that helped me dig deep for that solitude and find the tenacity to complete the words on these pages. To Muriel - for helping me find the Salt Spring Island connection and a room with a view to finish the edits to this story. And to Ron, for giving me the peaceful time to write and the experiences of Jazzman...

And finally, to my gifted and gracious daughter Jayda. This one is for you, my dear precious young woman and artist, and your "half-made moon". I promise it will always linger on our special river's edge whispering the stories that we told as mother and daughter.

Chapter One

Winter heaved around her tormented face and bulky, canary-colored parka, belligerently blowing snow into her eyes and across her cheeks, to the street, and then up, towards the lamp posts leading to the midnight blue above. She shuddered from the fierce gusts of cold, ravaged from head to toe with the season's cutting constant. Then black nails stretched to the sky, ones reaching from filthy hands that, in fragments of a better time, were as creamy as the half-made moon above.

"Please," she begged hoarsely. Her plea echoed around her haggard being and snarled hair, then disappeared over her shopping cart, laden with her only possessions, and into the snow-filled streets and headlights of late night traffic.

She closed her eyes.

Sometimes, she was able to grasp at a morsel of something that she remembered feeling good. Chamomile tea. Foaming baths with lavender. The touch of another. Skin touching skin. Sometimes, when the demons didn't lurk nearby, greedily and cruelly threatening to consume her, she would grasp onto these memories, albeit briefly, and she wouldn't feel as desperate. She stood still for a moment, perhaps two, and begged again for something that might warm her, if for only a moment.

"Please," she whispered again.

Instead, winter gasped around her, teasing hopelessness, and she shivered as she opened her eyes in that all too familiar look of defeat.

She bowed her head to shield herself from the wind as she continued on. Metal and rubber whined in unison for several blocks as she pushed her cart towards her home. Several times, wheels squeaked in protest as they sunk to the icy sidewalk and she would use the weight of her body to push backward and forward, and forward and backward, until they came free.

When her feet found the beginnings of Mission Bridge she stopped for a moment. Not from fatigue, for she was used to being tired. It was because another deep, raspy cough rattled her throat and her chest heaved, again and again, until hints of fresh air found her lungs. As she wiped her nose with the back of her hand, her eyes opened wide with fear.

"Maci-manitow!" she hissed in her second tongue.

Black nails under clenched fists punched at the empty night air. Rubber boots above frozen toes kicked hysterically and frantically this way and that.

"Maci-manitow!" she shrieked repeatedly. "Devils! I beg you, leave me!" she hissed in English.

Traffic slowed as curious drivers watched as the bright yellow parka bent and jerked, and the black rubber boots kicked here and there, and the snow blew this way and that as she fought off her own hallucinations, desperately pleading for them to leave.

“Go away! Leave me! I beg you, Devils!” she shrieked in a voice full of venom.

“Maci-manitow!” she cried out when she saw them turn to leave. Then she spat into the snow. “Filth!” she cried and spat over and over again, until they disappeared into the night.

She continued on, across the bridge, then down the river pathway that led to the Elbow River that led to her home. When she had discovered it, years ago now, she was preparing to die. The years of living on the streets and living in constant fear, the years of begging for a brush of reality, had consumed almost all of her strength. Thus, she hardly noticed the gifts of nature that she once would have embraced; the spectacular colors and frostings of fall and winter, the dreamy buds of spring and summer, and the glistening river that went on forever and forever, regardless of the season.

She parked her shopping cart in the exact spot that she always did, in a secluded, southeast corner of the bridge’s underground, under the concrete, beside her bed. Winter’s breath heaved again. Loose snow scattered angrily across the embankment, threatening more havoc. More spite. She shivered again as her glazed eyes timidly looked around her. Eastward and then westward. North and then south. Then towards the river’s edge. Until she was positive that the demon’s hadn’t followed her.

“Hmf,” she muttered hoarsely, a barely audible, but very real, grunt of relief. Then she pulled out a red blanket and then a large, green piece of fake fur from her cart and made her bed for the night.

When she was lucid she sometimes thought that summers were an easier hell to bare. The demons didn’t appear as frequently in the warmer months, although they still haunted her day and night as they so chose - real and tenacious shadows on her doorstep.

A memory of her last hospital stay flashes back from time to time. A doctor in a crisp white jacket was coldly explaining that stress might sometimes elevate the symptoms of schizophrenia. He was speaking slowly, pronouncing each word very carefully. As if she didn't understand English. As if she was a child. Sometimes, when she was biting cold, she would wonder if the stress from Calgary's eternal winters and its angry bursts of white skies and mean winds were just too much. Perhaps this was why she was getting worse instead of better? She could feel it. Sometimes, she wondered about finding her way back to Vancouver. She remembered that the winters were warmer there, even though the rain was relentless and the ocean air was cutting and oh so bitter.

Other flashes from that last stay in the psyche ward, a long time ago now, were infrequent, from time, or the disease, or the prescription drugs that the doctors told her would help. Still, when they appeared they were pronounced. Spending fierce mental and physical energies that brought the same hollow and despairing results. Hopeless pleas to decipher between truth and the demons. Clutching to delicate strings of the now, then plunging further and further into that eternal evil that only she could see. Merciful cries to be left alone. Gasping for oxygen from fear. Vomiting from the side effects of new medications. Feeling helpless and humiliated. Wanting to live. Begging to die.

And then, the tormenting nights in this sinister place.

The filth of the nurse's touch, the sticky salt on his saliva, the greasiness of his sweat - and what he did to her, again and again in that white room on that white bed.

This last image still filled her with such pain that her body would shudder and she would clutch her chest.

"Please," she would beg.

Years ago, she had been able to hide her demons from most of the world. The medications masked her disease - most of the time - and she had been diligent at hiding her suffering. For the most part, her life had been relatively normal. When she did have a relapse, only now and again, she would quietly check herself into the hospital. The doctors would prescribe Haldol, or Trillion, or some other medication, and eventually, she would return to the world in better form. Able to cope. Able to work. Able to love and laugh and do things that regular people do.

However, the last time she committed herself was substantially different. The old medication wasn't working, the new prescriptions didn't agree with her, and the doctors were clinical and aloof. As days blended into weeks, and weeks into months, she fought the battle of her lifetime. As she desperately clung to fragments of reality, gasping, always, for fresh air and clear thoughts, she also succumbed to the nurse's filthy touch.

And what he did to her, gain and again in that white room on that white bed.

His silver badge read "Nurse Christopher" but even in her drug-induced state, his eyes told her differently. She knew that he couldn't possibly be a child of God. His piercing eyes were void holes in his repulsive, savage face. She was positive that he was the devil himself. As she faded in and out of reality, she was no longer able to differentiate if Nurse Christopher was real - or a product of her disease.

Over the months, Nurse Christopher drugged her repeatedly, progressively becoming bolder and more abusive. One night, he did other things to her body, brutally ripping her apart, presenting pain that was so excruciating that she was certain that she had entered hell.

Until she could take it no more. She left the hospital in the middle of the night, as quietly as she had arrived. Almost immediately, she plummeted into a world that she had sometimes feared, but one that she had never known. Medication was replaced with alcohol and cold benches, dark alleys and glassy-eyes strangers, many reeking of stale cigarettes and alcohol, all smelling like sickness and death. Once in a while, she found a cold floor with a thin mattress and a blue or green or grey blanket, depending on the hostel, each one crusty with dry body fluids. More often, she rummaged for food, searched for warmth, and stood in line with a street full of others as cold and hungry as she, waiting to find food and shelter.

And daily, she ran from the demons, praying each time she felt their satanic breath on her back.

Please be merciful.

Please be merciful to me.

I want to embrace the truth.

The white buffalo has come to me.

I can see it through the fog.

I am on the river's edge, reaching for its strength.

I am on the river's edge, reaching for its powers.

I beg you now, to let me live in peace.

And without the evil storm, for it still follows me.

I want to live in peace.

Please give me hope.

Chapter Two

The regal brownstone hung proudly over the river's edge, an understated eloquence that sprawled over more than an acre of natural forest. It was almost always a topic of conversation for those enjoying Calgary's lush Elbow River pathway, primarily because it was one of the largest and most elegant properties on the river. Often, subtle "awes" were hushed at its enchanting splendor, sometimes followed with questions about who lived there, or how much the property might be worth with the city's booming real estate. Other times, whispers scattered across the water that it was the home of former golden boy architect and developer Marshall Stein. Or why he lived alone - and the tragic story of his family.

Ten years prior Marshall Stein had won a prestigious award for the development. Quoted in one of the most respected industry rags, he proudly called it “A Gift to My Family” and thus the property was unofficially named.

“Why did you call it ‘A Gift to My Family’ Mr. Stein?” the peppy young journalist had asked.

“My family is everything,” Marshall had replied gravely. “I was an orphan from the Prairies,” he went on to explain. “I grew up in several foster homes, and never had a family to celebrate. This will be sanctuary to my wife and son, and his children, and their children. ‘A Gift to My Family’ will allow us to celebrate everything that family means to me - to all of us - and to embrace our good fortune.”

However, that was ten years ago, and a decade later, the interior of the small mansion was an alarming contrast to its majestic exterior. His award, along with the many others that the President of Stein Morretti Architects and Developers had received over the years, had been buried in boxes in the basement for over two years. Marshall had dragged them home the day he sold out of his thriving business and disappeared from the world in which he had once thrived.

The collection of rare art and furniture breathed exceptional taste and an appreciation for the finer things in life, exactly what one might have expected. However, the contrast of grief was pungent in every corner of ‘A Gift to My Family’ as Marshall hid behind the very walls that he had created. Sometimes, he would find a morsel of solace in the breathtaking view of the river just outside his doors. In the winter, it sparkled a crystal fantasy in its finest form as Jack Frost’s slate was painted. In the warmer months, it glistened with the sun and danced with the moon as it flowed past a bragging borderline of untouched lushness of trees and wildflowers on its embankment. However, the hint of calm, or forgiveness, or whatever it was that Marshall might have grasped at when his green eyes fell to the beauty below would last only for a second, for always, this would take plunge him deep into his suffering.

It wasn’t quite the call from Afghanistan that took him to this place.

It was the call from Europe.

Often, Marshall would stare at a large silver framed photograph, past his own eyes to the wide spread grin of the young boy and the dancing eyes of the woman, and then to the white sand and the three pairs of sandaled feet. The photograph was taken almost twenty-five years ago, many years before Marshall's world had crumbled. But it was tangible proof that life once held hope and happiness.

Six months after his son Charlie's body was flown back from Afghanistan, his wife Sarah's casket arrived from Paris. Weeks later, Marshall sold his shares of the flourishing company to Tony Morretti, his business partner of almost thirty years - and his only friend. The day the multimillion dollar transaction closed, Marshall, now worth much more than the poor orphan from Saskatchewan had ever imagined possible, no longer cared about the money. He was ridden and damaged with guilt and despair, and the mansion's walls dripped with sorrow and loss and other emotions that Marshall was unable to comprehend. Gradually, he fell deeper and deeper into the darkness with each new god-awful day.

Marshall's disconnect from society was inevitable. In the beginning, his phone rang on occasion. Most often, it was Tony checking in on him. Sometimes, it was a condolence call, typically followed by a polite lunch or dinner invitation with an underlying hint of a business proposal. Word on the street traveled quickly that the golden boy had taken an early retirement and was up for grabs. However, as more and more invitations were declined and more and more telephone calls never returned, the Stein household eventually lapsed into solitude. Marshall only ventured out for coffee or groceries, when he ran out of scotch, or when he felt like he needed a doctor. He only ate when he needed to eat, when his body told him that he needed energy. His only contact with the outside world was when it was necessary. Marshall had all but disconnected himself from the world he once knew - except for Sarah, for Sarah was still everywhere.

The smell of her perfume still lingered in every drawer and around every corner. Her shawls and clothes and coats and scarves hung neatly in the closets, just as she had left them. Her pen and stationery sat side by side on her antique desk in her den. Often, Marshall envisioned her sitting at her desk and could vividly picture every detail of her porcelain face. Her deep-set blue eyes. Her cute, but slightly crooked nose. Her full pouting lips - lips that never really pouted. Often, he would picture her blonde head down and her long, slender fingers diligently penning new words. For as long as Marshall could remember, Sarah had connected to the world through her elegant scrawl, voicing well wishes and warm thoughts on thank you cards and greeting cards on her own personal stationery with her name engraved in fine gold print at the top of each page.

Sarah Stein

The white cashmere sash that Marshall had given her for Christmas many years back, the one that she had often wrapped around her neck as she played the piano, still lay on the piano bench, almost exactly where she had left it. Sometimes, Marshall would pick it up and press it against his face, and her scent would fill his nostrils, and he would feel like she was in the room. Sometimes, he would wrap the soft wool around his own broad shoulders and his green eyes would darken as he was consumed with one very vivid memory. It was a moment that Marshall had concluded as being the biggest mistake in his life - and he was unequivocally certain that it would haunt him in vigor for the rest of his life.

. . .

Sarah's long, slender fingers rested on the ivory keys of the grand piano in the parlor. She heard him enter the foyer and had turned to greet him as he stepped into the room.

"Hello," she whispered. Just "hello".

Her voice held no hint of accusation and Marshall was thankful for this. "Hi," he mumbled and smiled wanly. He leaned over and kissed her on the cheek, and as he did this he wondered, as he had done on many, many occasions, just how much she knew.

A heartbeat later, a song that Marshall vaguely remembered filled the parlor.

"Remember this one? Remember, we sang this one in Paris, hun?" Sarah's lips had formed that gentle smile that he so adored.

Marshall cocked his head to one side and put his hands in his pants pockets as he listened. He vaguely recalled singing the song around an old piano - and Sarah's cute little hat with the yellow flower embroidered on its side. And how adorable she had looked. But he couldn't remember the song.

A familiar heaviness found his chest. He moved to the patio doors that overlooked the dewy river below, and as his eyes spanned its lush beauty, he wondered whether Sarah was still grieving - as he was still grieving. Then he wondered - again - just how much she knew. As he turned toward his wife, he found her bright blues locked on his.

"Let's go back to Paris again?" she hushed in hope.

Marshall pulled his hands out of his pockets and rubbed his chiseled jaw. "You know how busy I am," he replied in an even and very matter-of-fact tone as he turned to face her. "Paris will have to wait until next year, Sarah. You and I will go next year. In the spring?"

Sarah's face had filled with "that look". He hadn't been able to pinpoint exactly what it meant, but it had shown its face frequently over the months. It had appeared sometime after the call from Afghanistan. Or was it before the call from Afghanistan? Marshall closed his eyes and dropped his chin to his chest.

"Marshall," Sarah began softly, "I thought I would come with you to Europe. On your next trip. We could window shop, and walk along the ocean, and sip on wine in quaint bistros along the way... We could sit by the fire at night and relish what we have. Remember that quaint little inn that we stayed at in Paris, Marshall?" she added in a whisper verging on a beg. "We can do this for Charlie," she added softly. "Charlie would have wanted us to be happy."

The room fell so quiet that Marshall could hear Sarah's breath, and then the brush of her shawl against the keyboards. Moments later, she stood behind him and wrapped her delicate arms around his chest, tenderly pushing her breasts into his back.

His nostrils filled with her scent, and for a moment, he thought of turning into her and holding her. Instead, he gently pulled her hands away and turned to face her.

The night's moon peaked through the French doors and onto Sarah's face and he was instantly taken aback by how fragile she looked at that very moment, and this made him angry. Then, rather than doing exactly what he needed to do, rather than doing exactly what Sarah had silently begged, rather than touching the woman that he had loved for so many years - like he used to touch her - Marshall spoke in a cold and unnatural tone.

"Sarah, my trip to Europe is four days of business! How would we enjoy Paris like that?" His face mocked ridicule. Then another reason, the real reason, filled his mind and he was consumed with guilt. "Besides!" he boomed as his eyes darkened in defensiveness, "Tony was hinting this very afternoon that Florida is next. We won the museum project. I'll have to fly there right before Europe. I'll be working and tired and tired of traveling!"

His voice had grown louder with each word, much louder than he had intended. Sarah took a tiny step backward. Her eyes locked on something outside the parlor doors and Marshall followed her gaze. A plump, orange-breasted Robin sat of the terrace wall, a tuft of twigs hanging from its beak.

"Spring always brings us such surprises," she whispered. "It teases its arrival, and we wait in anticipation, breathless for its gifts."

Sarah had always loved the turning of spring, the presents of summer, the colors of fall, even the threatening of winter's ice. Marshall had often mused how such a beautiful creature could embrace, or accept, whatever was around the corner. And how she was so strong. It was one of her qualities that he loved most.

When Sarah spoke again, her voice was even and collected. "I can't wait for you for another week - or another month. I've decided to go to Paris on my own."

"Go on your own?" Marshall scoffed. It was the most ridiculous thing that he had heard her say.

"Yes," she said fiercely as she lifted her chin. "I need to get away."

"When, exactly, do you plan to go on your own?" he questioned in a mocking tone.

Defiant eyes found his. "I've booked my flight. I leave day after tomorrow."

"Day after tomorrow?" Marshall exploded. "Day after tomorrow? I'm leaving for business again. I leave for New York day after tomorrow!"

"I'm quite aware of your trip to New York."

There was hardly an accusing tone in her voice, but Marshall sensed the accusation. "You can't leave day after tomorrow!" he retaliated. He couldn't believe what he was hearing.

"And pray, why not?"

Sarah's words reeked of sarcasm, but Marshall caught a glimmer of vulnerability. Sarah wasn't vulnerable. He took a step towards her. "Because..." he began, and then hesitated. At a loss for words, he rubbed his hand through his hair in frustration.

For a split second, Sarah's bright blue eyes hinted a sliver of hope and she lifted her slender hands, as if in offering.

"Because *why* Marshall?" she begged in whisper.

Marshall's eyes dropped to the Persian rug under his feet and then to the chocolate brown paws that had stretched out for an evening nap. The spoiled Himalayan had always been able to sleep through anything, he thought. How he hated that cat! "Because," he began slowly as he looked up to his wife. Sarah's face had turned to a profound picture of sadness and, although he wasn't quite sure why, this filled him with a stronger anger. "Because," he repeated again in a tone thick with impatience, "I won't be here! And someone has to look after that nasty cat!"

In an instant, the room exploded in a hot string of words. "You are a selfish, selfish fool!" Sarah's retaliation had turned her face a bright hue of pink. "Selfish! Selfish! Son of a bitch!" she hissed again, then turned and stormed out of the room. These were the first words Sarah had ever voiced with venom. Her next words grew louder and harsher with each step. "I'm taking poor Jazz with me, you fool. You selfish, selfish, selfish fool!"

"You're taking that damn cat to Europe?" Marshall sneered. "You're taking that damn spoiled cat to Europe! Now that has got to be the most absurd thing that I have ever heard you say!" he spat.

He couldn't believe it. He just couldn't believe it.

. . .

Marshall awoke from his nap on the sofa in the parlor to the sound of breaking glass.

"Shit," he grumbled knowingly as he opened his eyes, realizing that Jazz had likely pushed something into the sink - or onto the floor - again. "Shit! Jazz!" he shouted as he pulled himself up.

Jazz's outbursts and defiance had progressively worsened over the months, and Marshall was beginning to feel more resentful towards him than he cared to admit. How many times had he told Sarah that he didn't like cats? he thought as looked around the dusky room helplessly. At that very moment the faint beginnings of a song from the river below, the one that Marshall had learned to despise even more so than the signs of Jazz's destruction, filtered up and through the parlor door, and Marshall scowled. He knew that the inevitable would soon follow. He knew that at any moment that damn homeless person from the river would poison his world with her chants.

As the parlor's walls echoed the familiar verse a rawness and vulnerability consumed Marshall, and his body bent in anguish as he broke into a flood of tears.

Chapter Three

It wasn't the doorbell that pulled Marshall out of his sleep the next morning. It was a familiar muffled knocking, and it was coming from the hallway.

Marshall sleepily stumbled from the sofa to the hallway towards the bathroom. The moment he swung the door open, Jazz's blue eyes glared up at Marshall in defiance before he let out an obnoxious complaint and scurried between Marshall's legs and out of sight. Marshall perused the destruction. A shattered crystal scotch glass lay in every corner of the room. Tufts of toilet paper filled the bowl to beyond its rim. The better part of a dated Forbes magazine was strewn across the marble floor, shredded into thousands of tiny pieces. One quick glance reminded Marshall of the repetitive tale of Jazz's frequent demise.

"Shit!" he scowled, remembering the sound of breaking glass the night before. Jazz had somehow locked himself in the bathroom for the entire night. When the doorbell rang again Marshall's eyes widened slightly with surprise. His doorbell never rang. His eyes roamed from the mess on the floor towards the foyer as the doorbell rang again, and then again.

"I am coming!" he bellowed out, much louder than he had intended.

"You *are* alive!" Tony Morretti exclaimed sarcastically when Marshall opened the door.

Marshall's ensuing glare at his former business partner and only friend held little welcome. "What do you want?" he grumbled.

Tony was used to Marshall's impatience and downright rudeness. Despite this, he had a great deal of respect for Marshall's uncanny business sense, and had learned very early in their partnership that Marshall's talents would make them both a lot of money. Thus, Tony had mastered his ability to temper his retaliation - sometimes he even ignored Marshall's outbursts, as if they instantly evaporated into thin air. As if they had never occurred.

But this morning was different. For the past two years, Tony had made a point of phoning Marshall on a regular basis, to check up him, or to extend a heartfelt invite. However, more and more frequently, Marshall's phone went unanswered, and they had spoken rarely over the months. On the odd occasion that the two men did connect, their conversation was always short and abrupt. And it always oozed with Marshall's personality flaws and frame of mind.

Since the deaths of Charlie and Sarah, Tony had remained diligent at practicing patience and forgiveness - and his concern and compassion for his friend was genuine. However, after two years Tony was losing his patience. Enough was enough. What is *this*? he thought at this very moment. A man who had always been eloquent with his words and articulate with his dress looked and sounded unsightly. He couldn't believe what he saw, and the newfound sight of Marshall's digression fueled his anger. "What do I need?" he asked sarcastically as he raised his greying brow.

"I was just about to head out. You have a minute."

"A minute?" Tony repeated as he pushed his way around Marshall and through the foyer.

Over the years, the two men had created many a project, concluded many a deal, and shared many a drink in the parlor. As Marshall followed Tony to the very room that had become his personal hell, he glanced up to the grandfather clock. "I have to be downtown at City Hall for a ten o'clock meeting," he lied as he brushed back his long, unkempt salt and pepper hair with his fingers.

"Looking like that?" Tony grimaced. "You look like last month's buffet, and then some!" He shook his head. "Basta! I suggest you stop and get a haircut. You might think about getting a shave while you're at it," he retaliated. "And socks don't match," he added, noticing Marshall's lone black sock on his right foot. "I suggest that you call whomever it is that you are meeting and tell them that you'll be late. Marshall, I'm not joking when I say that you look like you've miraculously survived a natural disaster. You look like shit! Basta! One absolute mess!"

Marshall's brazen green eyes grew dark. "I don't remember inviting you in. And I don't need to take this crap from you. Especially first thing in the morning."

"Ten o'clock is certainly not *first* thing in the morning," Tony replied grimly as his eyes traveled from one corner of the parlor to the other. The coffee table was a clutter of empty frozen dinners and dirty dishes, a couple of empty scotch bottles, and stacks of unopened mail. The lid of the grand piano was covered with dirty towels, more unopened mail, stacks of newspapers, probably a six month's worth, he guessed, along with other paraphernalia. He ran his fingertips over the edge of the eloquently engraved redwood. As he lifted a thick blanket of dust, he whistled softly.

"Basta! Tu vive come un mail!" Tony hushed in his Italian tongue. "You live like a pig!" he repeated in English.

Over the years, the two men had also developed an inbred trust, along with an easy and open rapport; they had always said what they meant – and meant what they said.

"What the hell do you want?" Marshall's face had stiffened from embarrassment, but if Tony noticed, he didn't let on.

"This has got to be the most decadent table coaster I've ever seen," Tony continued in a hush as he brushed the dust from his hands. "What did you pay for it? It was over a couple hundred grand, wasn't it? Yes, I remember. You paid a fortune for this piece." He shook his head. Then his eyes fell to the three smiling faces in the silver-framed photograph, and he hesitated, in thought, before turning back to Marshall. Then his black-brown eyes pierced Marshall's before he spoke again.

"I left you at least a dozen messages in the past month. And I called four times yesterday."

"I've been busy."

"Sure Marshall. You've been busy."

Marshall's hand motioned to the foyer.

"You're not returning anyone's calls," Tony persisted. "No one has seen or heard from you. In months! And you're not here!" he added, raising his voice. "Because the Marshall Stein I once knew certainly couldn't live like this!"

"Your minute is up," Marshall replied coolly.

"I can't feel sorry for you anymore," Tony said cautiously, and very gravely. "I know it's been tough," he added, lowering his voice. "But man!" A look of disbelief filled his thin face as he shrugged helplessly. "Marshall. You are my friend. But it's been over two years! You've been living like this for more than two years! And you want to bet that I've got other things to do than drive to this pigsty on a Wednesday morning that is threatening snow in the middle of spring, when the rest of the world is working. Just to make sure that you are alive!"

Marshall's eyes opened in alarm with Tony's last words. Then he lifted his brow in a scowl. "Alive?" he sneered.

"I thought I might find you dead, Marshall," Tony replied grimly. "When I was driving here, I was wondering if I'd be calling 911!"

Besides muttering "911?" under his breath, Marshall was at a loss for words. "I've been batchin' it," he finally replied with a hint of dry humor as he managed to force a fake grin to his lips.

Tony ignored Marshall's attempt at lightness. He moved toward the patio doors and blindly looked down to the river below.

"I got an odd call yesterday," Tony finally said quietly.

"An *odd* call?"

"*She* called me."

"*Who* called you?"

Tony turned to face Marshall. "She's looking for Charlie," he shrugged. "She was hoping that you would know how to reach him."

It took several seconds for Marshall to process what Tony had just said, and when he did, his face turned ashen. She didn't know! he thought in astonishment.

"There's more," Tony warned, holding up the palm of his hand. "She's also looking for their kid."

Marshall's eyes widened in confusion. "Kid?"

"Apparently..." Tony hesitated. "Apparently she left their child with Charlie."

Marshall didn't understand. "Child? What are you talking about?"

Wide-eyed, Tony shook his head in disbelief.

Marshall scoffed. "You are telling me that the couple of the century had a kid," he belted out, but it sounded like more of a question that an accusation.

"That's her story, Marshall. That's why I am here."

The room fell very quiet for several seconds as the two men looked at one another for answers. Marshall spoke first.

"Now just how can a mother lose touch with her child?" he demanded.

"Look," Tony continued slowly with a great deal of kindness and compassion on his face. "She sounded legit, Marshall. It was..." he hesitated. "Man, it was an odd conversation. But she sounded real. And genuinely concerned. I told her that you had sold out. Retired, I think I said. And that I wasn't sure if I could find you."

"What the..."

"Look." Tony let out a sigh, obviously frustrated. He pulled off his glasses and rubbed his eyes. "Marshall," he continued. "I wasn't sure what to say. Quite frankly, the call shocked me – I didn't know where to begin..."

"Where to begin?" Marshall repeated hoarsely. "There is nowhere to begin!" he mocked ridicule. The whole story was bogus, he thought. It was a joke. A plea for help, or money, or something else. What could the bitch want now, after all of these years?

Tony held up both of his hands. "Look. Marshall. If she doesn't know about Charlie... if she really doesn't know what *happened* to Charlie... if they have a child out there? Well, this is a serious situation!"

None of it made any sense to Marshall, and his brilliant, yet fatigued and underworked mind spun in a million different directions as he tried to connect the dots. As an idea surfaced his eyes lit up marginally. "She must have known that Charlie took an assignment overseas."

Tony shook his head in uncertainty. "No idea."

"How old is this hypothetical kid?"

"I don't know. I didn't ask."

"You didn't ask?"

The words were harshly sarcastic, as was the norm for Marshall Stein's delivery when he was agitated or unhappy with what he was hearing. Tony, familiar with Marshall's ways, threw it back to him.

"Give me a break, my friend," he retaliated. "As I previously said, it was a short conversation. I didn't know how much to tell her. Nor did I question her."

Instantly, Marshall was desperate to believe that he had a grandchild. But it made no sense. "Did you ask her if this *hypothetical* missing child is a boy or a girl?" he asked.

Tony sensed an underlying glimpse of hope in Marshall's tone, or his eyes, or from the question that he has just asked, he wasn't sure. He shook his head grimly. "No."

Marshall moved to stand in-between Tony and the world outside. He looked down to the glistening river and budding foliage. But it was only Sarah's face that he saw. No, it wasn't Sarah's face. It was *her* face. "She must know about Sarah," he finally whispered, as if to himself.

"No," Tony replied quietly. "I was purposely vague. When I said I didn't know how to find Charlie, she asked if I could get her in touch with *either* you or Sarah."

"Well," Marshall replied, shrugging in indifference. "This just doesn't make any sense. Sarah would have known if Charlie had a kid. And Charlie would have most certainly told Sarah if she was a grandmother."

Tony cleared his throat. "Marshall, tell me that you didn't know?"

Marshall shook his head in silence.

"Marshall, Sarah never mentioned a thing?" Tony questioned in honesty, but it fell out of his mouth sounding more like an accusation.

Marshall shook his head again, more adamantly this time. Then he chuckled. "Of course not! You know that I hadn't talked to Charlie in years."

Tony knew the history of father and son Stein all too well. By the time Charlie left for university, the dissension between the two of them had escalated. Charlie Stein, Marshall's only child, had the world at his fingertips. He could have taken advantage of his quick mind, his boyish, handsome looks, and the fortune that Marshall had built. He could have joined the lucrative Stein Morretti team as Marshall's predecessor - as Marshall had hoped. Marshall had offered to pay for the best architectural school money could buy, and would have done anything to give his son what he never had. "He could have made miracles." Marshall used to voice frequently. "*They* could have made miracles," he'd just as often say.

Charlie's decision to become a journalist in third world countries where the political climate was hot and the environment deadly all but ended the father and son relationship. For years, neither of them had been able to see eye to eye on anything - until eventually they were no longer communicate without an ensuing argument. For years, Sarah had been the insistent glue that had tried to keep the small family together, but it was to no avail. By the time *that* woman had crept into the Stein family, the disparity between father and son was glaring - it had been almost a decade since Marshall and Charlie had spoken.

"This is absolutely ridiculous," Marshall belted out, suddenly emphatic that it was all a hoax. "The bitch has gone off the deep end. She was trouble from the beginning. She's probably into another stint of sweat lodges on one of the reserves, or some wacky spiritual retreat. Or she's spent all her money on one of those alternative-healing quacks. She didn't know when to stop! That's probably it. That *is* it!" Marshall concluded in a smirk. "She's spent all her money and is looking for a handout."

"I don't think so. No." Tony shook his head. "The woman could stand on her own two feet. You know that she wasn't a gold digger, Marshall. I don't think this has anything do with money. My instinct is telling me that this child is real."

"And what if your instinct is *wrong*?" Marshall asked sarcastically.

“Then I am wrong,” Tony shrugged his shoulders. “But this is too big to simply ignore. This could be a game-changer for you Marshall,” he added under his breath.

“Well,” Marshall retorted, bolder than he felt, “this is absurd. I’ll call her and get to the bottom of it all.”

“She didn’t leave a number. She’s calling me back tomorrow morning. At ten.”

Marshall swore under his breath. Then he opened his mouth to say something else, instead he stared silently at Tony for a moment, speechless. Then his eyes softened. With an unusual humbleness he asked very quietly, “So how did she sound?”

On the drive to Marshall’s Tony had wondered if he might be thrown this very question. He was hardly surprised. “She sounded...odd,” he replied grimly. “If I had to guess, I would say that she was sick. Her voice was very hoarse.”

“Sick!” Marshall mumbled and then headed towards the kitchen.

“So what’s next? What do you want me to do?” Tony asked as he trailed behind.

Marshall made a pot of coffee. He pulled two dirty mugs from a pile of dishes in the sink and rinsed them with warm water, setting them side by side on the countertop. Then he turned toward the messenger.

“Coffee?” he asked.

Tony looked at his watch and hesitated. He didn’t really have the time - he had already missed one meeting. “Sure,” he replied, grinning wanly. He pulled off his black suit jacket and loosened his tie. “Black,” he added as Jazz entered the room.

“What’s happened to him?” Tony asked as his eyes lit up in surprise.

Marshall glanced down to his foe. “What do you mean, what’s happened to him? He’s the damn cat that I was left with!”

"He looks worse than you! And what's wrong with his hair?" Tony's eyes widened as he reached down and touched the ends of Jazz's hair. "Shit!" he exclaimed. "What the...what is this?"

Marshall knelt down on one knee to take a closer look. Jazz's blue eyes stared up at him and let a cantankerous whine.

"He's fine," Marshall replied as he matched Jazz's stare. "His hair is just matted. I'll make an appointment to get him groomed." As he stood up and poured two cups of coffee, he remembered how diligent Sarah had been at brushing Jazz's hair and taking him for regular visits to the groomer.

Tony was now on both of his knees. "Man, he looks like he's been living on the street!"

"Soon," Marshall muttered under his breath as he looked down to Jazz's empty food dish. "He's probably just hungry. He's always hungry."

"Marshall. He's not just hungry. Look! He's losing his hair! And he's got some kind of rash all over his skin!"

Marshall knelt down again to get a closer look. What was left of the chocolate-brown and vanilla hair that had once covered Jazz's torso was now a haphazard collection of matted hair in-between patches of dark pink skin. The only parts of Jazz that looked healthy and normal were his thick, dark paws and his face. Marshall's indifference was quickly replaced with genuine concern when he saw what Tony saw.

"What the heck?" he exclaimed. "What the heck is that?"

That evening Marshall was physically and emotionally drained. Tony's unexpected visit and ensuing news had been unsettling and daunting, the Jazz scare had shaken him, and the veterinarian did nothing to lift Marshall's spirits.

"It's likely nerves," Dr. Isabel Simon replied grimly as she looked up to Marshall, perusing her client's disheveled presence in obvious disapproval.

"Nerves!" Marshall spat. "There is nothing nervous about that cat!"

The petite veterinarian frowned in disapproval. The poor cat was a pathetic picture of neglect - but his owner. Well! Pathetic was hardly the word! He looked like a dirty boar. Her eyes were icy cold as she handed Marshall a prescription. "I suspect that it is probably nerves, or neglect, but I've taken some blood tests," she explained. "If they show anything else I'll give you a call and we can get the little guy back in. Three times a day," she added, nodding to the prescription. "For ten days straight," she added firmly.

Then she turned to Jazz, who lay with wide eyes on the gurney, his torso buckled down in the most ridiculous looking straps. "Poor thing," she cooed as she unbuckled him and lifted him to her chest. "You'll be just fine," she whispered as she rubbed him affectionately under his chin before passing him to Marshall. Suddenly, she changed her mind. "Wait," she said, shaking her head. "I'm not sure if this will help him feel any better," she added as she strapped Jazz back into the gurney. Moments later she held an electric razor in her hand. When she had finished giving Jazz a traditional lion cut, shaving off all his hair, from his neck to the beginning of his paws, she reluctantly passed him back to Marshall.

"This is the worst case I've seen," she stated coldly. "I suggest next time you don't wait for months before bringing the poor guy in."

Marshall's eyes fell to the black and white linoleum floor.

"Poor thing," Dr. Simon said as Marshall carried Jazz through the doors to reception. "Make sure he takes care of you. It looks like you have suffered enough..."

At nine o'clock that evening, after taking his first shower in days, Marshall went in search of Jazz. As he climbed the winding staircase to the second floor, he remembered the cool reception at the clinic that afternoon. One word escaped his lips as he thought of Dr. Isabel Simon.

"Bitch," he mumbled under his breath. He had quietly voiced this one word a few times throughout that afternoon and evening.

The moment he entered the master bedroom his eyes fell upon the ugliest cat that he had ever laid eyes upon. And then his face softened. Jazz's pink-skinned body was curled up in a fetal position on Sarah's side of the bed.

"Hey, Jazzman," he whispered gently and wrapped his thick fingers around Jazz, lifted him to his chest and carried him down the stairs and into the kitchen.

Jazz wanted nothing to do with Marshall or the cold cream that Marshall rubbed on Jazz's back and sides, and then his stomach. However, despite a few minutes of struggle, the room eventually filled with the first compassion that it had in months.

"I washed your dishes," Marshall said very quietly as he set Jazz down in front of his clean food dish, now overflowing with fresh food.

Jazz, who now looked more like a rat than an elite bred feline of the 1920s, mewed pathetically at the smell of the fresh tuna. Then bright blue eyes looked up to Marshall as if in disbelief before he quickly devoured the first fresh tuna feast in over two years.

Later, Marshall searched every bathroom in the house for his own electric razor. He found it under a pile of clothes on the floor in the master bedroom. When he finished shaving off his three-month growth, he was surprised at how white he was, and how drawn and thin his face looked. Sarah would have told him to go to the doctor, he thought. Sarah would have known he wasn't well. Just like Sarah had known that something terrible had happened to Charlie. Even before that call...

That call came only six months before the call about Sarah.

"Mr. Stein, we have some very unfortunate news..."

Marshall shuddered as he entered the parlor, remembering how Sarah had buckled in anguish when he told her the news. And how he had held her as he desperately tried to shield her from the grief... As the cords of death entangled them, he felt her tears against his cheek, and then in his own blindness, realized that he too was crying.

The river's cool air was dancing through the French patio doors, and caressed Marshall tired face as he fell to the sofa and let out a hollow, shaky sigh. Blindly, he looked around the empty room and sighed again. His eyes darkened as he re-played the morning and Tony's news. He had always wondered why she hadn't been at Charlie's funeral. Before the funeral, he had assumed that they were still married. After the funeral, he had been too consumed with grief and guilt - and too embarrassed - to ask Sarah.

Still, if a child did exist, how could Charlie have kept such a secret from his mother - or from him? Impossible! he thought, shaking his head adamantly. And if there was a kid, *where* the *hell* could it be?

At precisely nine-forty-two the following morning, Marshall called Tony from his new mobile phone - the first purchase that he had made, besides the basics, in over two years.

"I need to talk to her," he instructed. "When she calls, give her my cell number. She needs to call me."

"Marshall..."

"Just do it Morretti. I doubt that this is legit," Marshall interrupted, "but I need to get to the bottom of it. If Charlie has a child out there, that child is my grandchild. And I need to find it."

Within twenty-four hours Marshall had concluded that the odds of this child existing were slim. Next to none. However, he also remembered Tony's words - and Tony was right. If a child did exist this could be one huge game-changer. And he simply couldn't turn his back on the possibility. He needed to know the truth. He was desperate to know the truth - and if he had his own flesh and blood existed...

"Marshall!" Tony replied impatiently. "Your cell phone has been disconnected for two years."

"I have a new number," Marshall snapped. "Just leaving the store."

"Great. That's great," Tony replied as he eyes widened marginally in surprise. "But Marshall, I just don't think that you should have any contact with her."

Almost nine years prior, Marshall's personal life had hit self-inflicted turmoil, and he had leaned on Tony, his only friend and his only confidant. Tony was a diplomatic and gentle soul, and respected Marshall's friendship as much as he did their thriving partnership. Thus, Tony never broke the cardinal rule. He never spoke of - or shared - one morsel of Marshall's private life with anyone. Not even with his own wife.

It was because of the secrets that Tony knew about Marshall's past that caused him valid concern at this very juncture. Marshall was already in bad form. And albeit Tony didn't know just how bad it was, he was positive of one thing. After all that had transpired over the years, he was positive that Marshall needed to stay as far away from *that* woman as possible. "I don't think you should talk to her, Stein. It's just not a good idea."

"Just do it. Get her number. But don't scare her away," Marshall instructed. Then he gave Tony his new number and ended the call.

Ten o'clock came and went, and then ten thirty. At two minutes before eleven, Marshall called Tony again.

"I haven't heard from her."

Marshall muttered something indecipherable.

"She'll call. I'll call you the moment I speak with her," Tony replied. Then realizing that this might be a golden opportunity he added, "I have a better idea," he continued. "Let's meet for lunch day today. On me. It would be great to just sit down and talk."

"The only thing I want to discuss is Charlie's hypothetical kid," Marshall retorted gruffly as he hung up the phone.

Marshall didn't have the opportunity to talk about "Charlie's hypothetical kid" that afternoon in late April. Or the following day. Or the one after that. However, with each day that he anticipated the call, a tiny morsel of what his life once was edged closer to normality.

Marshall slept in his own bed, rather than the sofa. He awoke early to the alarm, and read the newspapers that were delivered to his door over coffee and toast. He made a modest attempt to clean the “pigsty” that Tony had so bluntly referred to, and over the days filled several large black garbage bags with this and that. He was even diligent at rubbing the cold cream on the colder cat. He resented this last task a great deal, but his large hands were always very gentle.

Nevertheless, by the time Friday came and went, Marshall’s doubt and anticipation had grown to a brewing impatience. He called Tony again.

“She’ll be back,” Tony replied evenly. “She’s probably just busy and has disappeared for a few days.”

“The bitch was always good at disappearing!” Marshall shot back.

Then for several more silent and uneventful weeks, Marshall hibernated in his darkness as the river below him burst open with the gifts of spring.

Chapter Four

Rocky Mountain Estates was a thriving community development by Stein Morretti Architects & Developers. Located on the far, southwest corner of Calgary's newly annexed land on almost two full quarter sections, the comings and goings of builders and contractors were proof that the company had yet another success in its back pockets. By its second year of development, the Estates already housed some of the city's more prosperous. The two dozen already finished multimillion dollar homes, each on acre sections or more of land, bragged some of the finest. Mercedes, Jaguars, Hummers, and even a few Ferraris were samplings of the luxury vehicles that adorned many of the driveways and filled the garages.

The previous fall, Stein Morretti had planted over one thousand mature fir trees around the four quadrants of the Estates. With a steady track record for taking pride in the little extras that topped their developments over their competitors, the trees were tangible proof that Stein Marietta had once again taken no shortcuts. The multimillion dollar landscaping expense gave the community an established, mature aura, and the artisan-designed wrought iron and stone fences and gateways created a stately definition that Rocky Mountain Estates was *the* place to live.

Katy Fields almost enjoyed the mornings at the Estates. It was the least physical part of her day. Just so, she connected to the free gifts of Mother Nature. The large tree branches grounded her, and she felt protected from the world - and less exposed from her own losses. The mornings on the Estates also gave her a place to hide from the humiliation of the scandal. Just as welcoming, they gave her downtime from rambling, unsophisticated Rory Spradlum, the foreman that she was partnered with the day that she was hired.

Rory was in his mid-thirty's, had legs the size of tree trunks, and a deep voice that grated on her nerves. Daily, he would drop Katy off at one of the quadrants, and as she pruned a section of the firs, he would check up on the other crew members to ensure that they were on task. After lunch, Rory and Katy would crisscross the Estates in a five-ton Chevy the color of cherries with a bold red and platinum Stein Morretti logo painted on its doors, tending to the irrigation systems, or any other task that needed their attention.

However, despite her morning escape under nature's arms, the rest of the day was hardly what Katy had envisioned as a landscaper. Shoveling gravel? Using a pick axe to dig new irrigation trenches? Moving dirt and lifting rocks? Until her body ached, her muscles swelled and a ghastly build up of bile filled her throat? However, the hard reality was that Katy had no other options. She was officially broke and was doing everything physically possible to pull her weight - and just as diligent at hiding her struggles from the others. She promised herself daily that she would persevere and make it through the season. Even if it meant that her hands and feet would bleed from new blisters every day. Even if it meant she had to contend with the simple and annoying Rory Spradlum.

Most days, Rory bantered away about nothing in particular. Senseless, useless information. About what needed to be done next. About replacing valves and checking hoses. About the younger, lazier crews and how that generation didn't know how to work. Katy found both the man and his conversations unappealing - and a complete waste of time. He was uneducated redneck - and nothing more. In fact, she hardly acknowledged that he existed. She had little energy to make an attempt at conversation, any conversation, and rarely uttered a word - unless she was left with no choice. This particular sunny May morning was one of those occasions. Rory had asked her a pointed question, and Katy had no choice but to respond.

"Pardon me?"

"You from here?" the voice droned as he steered the shiny truck down the dirt road.

"Yes," she half-lied as she looked out the window and across the acres of underdeveloped land. Dead, flat land, she thought. A bunch of dirt that would soon come alive with households and couples and people that had control of their lives with plans and dreams and aspirations. It didn't matter any longer where she was from. She was here, and "here" was literally void of anything meaningful.

"Family?"

Instantly, Katy felt uncomfortable with the direction Rory was steering the conversation. She glanced at him quickly out of the corner of her eye. Tiny crow's feet under her bright orange baseball cap spoke her age as she frowned in disapproval.

"No. No family here," she finally replied thickly.

"Where 'da they live?"

Katy's thought of her mother. A small pang unfolded from the place that she had learned hurt the most, and she closed her eyes for a moment. She hadn't been to the West Coast or to visit her mother's grave for almost three years. She imagined her tombstone "Theresa Fields - Loving Mother and Wife", barren of flowers that she would have so loved. Then Katy's thick, dark brown brows furrowed under black eyes as she thought of her father. As her cheeks flushed under her baseball cap and chestnut brown hair, she lifted her chin slightly in defiance.

When she first heard the news that Si Fields had purposely and blindly deceived her, his only child, she felt blindsided. As if someone had sucker-punched her in the face, or kicked her in the stomach. It was unfathomable what he had done! And it had been almost two years since she had last spoken to him.

Except for Purple Waters, Si Fields' twenty-ninth best-selling novel, Katy hadn't a clue about how he was doing - and she knew that a couple of years can do a lot to an older man's body. She had started to hate herself for hating her father. That very spring, she was able to conclude that whatever Si Fields had done to her, and for whatever the reason, she needed to work hard at forgiving him, and just as hard at reconnecting with him.

"My father lives on the Gulf Islands," she answered reluctantly.

"Gulf Islands? In the Caribbean?"

"No," she replied dryly, thinking that she shouldn't be surprised that this simple man didn't know his geography. "Vancouver Coast."

"Oh yeah. Yeah. Think I heard of 'em."

For a minute, maybe two, Katy enjoyed the silence, and the privacy. However, Rory's next question surprised her even more.

"So what do you do in the winter?"

"The winter?" Katy repeated the two words in monotone as she thought what an odd question this was. It was hardly summer, she smirked. Then she quickly realized that winter would come quicker than the year past, or the year before that, and with it, the deliverance of snow – a tangible sign that her work at the Estates had come at an end.

She looked out the passenger window and up to the blue sky above, and in that instant accepted that soon, much sooner than she had calculated, she would have to find another job. One that would pay her rent. One that would continue to hide her scars and her failures and humiliation. She searched for an answer that sounded legitimate.

"For work," Rory added as his thick stubby fingers grabbed two large strawberries from a plastic container on the seat of the cabin, and he stuffed them both into his mouth. "Where do you work? In the winter?"

Katy scoffed aloud then. It was a tiny but obvious verbal protest, but because Rory was concentrating on the road and enjoying his mouthful of summer, he missed it.

What would this obtrusive red neck have said, she numbly wondered, if she told him the truth and handed him her real resume, instead of the fabricated one that she had used to get this job? What if she told him that not too long ago, she worked in Manhattan as a Publicist for a global leader in the environmental sector? Or that she was fired, disgraced, humbled and embarrassed - because of her loving father, the one who lived on the Gulf Islands. She was certain that he would have laughed out loud.

Or what if she told him about the fire only days after the scandal... She shook her head and a shaky sigh escaped her lips. It sounded ridiculous and pitiful all in one, she thought. Much more fabricated than the resume that sat somewhere in the offices of Stein Morretti.

"Bartend," she lied as her eyes vaguely followed a white rabbit scurrying into the ditch.

"Heard that there is good money in bar tending," Rory replied in between bites of strawberries.

Good money in bar tending? Katy privately smirked. "Sure," she replied as her eyes fell to Rory's mouth as he put another plump, moist berry between his lips. They looked sweet, she thought, even without sugar; she liked strawberries that were faintly dusted with those little white crystals.

Rory caught her expression out of the corner of his eye. "Hmm," he murmured as pink juice escaped the corner of his lips and trickled down his chin. "Go 'head," he offered in-between bites, "'ave one."

"Thanks. I'm not hungry." She reached down for her coffee mug, nestled between her feet on the floor and her duffle bag that held almost all of her worldly possessions: her lunch for the day and her wallet. Except for her small registered retirement savings account, her wallet held all of the money that Katy had until payday - forty-six dollars and thirty-seven cents in small bills and loose change. She knew this. She had counted it before she left for work that morning.

She wondered then if she just might find a job as a bartender, or if, at thirty-nine going on forty she was just too old to sling beer. Maybe she could buy a flattering black skirt? Her legs weren't that bad, and with a little bit of make-up, maybe she could hide her real age? Sure, she pondered, maybe she could find a job in a quiet lounge tucked away in the burbs where she would be less likely to bump into someone from her past. God forbid that, she'd thought. God forbid someone that she knew recognizing what had become of her life.

She tilted the plastic mug against her lips until her tongue felt the last of the lukewarm coffee. Suddenly, the silence in the cabin was unsettling. She turned to Rory.

"What do you do in the winter?" she asked.

In that familiar, slow and lazy voice, Rory Spradlum began his story.

He had been a figure skater, had made it pro, and had been the sweetheart pick for a medal at the 1992 Olympics - until he wrecked his knee.

"I was a small time hero from a small town in Southern Alberta. Then I tore all of the ligaments two months before the Olympics."

This surprised and bothered Katy at the same time. She sat up a little straighter as the Chevy crawled up a small dirt road to the north end of the development as Rory continued.

He had been a farm boy from Brooks, Alberta. By the time he was four, his natural talent for skating was obvious, and his parents encouraged and supported his gift. At twelve, he was competing across Canada, and throughout his career had achieved dozens of medals. It was the only life that he had known. Until the injury.

"You don't think I was born with these legs, now do ya?" he added, and a hearty chuckle filled the cabin.

Something pleasant filled Katy's chest from the sound of Rory's mirth, and she turned to respond. A crooked smile had found Rory's tanned and oddly rugged face.

"I have a garbage disposal and recycling business in the winter," he continued with a shrug. "It's okay. Don't know how to market myself, but it's not bad money. It's not great cash, but it keeps food on the table. Wife is a cashier at the drugstore part-time. We have four small kids, all under six," he added, "so she's a stay-at-home mom as much as the budget allows."

Katy's eyes widened slightly. She had hardly imagined Rory as a figure skater. But married and the father of four? Her eyes filled with something, a new kind of respect, or appreciation for the man, she wasn't quite sure. She opened her mouth to ask how old his children were, but Rory had something else to say.

"I'm not gay."

"I didn't..."

"Most people think male skaters are gay."

Katy laughed aloud. It was a short, but very real laugh - and the first that Rory had heard come from her throat. He turned and stared at her for a moment.

"Your eyes are alive," he said in that rubbing voice. "From your laughter," he added. "Your baby browns are alive!"

Katy wasn't sure that she had heard him right. She hoped that she hadn't heard him right. She reached down and placed the empty coffee thermos in her duffle bag.

"Your eyes usually look dead," he added, very matter-of-factly.

Rory's five short words threw off an alarm. Since Katy had returned to Calgary she had worked very hard at hiding from the world, and hiding her emotions. Still, this simple man had zoned in on her vagrant world - and with such accuracy! She was shocked. "Oh," she finally muttered awkwardly, "I'm just quiet..."

"Sure," Rory replied thickly. "Sure," he repeated seconds later, then, without skipping a heartbeat, popped another question. "So you married?"

Enough already. Please let it be, Katy silently begged.

"No."

"Kids?"

"No. No kids."

"No kids, huh?" he replied with sincere surprise in his voice. "What? Just didn't want them?"

"No," she said quickly. Too quickly. She remembered a tender moment from the past.

. . .

Brad lifted Katy's left hand, and then very gently, kissed the Tiffany Princess ring before putting it on her ring finger. He had just proposed, and she had just accepted. She felt loved and tingling. Euphoric.

"Someday soon," he whispered, "after the wedding, promise me something?"

The quaint Italian restaurant in Little Italy in Manhattan was hushed as every patron watched.

"Promise you what?" she asked softly.

"Promise me that we will make little Katys?"

"Little Katys?" she teased. "I thought you wanted a girl and a boy."

"I do. She will be a little Katy, and he will have your eyes."

. . .

Katy suddenly felt exhausted. "No, Rory. I just didn't want kids," she lied. Then she pulled her baseball cap down to hide her face and her eyes disappeared to the world outside.

For several minutes, the only sound from the cabin was the echo of the Chevy's tires spitting up gravel as they travelled to their next job. As Rory steered the five-ton to the edge of the northeast quadrant, his voice rattled above the engine.

"Amazing," he said thickly as he put the Chevy into park.

"What is amazing?"

"You know my name," he stated matter-of-factly as his large hand grabbed the last three strawberries in the plastic container.

Katy's brooding eyes lit up in surprise. Of course she knew his name!

Then, "'ere", the voice beside her droned.

Her eyes fell to a large ripe berry glistening between Rory's fingers. She hesitated before taking his offering. Then, mumbling a thanks, a tiny smile found her lips.

Chapter Five

Memories forged into Marshall's mind over the next several weeks as he continued to wait for the call. Often, Sarah's face was replaced with Christina's face, or Christina's face was replaced with Sarah's, depending on where he had allowed his mind to drift.

One morning, he awoke from a dream sobbing like a child and screaming for help. He had been making love to Sarah.

"I love you," she whispered huskily. "I love you," she hushed again as she lifted her head from his shoulders. But long blonde locks framed another face.

"You're not my wife!" he screamed. "Where is Sarah?"

"Marshall, it will be okay," Sarah whispered.

Sarah was sitting on the corner of the bed. She had been watching.

"Where is Charlie?" Marshall begged, breaking out into sobs.

Sarah bowed her head. He could see the silhouette of her tiny nose, and her full, pouting lips. "Charlie is dead, Marshall!" She was holding her swollen stomach.

Marshall's wild eyes fell from Sarah's pregnant stomach to the long blonde locks and supple breasts near his bare chest. "What did you do with Charlie?" he cried.

"Here. I have a gift for you, Marshall," Christina whispered, cradling an infant wrapped in a yellow blanket.

The dream haunted Marshall for the entire day, and he picked at it repeatedly as he desperately tried to recall every detail. By late afternoon, he had bludgeoned it to death, and was now uncertain which parts of it were real and which parts he might have fabricated in his analytical flurry to dissect the monster.

Later, he had an epiphany and found himself in frantically ripping open the boxes that he had brought home from his office the day he sold his shares of Stein Morretti. He couldn't remember the thin and quirky private investigator's name, but he was positive that he had kept his card. He finally found what he was looking for.

Thomas Sinclair, Private Investigator

Marshall reached the seventy-some year old on the third ring.

Thomas Sinclair vividly remembered his difficult and belligerent client, despite his aging memory.

"Retired, sir," Thomas declined immediately. "Almost five years ago. But I can give you a couple of other names."

Marshall insisted.

"Thomas, I don't want to start from scratch. You have a head start. You know the mother, which is half of the battle. And I have no desire, nor the time, to bring someone else up to speed. Besides, this is urgent. nAda you must recall that I pay generously?"

Thomas Sinclair certainly remembered the generosity of his client. Marshall Stein had paid well. So well in fact, that Thomas was able to take his wife on a few unexpected vacations. He also *vaguely* remembered the case. Marshall Stein, a married man and a father, had been devastated because he had had an affair with a younger woman who was now sleeping with his son. Eventually marrying his son.

Still, more vivid however was his client's belligerence, and Thomas just didn't want to go *there* again.

"Mr. Stein, I don't have any of the files," he replied in truth. "I destroyed everything when I retired. Went into the shredder."

Marshall wouldn't let up. Years ago the quirky little man had been successful with exactly what he had been hired to do. Marshall knew that if anyone could find the missing child, or at least the child's mother, Thomas Sinclair was the man. He also recalled how Thomas doted on his wife, and suspected that a few words might influence the old guy's decision.

"How does a five thousand dollar, cash under the table retainer sound?" he bargained with a great deal of confidence. "I'll also give you another twenty-five thousand the moment you deliver me the kid."

Thomas silently gasped. The retainer was prize enough, but another twenty-five thousand more for one job? He could hardly contain his surprise, but he was able to maintain his composure and played a little game. He hummed and hawed, and hawed and hummed before "conditionally" agreeing to meet Marshall the very next morning at a twenty-four hour breakfast stop a few blocks east of Marshall's home.

The following morning Marshall placed a white envelope full of cash on the linoleum table in front of Thomas Sinclair - even before their coffee was poured. Then, over two plates of bacon and eggs, Marshall talked and Thomas listened intently. Finally, when Marshall appeared done with his story, Thomas sat back in the hard vinyl booth and put his small, spindly hands on the table.

"It sounds like a very tough case, Mr. Stein," he began as his filmy, bloodshot eyes found his client's. But he very much liked the sight of the envelope with his retainer beside the salt and pepper shakers, so his words came out slow as he carefully processed what to say.

"Mr. Stein, sir, if you have told me everything that you know," he continued cautiously, "then it's near a dead end. You say that there was no mention of a child in Charlie's will. You don't know how old this child might be, its name, or even whether it's a boy or girl. And you can't even hypothesize where the child was born." Thomas cleared his throat. "Furthermore, you don't know the name the mother was using when she gave birth - if she did give birth! Or the alias she may be using today! Or where she lives, where she works, or even how long ago it was that she left Charlie and the kid. Mr. Stein," he added, shaking his head gravely, "you don't even know for certain that this child exists!"

Marshall's jaw tightened. "I know the child exists."

"Well, sir, is there something that I missed? You told me..."

"Look," Marshall interrupted as he leaned across the table. "I will confirm one thing. I have a grandchild out there - somewhere. I am absolutely certain of this, and I need you to find it."

Thomas paused. There was a hint of desperation, or something else, in Marshall's eyes, and this made Thomas feel uncomfortable. This was certainly not the same man that he had worked for almost a decade prior. "Mr. Stein," he began very slowly, as if he was talking to a young child, "the last time was quite different. If you recall, you provided me with the first connecting threads. You had an address. Place of employment. Etcetera! Etcetera! But my goodness!" A breathless sigh of exasperation fell out of Thomas' mouth. "This time we don't even know what city to start in. My goodness, I can't imagine finding a fresh trail!"

Thomas' last words were spoken with both sincerity and conviction. He had already asked himself a number of realistic and pressing questions. Where on earth would he begin to look for this child, or its mother, with the little information that he had? And how the heck could he begin to look for a child that might not exist - even if his client was telling him otherwise? For a brief moment, he thought of thanking Marshall for breakfast and declining the assignment.

However, it was apparent that Marshall was a broken man - and Thomas was deeply moved by what he saw, and the drastic change in his client. Marshall's once very handsome face was now drawn, almost white. His remarkable green eyes, eyes that used to speak with authority and life, were now dark and direly unhappy. This was certainly a different man than the one that Thomas had remembered, and for a moment, he actually felt Marshall's pain. The deaths of his family had changed him, Thomas concluded sadly. But how could the death of a family not change a man? He shuddered. He couldn't imagine! How could possibly say no to this man?

Also, Thomas very much liked the looks of the envelope on the table - and he had already spent the money. He would use the five thousand dollar "gift" to take his wife Cecelia on a holiday, somewhere warm, where the humid air would help her arthritis.

"Sir," he continued with a sigh, "if you can assure me that you understand that our odds are very slim, I'll take the case. But I need you to reassure me that this is clear, okay?"

"Of course!" Marshall nodded.

"I'll start from the beginning, sir," Thomas started in a compassionate tone. "Let me see what I can do." He smiled gently then. It was a large display that pronounced his yellow teeth and dark pink gums, contrasting his brown synthetic, wool-look-alike suit jacket. "But I have many questions that you need to help me answer."

Marshall's eyes flickered, but this time Thomas didn't catch the gleam of hope. He was busy pulling out a note pad and pen from his vinyl briefcase. And as he mentally prepared the questions for Marshall, his recollection of the woman slowly became clearer. She was certainly a looker. Tall and willowy, with a long blonde mane of hair and an exquisite face. He also recalled her dark side. She was borderline psychotic, at least this is what he had surmised back then. She had also gone by several different aliases, and yes, yes, he was remembering... His quest had taken him from sweat lodges on native reserves to alternative medicine camps, and then some as he followed her trail.

“Okay,” he began in a matter-of-fact tone as he looked back up to Marshall. “Let's start with the wedding.”

“The wedding!” Marshall sounded surprised.

Thomas explained what they were about to do.

“We are going to cover everything, sir. Some of it might be somewhat... umm...”

“Fine. I get it Thomas,” Marshall retorted impatiently.

Thomas cleared his throat. “So, tell me again. Your wife never mentioned that the two had actually wed?”

Marshall shook his head adamantly. “No. That's not what I said. What I said was that Sarah told me they married on Valentine's Day.”

“Right.” Thomas scratched his chin. “So your wife knew about the wedding, but you don't think that she was aware of the child?”

Marshall shook his head. "She couldn't have known about the child. She would have told me."

Thomas cleared his throat again. “Could it be possible that she did know, but because of your, well, because of your relationship with Charlie, that perhaps she purposely kept this piece of information from you?”

Marshall had wondered this exact thing several times over the past few weeks, but each time he came to the same conclusion. Sarah wouldn't have hidden something this significant! He shook his head again. “No way,” he replied with too much confidence.

"Okay. Okay," Thomas mumbled as he wrote on his note pad. Then, "Have you gone through all of your wife's things, Mr. Stein?"

Marshall closed his eyes for a brief instant. How he dreaded this task. He had avoided for over two years. Every single one of Sarah's things, even her favorite hat, lay exactly as she had left them.

"Some," he finally replied. "Some," he lied. "Only some."

"Maybe that's where you can start?" Thomas Sinclair suggested. "You might find something that we can use?"

As Marshall hesitated it suddenly dawned on Thomas how difficult this would be for anyone, packing up the things of a loved one who has passed. "Perhaps you can get someone to help you with this, sir? It might make it easier for you?" he offered with compassion.

"*That* will not be necessary!" Marshall snapped back. "I'll see what I can do," he replied quickly. However, he hardly suspected that Sarah's things would divulge anything of importance. "I'll see what I can find," he added, "but I doubt there will be anything there."

"Good!" Thomas continued with more enthusiasm than he felt. "Good!" he repeated. "Let's go back to the mother for a moment."

Marshall grimaced. "Hardly a mother, I would think."

Thomas ignored the sarcasm. "You said that she would be thirty-five or thirty-six years old today?"

"Yes," Marshall answered as his eyes fell to Thomas' chicken scratch notes.

"Which one is it?"

"I'm not sure," Marshall admitted.

Thomas thought for a moment. "What did you say she did for a living? Forgive me. I can't remember."

"She was an editor for a small rag."

"Rag?" Thomas asked naively.

"A magazine."

"Oh, of course!" Thomas replied with a silly grin. "Forgive me, my memory is fading. Do you remember which one?"

Marshall tried to remember. "I don't remember," he finally replied. "You were the one to tell me that it was owned by a large company out east. But she worked out of Vancouver. That's where she lived when I met her."

It was Thomas' turn to hesitate. If recollection served him correctly, he had told Marshall that she had used several different addresses and just as many aliases. He thought then, just as he had done so many years ago now, that lust breeds many crazy things and that a wise and articulate man like Marshall just didn't want to remember the truth. But Thomas didn't rebut. It wasn't worth the time. He changed the subject with another question.

"So, sir. When she phoned your partner, uh, Tony? It is Tony, isn't it? Is it correct to say that he didn't know where she was calling from?"

"That's correct," Marshall agreed. "Tony said the conversation was hardly a minute. He didn't ask, and she didn't offer. She could have been calling from anywhere."

"That certainly doesn't help us at all!"

"No," Marshall muttered dryly.

"Okay." Thomas paused. Then he had another thought. "Any idea if she took Charlie's last name? Your last name?"

"No idea."

Thomas scratched his chin. "I am trying to very hard to remember what alias' she used, but age is against me," he added sheepishly. "Do you remember any of them?"

Marshall smirked as old anger surfaced. "The woman I knew went by Christina Shore. You were the one to tell me that she'd gone under several other names! Beth something or other. Courtney Goodman, or Goodall. Shit, it was a crazy labyrinth of lies and deceptions."

It had been eight or nine years, maybe even ten, since Thomas had worked on the case. Time, age, and all the other cases in between this case and his retirement had muddled his memory. He recalled uncovering a whole other life to the one that Marshall Stein had known as Christina Shore, but for the life of him, her alias came up blank. He wrinkled his nose and sighed in frustration. "I'll be darned," he muttered, half to himself. He was truly starting from scratch. "I need more leads," he said as he looked up to Marshall. "Let's look at this in a different light. Let's start with the basics. What about family?" he asked. "*Her* family," he quickly added.

"Her family?" Marshall scoffed. "Christina's mother lived on the streets. She raised Christina and her kid sister and brother working as a prostitute. They all had a different father. And her brother was in some penitentiary for manslaughter."

"Yes, yes, now I remember. And what about her kid sister?"

"Kid sister? She was probably eighteen or so at the time. Christina was supporting her. I think that the kid had been into drugs or alcohol since adolescence. I'm not sure, but I think that it was you that told me that she had a serious drug or alcohol abuse problem."

"Yes. Didn't I find her in an expensive drug rehab?"

Marshall nodded. "I think you did."

"Vancouver, wasn't it? Yes, it was Vancouver," Thomas exclaimed. "Now I remember! I wondered how Christina could have paid for a stint like that. Hard enough just feeding a kid sister on an editor's salary."

"That was always the odd part," Marshall replied quietly as another memory returned. "I never knew exactly where her money came from, but she appeared to do okay. She did more than okay," he added sarcastically. "She told me that she had several writing contracts to subsidize her income."

"She was an editor but was her writing worthy?" Thomas asked with a hint of suspicion.

"Don't know." Marshall shrugged. "I never read a thing she wrote."

"Probably got by on her looks. She was most definitely a beauty!"

In the early days, Marshall himself had sometimes wondered if men had indeed paid Christina's way. It was a tiny, but nagging suspicion, even though she had never once asked him for money. Later, when she married Charlie, a "poor, traveling journalist", Marshall's suspicion was put to rest. "Anything is possible," he replied dryly, "but I highly doubt *that*."

"Any idea which slammer the brother was in?"

"Hell no!" Marshall scoffed. "I knew her for three months. I never met her family."

Thomas hesitated. "What about your family, sir? I mean *other* then Sarah and Charlie," he added awkwardly.

Marshall did not flinch. "There is no other family."

Thomas cleared his throat, remembering too late that Marshall was an orphan. "That's right. I remember now. I apologize. But did Sarah have any relatives? Perhaps they took..."

"Look!" Marshall interrupted impatiently. "Let's not waste any time *there*!" He leaned across the booth toward Thomas. "I grew up in seven or eight different foster homes. Sarah grew up in Europe. She was the youngest of nine brothers and sisters by eleven years. The ones that are, or *were* still alive, lived in different parts of Europe. Sarah hadn't talked to them in years."

Thomas struggled for a moment with the stark reality of his client's empty life. He thought of his own family; a wife of almost fifty-one years, six children, nineteen grandchildren, and another on the way. He couldn't imagine life without them. Any of them! He nervously cleared his throat again before posing the next question. "Any chance Charlie left the kid with cousins in Europe?"

"Cousins in Europe?" Marshall's voice was high and strained. Every single one of Charlie's aunts and uncles, Sarah's brothers and sisters, had disconnected themselves from Sarah the day she married Marshall. "You're on the wrong track now, Thomas! As far as I know there wasn't one family member in Europe that even knew that Charlie was born."

Thomas' face turned to one of intense disbelief. He could not hide his surprise.

If Marshall noticed, he didn't let on. "Sarah was as disconnected from her family as I was from mine," he explained in a stoic, matter-of-fact tone.

Thomas looked down to his note pad. Marshall's admittance had left him feeling odd and uncomfortable. It just wasn't natural, he thought, what this man was telling him! He fidgeted with his pen for a moment. Then he looked at his watch. "Oh my!" he exclaimed. "We are running out of time. I have to pick my wife up at the hair salon shortly."

Marshall looked up to the large oval clock above the cash register and his eyes lit up in surprise. They had been there for almost two hours. How fast time goes by when one is using their mind, he thought. He looked out the window and wondered how much time he had wasted in his lifetime.

"Okay. Umm. Okay. Umm." Thomas repeated, scratching his chin.

Suddenly, the little man and his little sound annoyed Marshall a great deal. He was used to getting things done quickly and efficiently. "What else do you need from me today Thomas?" he asked gruffly. "I would like to get this meeting over with."

Despite his client's rudeness, Thomas still felt compassion for the man sitting across from him at the table. His glassy eyes looked to Marshall's with kindness, and his next words spoken with a great deal of patience. "Mr. Stein, just a couple more minutes? We need a couple more minutes. Can we touch on your son for a moment?" He shrugged as he asked this last question, as if in apology.

"What about my son?"

"Let's start with his full name?"

Marshall looked out the window. "Charles Marshall Stein," he replied.

"And his date of birth?"

"Date of birth?" Marshall repeated in a tone of question. He and Sarah were married in 1975. Charlie was born two years later. "1977," he said flatly. "September 1977."

"September?" Thomas repeated to cue the man in front of him that "September" simply wasn't enough of an answer.

Silence beckoned. "What day in...?" Thomas prodded.

"Yes," Marshall interrupted. "It was September," he added as his eyes lit up slightly.

. . .

"Our beautiful boy. And born on the first day of fall," Sarah had cooed from the hospital bed the day Charlie was born.

. . .

She had looked so beautiful.

So proud.

So much like a mother.

Marshall closed his eyes for a moment. "The 22nd," he said thickly. "It was September 22nd, 1977."

Thomas jotted down the date. "And when did he leave for Afghanistan?"

Marshall's brow wrinkled in thought. He was getting tired. He was beginning to feel frustrated. He had already told Thomas the little he knew about Charlie's assignment in the Far East. "August," he replied with a look of impatience. "No. September. 2001."

Thomas was big on birthdays. He quickly calculated that Charlie Stein traveled to his death on the month, perhaps even the exact day of his 34th birthday. "Then Charlie had custody of the child before that trip? He must have left it with someone before he left for Afghanistan."

"Of course he left the child with someone before he left for Afghanistan!" Marshall shouted. "No one in their right mind would take a kid to a war zone!"

Thomas looked around the room in embarrassment to see how much attention their table had demanded, but the only eyes boring into his were those of the matronly-looking cashier. She was shaking her head back and forth and pointing one finger to her ear. Thomas nodded apologetically and smiled, then he turned back to the table. Without question, this was a complicated case. But he certainly hadn't meant to imply that a father, especially Marshall Stein's own son, would take his child to a war. "Of course not! I was simply thinking aloud."

"I am sure you were," Marshall mumbled.

Thomas dug in again. "Forgive my naivety, but I need to know. Was Charlie covering the war?" It was an honest question, Thomas thought. For all he knew, Charlie could have been writing a story on the culture.

Marshall nodded.

"That's gotta be a tough thing, sir, losing a child in a war," Thomas offered gently. He couldn't imagine such a thing. "I'm very sorry, Mr. Stein."

Marshall's demeanor imploded with Thomas' words. He ran his fingers through his salt and pepper hair and breathed in. Then with a tight jaw, his next words came out very evenly. "Thomas, if you want to set the record absolutely straight, Charlie died in a helicopter crash. He had hitched a ride in a transport chopper with a private contractor. He was in Kabul, and wanted to get to the city of Kandahar, where the troops were stationed. The chopper crashed in a severe dust storm. Apparently it sprung up out of nowhere. Everybody on board died. The pilot and all three passengers."

Marshall shrugged and leaned back in the booth. "That's it. It is that simple. So one can't go off on a tangent and fabricate some heroic story that Charlie died a hero, stepping on a mine saving a child, or getting shot to death defending his country."

Thomas inwardly gasped. "That hardly matters! He was doing a brave job, sir, regardless of how he died."

"Just wanted to set the record straight." Marshall replied stoically. Then without a skipping a beat added, "What else do you need today? We are now officially out of time."

Thomas squirmed in the vinyl booth. He was taken aback by the asshole's ability to turn on and off like a light switch. His compassion for the man was still there, but that didn't mean that he had to like him. "Just a couple more questions..." He cleared his throat. "Yes. Yes!" he remembered. "Any idea which publication Charlie worked for on this assignment?"

"I don't know. Could have been Time Magazine? Maybe the New Yorker?" Marshall recalled someone, probably Sarah, mentioning that Charlie had done a war story for the New Yorker.

"His bank accounts might tell us this," Thomas replied quietly, and then he scribbled a reminder on his note pad.

"Bank accounts! Those would be impossible to find."

"But Charlie had other assignments, didn't he?"

"Of course he had other assignments, Thomas! He was a freelance journalist!"

Again, Thomas barreled past the man's arrogance. "Where was Charlie's home base?"

"He lived in Hong Kong for a year, I think. And South Africa, at least for a while..." Marshall tried to remember the things Sarah had shared with him...

"Where was he living when he left for Afghanistan?"

Marshall's eyes shifted uncomfortably. "I'm not sure. I know that he had a condo in Vancouver. But I'm not sure if that was where he was living at the time."

"Any chance you have the address?"

"Address?" Marshall repeated in scorn, shaking his head.

Thomas suddenly longed for the warmth of his home. Yearned for some of his wife's homemade apple pie and a cup of hot tea. This meeting had exhausted him. This man had fatigued and frustrated him. He needed comfort food and love. "Didn't suspect that you would remember," he replied dryly and with as much diplomacy as he could muster.

Marshall caught Thomas' sarcasm. He sat up a little straighter in the vinyl booth and clasped his hands together. "I might be able to find it back at the house," he admitted, remembering the bankers boxes that held what was left of Charlie's life. "I'll look when I get home. I think it was in False Creek, overlooking Granville Island," he added, vaguely remembering Sarah telling him about Charlie's view at False Creek. Maybe it was the estate lawyer, after Charlie's death. He wasn't sure.

Thomas quickly scribbled something in his notepad before looking back up to Marshall. "Good. That's good. Now, I'll need you to do some homework." He hesitated for a moment on how best to proceed. "Maybe I can email you a list of questions?"

"I doubt that will work. I don't use my computer."

For the first time that morning, Thomas made no attempt to hide his surprise. "No computer! Well!" Even his old fingers were proficient on a computer, he thought, thanks to his grandchildren's patience, tutorials and help with troubleshooting. "Okay then. I'll write the questions down for you. Now. Before I go. I might have more later, but we can start with these... I need Charlie's last address in Vancouver," he continued as he began a list in his notepad. "I also need his social insurance number. Insurance policies. Medical records. Bank accounts. *All* of them," he emphasized, looking up toward Marshall briefly. "I need his T4's. All of them. Also, a list of jobs - *any* and *all* of them. Including where he was stationed and company names."

Marshall looked overwhelmed as Thomas ripped the piece of paper from his notepad and pushed it across the table. "Wait," Thomas exclaimed, and pulled the list back towards his edge of the table. "I'll also need the estate lawyer's name. And," he scribbled fervently, "friends. Any friends that he might have kept in touch with . Including their phone numbers."

"Friends!" Marshall muttered helplessly. "You know that Charlie and I hadn't spoken in years! I don't know his friends!" he spat.

It was the first time during the meeting that Thomas looked at a loss for words. His jaw dropped and his filmy eyes filled with surprise. "What about friends before that, Mr. Stein?" he finally asked. "University buddies? Friends of the family?"

Marshall's eyes grew distant and Thomas' impatience thinned. "Look, Mr. Stein. I need your help. I need your cooperation. I need anything from you that might give me a warm lead. What about friends that came to Charlie's funeral?"

Awkward silence filled their space for several seconds as they two men looked at one another for answers. Thomas finally spoke again, his voice almost a whisper. "Sir. There must have been friends at your son's funeral?"

Marshall's eyes flickered dully for a moment. "I'll see what I can find," he replied.

In reality, Marshall doubted that he would find anything. Several friends of Charlie's had paid their respects at his funeral. However, he had been too consumed with his own world to pay them any attention. He had left that up to Sarah.

"Yes. Please. See what you can find," Thomas replied. "I'll begin on my end," he added. "In the meantime, perhaps once you go through Sarah's things something else may surface."

Marshall nodded. However, the thought of going through Sarah's things, the thought of digging through her life, left a sickly feeling in the pit of his stomach. His eyes fell to Thomas' list, then to the salt and pepper shakers in the middle of the table. He couldn't wait to get home and have a nap.

As the two men were nearing Marshall's SUV in the parking lot, Thomas's popped the question Marshall had been waiting for.

"I need to ask you one last thing sir. It just might help. When was the last time you saw her. I mean, Christina?"

Marshall didn't hesitate. "New York," he answered coldly as he clicked the key lock of his Lexus.

Ten minutes later he fell to the sofa in the parlor, however, neither sleep nor solitude showed their faces. Just as Marshall was dozing off, the sound of breaking glass pulled him wide awake and his eyes fell to the scene of the crime. Chocolate brown paws jumped from the corner of the piano lid as Jazz let out an obnoxious complaint before scurrying out of the room.

"What have you done now? You spoiled ass!" Marshall bellowed as he pulled himself off of the sofa. "Ouch!" he instantly exclaimed as he stepped on a large piece of glass. Blood oozed from the arch of his foot and onto the hardwood floors.

Outraged, Marshall chased Jazz across the hardwood, across the light Persian carpet, through the dining room, and then across the marble kitchen floors, the whole while screaming. "You're out! Out! You are going to the pound you evil thing! You are out you spoiled ass!" he kept shouting.

Jazz hissed from under the kitchen table and then scurried between Marshall's legs and out of sight.

Marshall wrapped paper towel around his wound and held it together with tape, for he couldn't find a Band-Aid. Then he limped from room to room with the roll of paper towel and a bottle of Fantastic as he attempted to clean up the blood. When he reached the dining room he turned on the lights to find lively walls of original paintings and a magnificent dining room table and twelve matching chairs. As he tried to remember where Sarah had found the exquisite antique he realized that he hadn't eaten around that table, he hadn't even set foot in that room, since the day of Sarah's funeral. His face was drawn and gray as he wiped up a few blood splatters on the hardwood floor before limping back to the parlor.

As he entered the parlor his eyes fell to several large blood spots on the Persian carpet, and he exploded again in rage. "You're out! Out! Out!" he shouted at the top of his lungs as he scrubbed and scrubbed and scrubbed with the same results. The carpet was ruined. "Times trouble by one hundred," he shrieked when he realized this. "To the pound!" he threatened. "You're out! Out! Out! You damn spoiled ass!" he cried repeatedly. Never before had Marshall felt so hostile or out of control.

By the time the sun had begun to set, "A Gift to My Family" had turned into one of perpetual silence. Marshall slept in the parlor. Jazz slept under the master bed, directly below Sarah's pillow. It was always where Jazz disappeared when Marshall was on the attack.

At just before midnight Marshall awoke and slowly opened his eyes. His foot was throbbing. He sat up and looked down to his feet. Blood had oozed from his wound through the paper towel. He wondered if he needed stitches. He was certain that he needed painkillers and tried to remember where they might be. Then his eyes roamed from the piano to the silver picture frame that now lay shattered, face down, on the floor. He hadn't been able to look at the photograph that afternoon. He didn't want to know if the broken glass had ruined his favorite family photo.

He stood up and hopped across the parlor. Then he reached down and gently lifted the frame from the floor and held it up to his eyes. The photograph held a younger Sarah; her honey-colored hair fell in wisps around her shoulders. At her side was a handsome boy, about four years old. Next to the child stood a younger Marshall. They all wore beach shorts and T-shirts and were tanned and smiling from ear to ear.

The glass had dug a long vertical line into the photograph, dividing Marshall from Sarah and Charlie. As if separating him from his family, he instantly thought. His eyes grew moist as he peered into Sarah's eyes, and then his son's, willing himself back to that moment. He lovingly caressed their faces with his fingers, and then their smiles. Finally, he fell back into the sofa, staring at the photograph as he tried to remember.

For years, Marshall had tried to recall exactly when the picture had been taken, and what beach held the white sand. After Charlie's funeral, he had wanted to ask Sarah this very question. But he was too embarrassed to admit that he didn't remember such a thing. He knew that they had taken a trip to Hawaii. He remembered how proud he had been to stand on that beach with his beautiful wife and child. He also remembered vividly that this was their first family vacation. It was their *only* family vacation. Marshall had always been too busy.

Without warning, the song from the river pulled Marshall into the present and he scowled in disapproval. How he hated the chants. They made him feel more vulnerable than he could allow himself to feel. Sometimes, they made him feel so angry that he would stand on the terrace and scream as loudly as he possibly could. "Quiet!" he would shriek like a crazy man. "Quiet!" he would beg, but his pleading voice always traveled unheard across the river, disappearing into the night.

Marshall unlocked the patio doors and hopped onto the terrace and around the empty flowerpots and abandoned wrought iron furniture. When he neared the southwest edge of the stone wall he tilted his head towards the bridge, certain that this was where the chant-like song originated. Then he fell against the coolness of the terrace wall and slid to a fetal position. Tears spilled down his drawn face and onto his crumpled shirt; they were silent, mute droplets, but released after harboring so much pain - and for so long - they fell with a relentless tenacity. He laid in silence for a very long time, long after the song from the river below had ended. Finally, he lifted his head and looked up, towards the north and the city skyline. Swollen eyes traveled across the brightly lit landscape: the Calgary Tower, Bankers Hall, the Chevron Building, to other familiar skyscrapers that stood tall and stately, some of them Marshall's very own creations. Many of the buildings were as familiar to Marshall as the back of his hand, for Stein Morretti had been a key developer of the City for almost three decades. And somehow, this sight gave Marshall some solace.

He wiped his damp cheeks with the palms of his hands. Then he wiped the corners of his mouth, and then his eyes. He sighed and looked again.

The skyline looked remarkably beautiful, he thought.

Strong and vibrant.

Just like Sarah.

Chapter Six

Had it not been for that first chance encounter with Christina, the clandestine meetings that followed, and the sensuous teasing that had made him feel alive and young again, Marshall would have remained absolutely faithful to Sarah. He was certain of this. Sarah wouldn't have gone to Paris by herself, or have been driving down the freeway late at night by herself, or have had to worry about the headlights from the oncoming semi, or the driver that had fallen asleep at the wheel. Sarah would still be alive today, enjoying the gifts of spring that she so embraced. For she wouldn't have needed to change her world, the world that Marshall had destroyed.

Since Sarah's death, Marshall's anger and despair held fast, eventually taking him into a deeper depression. He was convinced that these feelings had settled to stay, and they felt like quick sand in the pit of his stomach.

From the beginning, Christina's open and raw passion bred Marshall's thirst for more and more. He became addicted to her scent, craved her touch, and felt deprived of life when he couldn't be with her. The day that she had said goodbye to him in the hotel room of The Plaza Hotel, he couldn't imagine not having her in his life, and lived the life of a desperate and jilted lover for a very long time afterward. When he finally accepted that Christina was gone and that she was with his very own son, his thirst for more of the same led to several other women.

At first, he had been very careful and discreet about his philandering lifestyle. He couldn't possibly hurt Sarah. However, as time progressed and new women entered Marshall's life, he became subconsciously reckless. He traveled more frequently, and often planned his trips and infidelity on the spur of the moment. Sometimes he had legitimate business to deal with, and by day would check in on partners and projects. In the evenings he rendezvoused with a blonde or brunette that didn't mind sporadic encounters of fine wine, five star hotels and shopping sprees that were always topped with clandestine sex.

The morning Marshall received the call from Paris, nine days after Sarah and Jazz had flown to Europe, he was in bed in a hotel room in Florida, quite enjoying the flight attendant that he was with and what she was doing to him. The call came at the most inopportune moment, but Marshall sat up instantly and reached for the phone. Its shrill ring had cracked open the room at half past two in the morning and it had sent a shiver down Marshall's spine as he looked at the clock on the night table.

. . .

"It's almost two-thirty," Marshall said in alarm.

"They can leave a message," the flight attendant whispered as her hands caressed him under the sheets.

"It's almost two-thirty in the morning!" Marshall repeated, much louder this time. As he put the receiver to his ear, he was certain that any news at this hour had to mean that something was terribly wrong.

. . .

Marshall procrastinated with the task of going through Sarah's things for three solid days. He knew it needed to be done, and it was on his mind night and day and day and night. Quite simply, he had walked by Sarah's desk and drawers and other things for over two years now. What difference would a few more days make? he had reasoned. And where, exactly, did he start, he pondered, helplessness and dread thick in his chest.

The following Monday, he awoke with the alarm at precisely six o'clock, and a long, hollow sigh fell from his lips. "Well," he said as he lifted his head off the pillow. Jazz, who had been sleeping on Sarah's pillow, opened his eyes. Subconsciously, Marshall reached out to pet him, but Jazz hissed with a vengeance before scurrying off the bed and out of the room.

Marshall lay and stared at Sarah's pillow for a moment. Then he leaned over and pressed his nose into its softness, breathed in again and then again as he inhaled any hint of her scent that she might have left behind.

Finally, he pulled himself up from the bed and dressed. A pair of old jeans and a ratty golf shirt the color of his eyes that Sarah had bought for him years and years ago.

"Well," he said again as he stood in the middle of the bedroom.

This one word was Marshall's reiteration that this morning was *the* morning.

Half an hour later he was on his hands and knees beside Sarah's antique desk, its contents now scattered across the floor. He found her stationery and greeting cards. He found her ball point pens and little Post-it notes, some of them blank, and others with a handwriting that he recognized so well. He actually grinned as he remembered how the pink, yellow and green Post-it notes had forever been

Sarah's way of reminding herself of something; he'd forgotten how he used to find them on the fridge and mirrors or next to the telephone.

As Marshall haphazardly put everything back in Sarah's desk he was positive of two things. There was nothing here pertaining to Charlie. And there was certainly no hint of a child.

Marshall's search continued in the basement storage room. He would have started in this room, for he was relatively sure that whatever might be left of Charlie was stored in here. But he had always hated this room. It left him with that unsettling feeling – even when Sarah was still alive he had avoided it. It reeked of a mess, he thought, even though it was very tidy. It held signs of life and aging, packed high with memories, hardly tangible signs of the past, he thought. It was also packed tight with at least two hundred bankers boxes, boxes that Sarah had carefully packed and then marked and stored over the years.

He flicked on the light switch and stood in the doorway for several seconds as his eyes glazed over. There were rows and rows of boxes. Hundreds of them! He instantly felt overwhelmed. After a few minutes of just standing and processing, the only comfort that Marshall could find is that every box was labeled with Sarah's neat printing in a thick black felt pen.

PHOTOGRAPHS: 1970S TO 1980S

PHOTOGRAPHS: 1990S

PHOTOGRAPHS: 2000

STUFFED ANIMALS

WRAPPING PAPER AND SUPPLIES

SARAH AND MARSHALL: WEDDING

SARAH AND MARSHALL: MISC.

SARAH: CHILDHOOD

Marshall knew that the absent box marked 'Marshall:Childhood' was not an oversight. Simply, Marshall didn't have one photograph from his youth. When they first married, Sarah would often tease him lovingly.

. . .

"If I could draw, I'd draw a boxful of pictures of the little boy named Marshall," she would say lovingly and playfully.

"But you can't draw," he would reply in tease.

"Yes, but if I could, I know exactly how you would look. You would have been adorable."

"Adorable?" Marshall would repeat. No one had ever before called Marshall adorable, and he liked the way it sounded.

"Yes. You would have been a very adorable, very handsome little boy. I'm certain. And when we have a child, if it's a boy, I hope that he looks exactly like you looked when you were a boy. That's how certain I am."

. . .

Eventually, Marshall reluctantly stepped into the room and continued reading. Occasionally, his lips would move as he voiced the words aloud. Finally, his eyes fell upon nine or ten boxes, stacked one on one, side by side:

CHARLIE: INFANCY

CHARLIE: CHILDHOOD

CHARLIE: SCHOOL (GRADES 1-6)

CHARLIE: SCHOOL (GRADES 7-12)

CHARLIE: UNIVERSITY OF BRITISH COLUMBIA

And then...

CHARLIE: 2001...

"Well," he muttered as he reached for the box labelled "Charlie: 2001...", hardly surprised that it read what it did, opposed to something more direct. Sarah had always been good with words.

This box was much heavier than he had anticipated, and he struggled to wedge it out from the others before carrying it up the stairs and into the parlor. It held legal documents, bank accounts, employment contracts and a death certificate. Marshall paused when his eyes read the official print at the top of the paper. It also held real estate transactions and more legal documents, including Charlie's will.

Marshall was surprised at the contents of the will - or lack thereof. Dated February 1998, it was as simple and straightforward as any will might be, and Charlie's entire estate was left to his mother, Sarah Melanie Stein. And there was no mention - whatsoever - of a wife *or* a child. As Marshall placed the document back into the white manila envelope and put it to the side for Thomas, he tried to pull a year from his mind.

How many years had it been since he last saw Christina? he wondered. Although he couldn't recall the year, he knew that it was in the middle of December. It was his birthday. Marshall closed his eyes.

. . .

She jumped from the bed playfully, and her long honey hair fell over her bare breasts and down her back. As she stood in the middle of their hotel room, he could hardly believe her beauty.

"I have a present for you Marshall..." she whispered in a deep, teasing voice.

"A present?"

"Yes, a present," she teased. And you must open it."

Oh, how gorgeous and fresh and exhilarating this woman, he thought. He could hardly wait to hold her again. "Oh," he said teasingly. "And what might this present be for?"

"It's a birthday present, Spunk."

He had never known why she had called him Spunk, for she would never tell him, even though he had asked her several times. Still, he loved it. He loved it and he loved her. He didn't remember feeling so light and so full at the same time. So alive and vibrant. And so young. "How did you know it was my birthday?"

"I have my ways..."

It was December 17th, 1997. They had already spent three full days in one of the penthouse suites in The Plaza Hotel across from Central Park. Marshall couldn't imagine being anywhere else.

Her creamy and delicate hands handed him a tiny box wrapped in silver paper. "Here," she whispered huskily. "This is for you. Happy birthday Spunk," she hushed.

As he took it from her hands, he saw that her eyes were moist. He should buy her a gift, he thought suddenly. Something to prove that he loved her. Yes, perhaps a gift that would stop her from disappearing for days at a time..."What could it be?" he asked with a teasing smile on his face as he gently shook the tiny package.

"It's not breakable," she whispered, curling up beside him on the bed. Her golden mane teased his arm and he inhaled, to hold her scent.

"It's not breakable?" he whispered back.

"No, I don't give presents that are breakable...life is too delicate."

His eyes were full of emotion and love and want for her again, even though he had just had her. But even more so, they held a curiosity for the woman before him that he had known for only three months. She had enchanted him with her ways and made him feel alive. And she fueled his curiosity with each odd expression or saying that she shared. "Why don't you give presents that are breakable?" he asked with a boyish and inquisitive look on his face. He didn't quite understand what she was saying, and he needed to know.

She shrugged her soft, supple shoulders and pulled her hair away from her flushed face. "Because, if they are as tender as the heart - and they shatter - then their memories are ruined."

Marshall didn't understand what she was meant. "What do you mean by that?"

"Oh, Marshall," she said softly, and then leaned down and kissed him gently on his lips. "Please open your present!"

Inside was a white gold buffalo about the diameter of a quarter. It hung from a long black silk chain. Marshall carefully pulled it out of the box and held it up towards the light on the nightstand.

"It's a white buffalo, and it is for life," she began softly in a story-like whisper. "It'll bring you a good life," she continued, and then began her explanation. "The chance of a white buffalo being born is one in a million. It's a rarity and a sign to the Native Americans. They believe that all buffalo are the providers of good things," she continued. "They represent a peaceful, wholesome life. And they also bestow great curing powers. In the contemporary sun dance, they also radiate power. And look," she added as she leaned toward him and clasped her look-alike pendant between her fingers. "You have already kissed this with love many, many times, Marshall. For us, our pendants will be symbolic of our rare and eternal love for one another, wherever life takes us."

Marshall's eyes were moist. He leaned over and kissed her, whispering a simple but heartfelt "thank you".

"I have something else for you," she said as laid her head on his chest, and curled her breasts into his side.

"Another present?" Marshall asked as clasped the buffalo in one hand and with the other began stroking her hair.

She didn't respond, and the room fell silent, and Marshall could hear the cars and taxis and horse-pulled carriages from Park Avenue below. Instinct told him that her mood had changed, like it sometimes did, and he lay very still as he waited for her to say or do something. Finally, she turned her head and looked up into his eyes. He realized that she had grown dark. He knew this look. He knew very little about this woman, but he had seen this look before, had felt its presence. It had only shown its face a few times and always at the oddest of occasions. However, something told Marshall that this time it was different. He sensed its escalation. He fell back to the pillow in silence. He knew he must listen.

"Something happened today…" she began.

"What do you mean, something happened today?"

She moved to the edge of the bed. The old but eloquent hotel room held an awkward silence for several seconds as Marshall waited for her to speak again.

Finally, she whispered. "I believe that something beautiful happened today, Marshall."

"Something beautiful!" Marshall was beginning to feel quite relieved. He did not like problems.

"Yes, and once I've finished explaining I will go and pack my things."

. . .

As another memory surfaced, Marshall's eyes opened wide in conclusion. Sarah had told him that Charlie and Christina had married on Valentine's Day in 1998. How had he forgotten this? Suddenly he recalled this conversation explicitly, even remembering how he had privately scoffed when he had calculated that the two had married less than two months after they had bumped into one another at Macy's. Two months after she had slept with Marshall! Thus, if Charlie wrote his will in February of 1998, and with no mention of Christina, this meant that they would have divorced before this date. This meant that they had been married for less than a year.

By eleven o'clock that morning, Marshall had ripped apart every box marked "Charlie", but to find nothing more of relevance or that would help Thomas with the case. He called Thomas only minutes later and gave him the news. "I've only found the statistical information on Charlie," he said a very matter-of-fact tone.

"Statistical information?" Thomas repeated in a question, mildly taken aback by Marshall's choice of words.

"Vancouver address. Will. Bank accounts. Most were with the files the estate lawyer put together. I also have that lawyer's name and number. But nothing else."

"Well," Thomas Sinclair replied grimly. "That's not good news. I'll start with the lawyer. The public records I sourced reveal nothing whatsoever about the child. According to Revenue Canada, Charlie never claimed a dependent on his taxes. Apparently, according to them, he was four years behind in filing his taxes. This could be the problem."

Marshall remembered Sarah telling him that Charlie had never been good with filing his taxes on time. This would likely explain why there was no mention of a wife or a child. "So where do we go from here?" he asked.

"I think I'll need to take a day trip to Vancouver," Thomas replied. "Charlie's neighbors might know something – if they're still around. It's a long shot. In this day and age, four or five years doesn't help our memories. I certainly know that!" he added with a chuckle. "And any neighbors that may have known Charlie could have moved on. The world continues to change, Mr. Stein, it continues to change..."

Will it change? Marshall silently asked himself as Thomas continued.

"I'll book flights to Vancouver for tomorrow," Thomas continued. "Maybe I'll take the wife and make a couple days trip out of it. The ocean air might be good for her arthritis."

"There are a couple more places I can look," Marshall offered reluctantly as he envisioned the remaining boxes in the storage room.

"Oh?"

"Let me know where you are staying. If I find anything over the next couple of days, I'll give you a call."

"Yes, think I'll take the wife," Thomas voiced his decision out loud. "And of course, we'll stay at The Holiday Inn," he added matter-of-factly. "Rates are reasonable. And I would hope they still have that wonderful free breakfast buffet. Last time I was there, gosh, it must have been six, maybe seven years ago now. But I usually stayed there for days at a time. Had quite the case at one point. Middle-aged stock broker just up and left his wife. Well-known fellow in Edmonton. Married and two kids. Wife suspected something was up, and boy, was she was right. Found him shacked up with a seventeen year old male from Mexico. The two had built a profitable ring of child porno. One of the toughest jobs, telling her the news. Nevertheless, The Inn was my hideaway after the long days of sniffing his trail. And it was always a good deal - especially with the free breakfast buffet."

Marshall grimaced as he listened, recalling how Thomas used to like to talk about his cases. He never went into depth, just bits and pieces of information that he didn't consider "classified". However, Marshall had no desire to hear about Thomas' cases, or free breakfasts, good deals at The Holiday Inn - or anything else for that matter.

"I have done a great deal of business in Vancouver as well," Marshall replied dryly. "Why don't you and your wife stay at The Bayshore Hotel? It's much more comfortable - and its in a different league for a few extra dollars."

"The Bayshore!" Thomas exclaimed. "With the rates they charge! Don't think so, Mr. Stein!"

Marshall thought of the five thousand dollars that he had already paid Thomas Sinclair. He just about opened his mouth to suggest to the man that two hundred dollars a night was just a fraction of what the Private Detective would make if he did what he had hired him to do. Instead, compassion suddenly fell from the sky and landed right on Marshall lap as he imagined seventy-some year-old Cecelia Sinclair. Her frailness, and, her thin head of over-processed purple-white hair and crooked, arthritis-ridden fingers.

"Stay at The Bayshore, Thomas. Your wife will enjoy it. Put a couple of nights on me. And tell them that you want a suite. Better yet, I used to have an account there. I'll call them for you."

"Well! That's very kind of you, sir! Thank you!" Thomas Sinclair exclaimed.

"But you damn well better bring me what I am paying you for!" Marshall exploded before hanging up the phone.

Chapter Seven

Rocky Mountain Estates wasn't the only connect between Katy Fields and Marshall Stein. Katy's balcony hung over the same river as Marshall's, but she lived on its west side of the Elbow River, opposed to its east side, in a dilapidated three-story walk-up that hung like a worn out madam on the edge of the river.

The instant she saw the "For Rent" sign hanging from the peeling brown fence she hardly noticed the pile of tattered furniture and bottles piled high against the side wall for the taking. Or the homeless that crawled into the garbage bins for sleep or food or whatever else the filth-ridden steel walls could offer. Or the peeling plaster in the hallways, or the cigarette burns that polka-dotted the burnt orange shag carpet in the apartment. Or the 1920s style kitchen and bathroom combo that smelled of rust and leaking pipes. She hardly noticed her soon to be neighbors, from cheap call girls on the first floor to the ghastly thin heroin addict who lived right next door. Nor did she notice Norm, the grossly overweight property manager with a bulging stomach to his knees, the perpetual smell of alcohol on his breath, or his hungry eyes, and how he looked at her.

Unequivocally, Unit 222 was a long way from where Katy had come. She found the apartment days after returning to Calgary from New York City, days after the scandal broke wide open, days after the fire lit up Chelsea on that bitterly cold and humid winter's night. By the time she landed on Canadian soil, the odd throbbing in her head and the heaviness of her heart were constants, and she was emotionally and physically a mess.

The moment her bloodshot, sleepless eyes had looked past the five hundred square feet of poverty and the cracked glass door that led to a rusting wrought iron balcony, she felt the lure of the frozen river and its crystal blanket. She could *almost* see the poplars and scatter of wildflowers that would spill over its embankment in the summer. And she had barely blinked an eye as she handed a wheezing Norm several crisp one hundred and fifty dollar bills.

"When can I move in?" she had asked.

In better form, if without the pounding in her head and the heaviness in her heart, Katy would have known that she needed something good to hang on to. Something to give her some teeth. A place to disappear from a world that had betrayed her and left her raw. Oblivious to what she *really* needed, this downtrodden apartment and its neighboring river, regardless of the season, would, in fact, eventually deliver the gifts that would take her to a better place.

It took Katy a long while to come to grips with the fact that she would never again work in her profession - as her reputation was destroyed. The release of her father's most recent fiction Purple Waters made certain of that! It was Number One on the New York Times Bestsellers list for almost fifty weeks, probably because it was written by the well-known author that never left his readers disappointed. Possibly due to scandal and the coverage that it created. A cold hard fact was that her father had stolen sensitive information from her computer that made for a plot that was one of his best fictions yet. A cold hard fact was that because of her relationship to the author no one would ever believe that she had nothing to do with the leak. And a cold hard fact was that, in the beginning, Katy was certain that she would *never* be able to come to terms with this betrayal.

Katy also desperately needed to deal with the loss of Brad - and the raging fire. Sometimes, she would wake up screaming from a bed of sweat-drenched sheets, the plaster walls echoing her pleas. "Brad! Brad! Brad!" she would cry out, and her begs bounced off the walls and ceilings of her bedroom, always leaving her gasping for morning. Often, she would sit on her balcony after these dreams and wait for the sunrise. Its arrival would give her proof that there was another day around the corner, and another chance to find resolve. And sometimes, she would hear the song from the river below, and she would close her eyes and embrace its message.

By the following spring, when the last of the river's icy blanket was replaced with rain showers and a trickling rivulet below, Katy was still raw and still exposed. However, the grief and numbness that had consumed her from Brad's disappearance in the fire was gradually replaced with anger, and then acceptance. And although she sometimes still missed him dearly, her heart was not as heavy.

Also, sometime that spring, between the fierce snowstorms and gray skies and when tulips began shyly showed their crowns, Katy began to do what her father did best. Writing allowed her to disappear from reality and fabricate her day, and it was a welcome release. Often, she pounded away at her keyboard from dawn until the arrival of another sunrise, and with this escape, she had begun to evolve into a different woman. A more accepting and more resilient woman. And a more forgiving woman.

This growth allowed Katy to carefully process other thoughts, and she able to focus better energy on the issues with her father. Simply, by this point in Katy'a growth a a woman mature, she had concluded that there just had to be an explanation about the scandal and Purple Waters. For the Si Fields that Katy knew - although pumped with ego and almost always high on scotch - had enough pride and integrity to fill the Pacific Ocean repeatedly. Katy was certain that he wouldn't have purposely hurt her or ruined her career. It made no sense! Si Field's was also the only family that she had left, and she needed resolve more so than ever and would soon need to try to reconnect...

By the following spring, Katy had been on Canadian soil for over a year and a half, and she was running out of money. After several sleepless weeks of tossing and turning, unsure of where to go or what to do to make a living, she made a hard decision. She fabricated a resume, purchased a secondhand mountain bike, and after searching several job sites on the internet, cycled to Rocky Mountain Estates to apply for a job as a landscaper. She had concluded that the fresh air and exercise might clear her head and allow her a few more months to write, until she decided what was next. When she landed the job her first question was "What was next?"

So what *was* next? she wondered again this very afternoon as an anxious wind skittered recklessly across the Estates, blowing dirt into her face and mouth. She wiped her tongue and then her lips with the back of her glove. Then she gripped the shovel tightly and continued to dig.

But her hands ached and her arms felt unusually heavy, and her feet throbbed under her boots. Minutes later the familiar ghastly buildup of bile crawled into her throat, and she dropped the shovel in exhaustion. Letting out a forlorn sigh, she looked up to the sky. The fatigue, or wind, or perhaps other thoughts that just wouldn't leave her had put her into a major funk, and silently, she begged for something. A sign, a break, perhaps even a miracle, to take her forward, beyond this shit-ass existence that she had made of her life. Her eyes traveled across the dark sky as she searched for the sun. Finally, when she realized that any chance of summer was hidden deep in the turmoil above, her eyes darkened as she spotted a large, dark gray mast of cloud threatening the west horizon, and she hoped it wouldn't rain. But it was raining! she thought. Even when it was sunny it felt as if it was raining!

As she began digging again, Rory's words wouldn't leave her, and for the first time in thirty-nine years, she realized how frightened she was of the truth.

"What do you do in the winter?"

"For work, what do you do in the winter?"

This question had forced Katy to look to the future, instead of the past - an exercise that she wasn't yet prepared to conquer.

"Why are you digging *there* woman?"

Katy looked up in surprise. Rory had left an hour earlier to fix a broken valve that she discovered that very morning. She had thought that he would be gone much longer. She opened her mouth to explain, but Rory's impatient was glaring.

"Shit, Katy! The point is over *here*," he said pointing about two feet from where she stood.

"Shit," she mumbled under her breath. "I thought this was the mark," she said, pointing to a pink flag in the ground near the hole that she was digging.

"That's from last year, Katy!"

It was the first time Rory's voice reeked with annoyance. "Geez, woman, you're makin' too much work for us!"

Instantly, Katy filled with frustration. It was a challenge keeping up with the rest of the crew. They were all bigger and younger than she was, and most of them men, and she was tired and sore. She needed to pay closer attention, she thought. She inhaled deeply as unwelcome tears filled her eyes.

Rory missed the salt and soot that rolled down her cheekbones and onto her lips, for her head was turned toward to the pink flag, and her defeat was hidden under her pumpkin-orange baseball cap. Still, he could see that her stature had imploded. Her square shoulders had fallen. He sensed her helplessness, or fatigue, and realized that she probably needed a break. His face softened. he opened his mouth to suggest that they take a break, but Katy spoke first.

"I need a coffee," she said, quickly brushing her cheek and her lips with the back of her glove. She had tried to sound strong and tough. However, the blisters on her heels and toes were unbearable. She could feel the blood seeping through her socks. She knelt down, unlaced her boots, and gently pulled her boots off, and then her socks.

"Man!" Rory whistled. "What happened to your foot?"

She looked down to the small, but open bleeding sores and shrugged. As if to say "no big deal". But she knew what Rory was referring to. The scar on her foot was now a part of her. Sometimes, not always, she almost forgot that it was there. It was a deep reddish-purple bubble of healed burn, covering her arch and spreading to her little toe. "It's just a burn," she replied nonchalantly. "It's the blisters that are hurting," she adding, shrugging. "I just need my feet to get air for a sec."

"I have some Polysporin and fresh Band-Aids in the first aid kit," Rory offered.

"No," she shook her head. "Not necessary."

"Let's put a Band-Aid on it," Rory said in a fatherly tone. Moments later he handed her a tub of Polysporin and four small Band-Aids that he pulled from the first aid kit from the back of the Chevy.

"Thanks."

She bandaged up quickly, as quickly as she was able, and pulled on her boots.

"Let's grab a coffee," Rory offered, adding, "I'll buy. I need real coffee today. Let's go to Starbucks. It's gonna pour," he added as he glanced up to the dark mast above. "No one will miss us."

As the Chevy purred down the freeway Katy remembered something. "I forgot to tell you. It looks like something might be wrong with the trees on the southeast quadrant. I noticed it when I was pruning them this morning."

"Which trees?"

"All of the ones on the farthest edge of the property. I think they are in trouble."

"What kind of trouble?"

"At least half of this tree's new needles are curling. Also, many of the older needles are turning a brownish or purplish color." She thought that she had seen the color change last week, but it was so slight, she had ignored it, thinking that it was fertilizer.

Rory glanced at her out of the corner of this eye. “Fertilizer. Probably a reaction. They were fertilized ‘bout a month ago. They’ll pick up.”

Katy hesitated, for fear of sounding like a know-it-all, or ridiculously stupid, she wasn’t sure. “I don’t think so,” she responded cautiously. Instinct and experience told her that she was probably right. She struggled to find an easy explanation, but when one didn’t come, she mumbled something about research on environmental contamination.

“Research?” Rory asked suspiciously. “What kind’a research?”

Katy hesitated again. The very last thing she wanted to do that afternoon, or any afternoon for that matter, was to explain her career, or how it had failed. It would be too painful and embarrassing. And it would consume energy - energy that she didn’t have to waste.

“It doesn’t matter,” she finally retorted in a tone that sounded more impatient then she had intended. “But Rory, I think that someone else should take a look.”

Rory’s face filled with a slight annoyance, or frustration, with her vague answer. “Doesn’t sound like anything much to me!” he retorted with a shrug.

“Look,” she snapped back. “If these were my trees, which they are not, I would have someone qualified to look at them. Test the dirt. I think that they might have been poisoned!”

Rory jerked his head towards Katy. “Poisoned! How would you know what to look for?” he asked with squinted eyes.

Katy hesitated. “Just trust me? I’ve been here before,” adding, “different story, same problem.”

It wasn’t how Katy had poised the question - or its magnitude. It was both the frustration *and* the sincerity that Rory heard in her voice, and he sensed that he should trust her. “Okay,” he said. Just “Okay”.

"I'm sure it's either poison, or some sort of environmental contamination," she added.

Rory's eyes opened wide in surprise. Then he whistled softly. "Shit, man. Don't think anyone at the Estates wants to hear that their multimillion dollar investment is in trouble."

"Multimillion?"

"Yeah. Stein Morretti has always spent a whack of dough on the landscaping. For show. Hardly think they give a shit 'bout them trees, but I know they spent a whack of dough on the landscaping. I think I heard someone say that it had already hit over two mil."

Katy's eyes widened at the estimated cost. She'd had no idea.

"Did you notice any problem on the other quadrants?"

"No," Katy replied slowly, and then shrugged. "But I wasn't looking. Besides, it has been three days since I've been on the southwest end. Three days can do a lot..."

"Let's get our coffee, and then we'll take a look at the other sections. Maybe we need to go and tell Randy."

"Randy?"

"Chief Foreman."

"Of course!" she said, remembering the good-looking but nervous and apparently anxious Randy, and the initial doubt in his eyes when she had applied for the job. "So," he had said dryly after he had finished glancing over her resume, "are you an admin assistant turned landscaper or a landscaper turned admin assistant?"

Katy remembered wondering if Randy was being sarcastic or trying to be funny. Regardless, there was no question that when Randy heard that the Estates' two million dollars worth of trees might be in danger that this would raise his anxiety level.

But what if I am wrong? she wondered as Rory steered the five-ton down towards the outdoor mall on the edge of town. And how was Randy going to react when *she* delivered such a thing?

"Look," she said quietly, "I shouldn't have said anything. I'm only guessing."

As Rory shut off the engine, his voice filled the cabin air with accusation. "Sounds to me that those bar tending jobs in the winter have taught you quite a bit more than how to make a Margarita," he said coolly. Before Katy could respond, he slammed his door shut, and his thick legs plodded toward the entrance to the coffee shop.

Within an hour, they had toured the three other quadrants. As both sets of eyes surveyed the tree wells, and often, the slightly yellowed treetops, they would both shake their heads in concern.

Stein Morretti's offices were bustling with builders and contractors, and the telephones were a constant. The young receptionist looked frustrated and unaware of their arrival as she answered the busy switchboard

"I need to see Randy," Rory explained as the pretty, young receptionist stopped them in their tracks, with a glare young, but accusing.

"And you are?" she asked as she ended a telephone call, and with more conviction in her voice than her years.

"I'm Rory, Landscape Foreman…" Rory started to explain just as Randy appeared around the corner with a pile of file folders in his arms.

"Yo! Randy!" Rory belted, raising his hand to get his boss's attention.

"I'm in the middle…" Randy began, shaking his head. "On a deadline…"

"I think you need to hear this," Rory replied gravely.

Recognizing some sense of urgency, Randy motioned them to a small meeting room down the hall from reception. As he listened to their concerns a look of impatience filled his eyes.

"Its the fertilizer," he replied nonchalantly.

Katy shook her head. "I don't think so... I am not positive, but I think it might be worth you taking a look. I think that there is a possibility that the firs have been poisoned."

Randy sighed dramatically. "I'm meeting with Tony later today. I'll pass it on," he added nonchalantly, as if it was nothing. Then Katy and Rory were dismissed with the wave of his hand as he answered a call from his mobile.

At about four that afternoon, Katy and Rory were installing a new irrigation pipe of the southeast quadrant when Randy's cherry-red Jeep with a red and platinum "Stein Morretti" logo on its doors pulled up.

"Yo!" Rory hollered as he pulled himself up from the dirt.

Randy didn't take the time to make formal introductions, except for, "This is Tony Morretti. The boss. We've got a busy afternoon and we have one minute."

"So what's going on?" the Morretti of Stein Morretti asked Rory.

"She can explain," Rory replied dryly, motioning to Katy.

Instantly, Katy felt unnerved. "I'm *not* positive," she began cautiously as she motioned towards the nearest fir. "It's slight - but look closely. Some of the needles are turning a brownish and purplish color. It's very faint. Here! Look!"

Her hand pointed to the midsection of the tree closest to her. She reached for a branch with new growth "These new needles are growing with a slight curl to them. A sign that they aren't healthy. We inspected the other three quadrants and many of the other trees are showing all of the same signs."

Tony took off his glasses and moved closer to Katy to get a better look. He squinted as his hand grabbed the same branch Katy was holding. He looked very closely and then took a step abc before studying the bearer of bad news with a great deal of cynicism spread across his face.

"This is not from the fertilizer," Katy plodded.

"Then what the hell do you suggest it is from?" Tony asked with squinty eyes.

"It is from some other chemical, I would guess."

"Are you implying the dirt is bad?"

"Perhaps."

"Are you implying that it's bad like polluted?" Tony's eyes had narrowed to slits.

"I am saying that I think you should get a soil test, just to make sure."

"A dirt test!" Randy exploded. "All the environmental testing was done over two years ago. This land is clean as a whistle!"

"Look," Katy said acs calmly and evenly s possible. "I'm not an expert in this. But I have seen it before..." As she spoke, she realized how unconvincing she sounded.

"Jeez!" Randy exploded, turning to Tony. "I don't have the time..."

Tony held up his hands. "I'd like to hear what she has to say," he said calmly, but his eyes still held the same look of doubt from moments before. "You're not an expert but you've seen it before? What exactly does that mean? What exactly *is* your experience with poisoned trees?"

What a ridiculous way to phrase the question Katy thought, instantly realizing that the only way to get out from under was to expose herself by qualifying her story. "I have an undergrad in Environmental Planning and Horticulture," she replied.

She could feel Rory shuffle in his boots. She purposely avoided looking in his direction and maintained her focus on Tony.

"From where?"

"Princeton."

"Shit!" Rory muttered under his breath. Katy guessed that her last comment had topped the day. She looked his way to find his eyes, as if to explain, but his head was down and he was shaking his head in disbelief.

"Princeton?" Tony exclaimed. "Know it well. My son is at Princeton."

And that was that. A minute later Randy and Tony were speeding away down the dirt road, and Katy and Rory continued in silence and connected the valve.

"There," Katy said, when they were done. She stood up and rubbed her hands together to warm them. It was getting chilly. She looked up to the sky. It was now a full, grayish-black mass.

"It feels like it might snow," she said, half to herself, but loud enough to get a response from Rory.

Rory ignored her. Instead, he began hastily collecting the tools that were scattered on the ground and throwing them into the toolbox.

"Man," she muttered quietly, under her breath. She shouldn't have mentioned a thing. One way or another, the trees would survive, or they wouldn't. "Man," she whispered again, angry at herself for opening up Pandora's Box. As she took a deep breath and began to help Rory the sky, as if grumbling from the weight of the day, belted in complaining thunder. Then without another warning a heavy downpour dropped from the darkness.

Chapter Eight

The door to the room with the boxes marked Charlie and Sarah and Marshall remained closed until ten o'clock the following evening. Quite simply, Marshall procrastinated and then delayed some more until the eleventh hour neared. Thomas was on standby for Marshall's call, be it good news or bad.

This time Marshall began in the corner of the storage room with the boxes marked "Sarah", and for almost four solid hours he dug through them one by one. He found music sheets and greeting cards, newspaper announcements bragging births, tin cans overflowing with buttons and beads, old costume jewelry and hats and musty mink collars.

When he found a silky red dress in a clear plastic bag and he instantly recognized it as something oddly familiar. He unzipped the bag and his fingers curled themselves around the silky, soft material. He gently pulled it out of the bag and held it up to his nose. It still smelled of Sarah, he thought whimsically, and then he held it up to the light. As his eyes fell from the delicate straps to the dancing neckline to the whimsical hem he tried to envision how Sarah had looked in it, or where she might have worn it, but his mind drew a blank. Then he wondered why she had boxed this very dress in the storage room when all of her other clothes were still hanging in her closet...

These questions left Marshall feeling unsettled and empty. His eyes were dark and vague as he folded the dress and then caressed it, once, and then again, before placing back in the bag with the zipper. Then for several minutes he sat very still and stared at nothing in particular as he tried to find the willingness to continue.

By two o'clock the following morning Marshall was still empty handed; he hadn't found one piece of information that would take him closer to Charlie's child. Mentally and physically exhausted, he limped upstairs to the master bedroom, fell asleep within minutes, and slept for five solid hours. He would have slept longer, he tried to sleep longer, but at just before seven, a soft but insistent knocking awoke him.

Knock knock.

Knock knock knock knock.

Marshall opened his eyes and groaned as he envisioned the relentless cat sitting on the other side of the door. He pulled the thin blanket over his head and tried to go back to sleep, but Jazz knocked again, and then again. Scowling, Marshall crawled out of bed and limped across the floor toward the very door that Jazz sat behind. Just as his hand touched the door knob he changed his mind.

He had a shower, brushed his teeth, and doctored and dressed his seeping wound with the bandages and gauze that he had eventually found. He changed the sheets on the bed. He tossed the dirty linens and strewn towels into the hamper. He opened the blinds and windows to let in fresh air. He even dusted the tops of the dressers and night tables with the orange oil that Sarah had always used. It took him a few minutes to find it, but it was exactly where she had left it, under the bathroom vanity.

The entire time Marshall whistled a tune he didn't know. He hadn't whistled for years and found an odd comfort in the sound, in part because it droned out the tenacious cat.

Knock knock.

Knock knock knock.

Eventually, the knocking subsided and Marshall smiled in satisfaction. The cat had run out of piss and vinegar, he thought, quite pleased with himself. When he opened the door, Jazz was nowhere to been seen. Marshall guessed that Jazz would eventually pay him back in one shape or form. He couldn't have been more correct.

As Marshall made a pot of coffee he placed a call to The Bayshore Inn. The front desk transferred his call to the Sinclair's room and an older woman's voice answered the telephone on its first ring.

"Good morning!"

"Yes, good morning. It's Marshall Stein. Is Thomas there?"

"Oh," the woman gushed, "this is Cecelia Sinclair, Mr. Stein. Thank you so kindly for your gift," she bubbled. "Thank you so very much! It's quite a lovely hotel! I'll get my husband for you. Thank you again Mr. Stein!"

"You are welcome," Marshall replied, but he wasn't sure who heard his words, for Thomas spoke into the phone almost instantly. "Well, Mr. Stein, you must have found something!"

"No. No, I haven't. What about you?"

"Mr. Stein, we only arrived yesterday afternoon. Changed our flights. I have hardly had a chance to pee!"

"Oh." Marshall sounded disappointed.

"We're going for breakfast. We are told they have a wonderful buffet downstairs. It's not free, mind you, like the Inn, but Cecelia has her heart set on the feast. Then we will go for a short stroll on the Sea Wall and then I am dropping her off to visit..."

"That's fine!" Marshall interrupted. "I don't need to hear your itinerary. I didn't realize that you only just got there."

"Today is Friday. We last spoke on Tuesday. I said that I would leave Wednesday, but we didn't leave until yesterday. I changed the hotel booking, so no need to worry about that. You see, our granddaughter..."

"That's fine. Fine." Marshall interrupted again. He had never had time for petty details. "Just call me the moment you have any news."

"Yes, of course. But I should warn you, we are here until Tuesday. I booked a few extra couple of days. I thought, seeing as we are here we might as well take some time to enjoy it. Cecilia heard about this lovely tea house on Robson Street. Or perhaps it is Bernard Street? I must check this. Nevertheless, I also have my heart set on visiting some of the pawn shops. It's been a bit of hobby of mine since I retired, so I suppose..."

Marshall's eyes opened wide in disbelief. "Thomas! You don't need to give me your life story! I'm simply looking for some answers. Call me when you have them."

"Yes, I understand," Thomas explained, "but I'll be working on and off between now and Tuesday afternoon when we have to leave for the airport. I am simply telling you this so that you don't worry if you don't hear from me right away."

"Fine. Got it." Marshall replied and hung up the phone.

Moments later, a sharp ringing filled the air. Marshall's telephone hardly rang anymore, and the sound made him jump. It was Thomas, now sounding flustered and very apologetic. "Mr. Stein, I apologize for disturbing you. But I should explain to you that we are checking out of this hotel tomorrow morning. Not that we aren't enjoying it here. We most certainly are. You have quite the taste, sir! But we don't want to take advantage of a good thing. However, rest assured that you can find us at The Holiday Inn on Broadway."

Just as Marshall hung up the phone, Jazz entered the kitchen and let out a loud complaint as he neared his empty food dish. Marshall looked down to the cat, then to the dish and then to the floor. Then his gaze fell to his injured foot and his eyes lit up in anger.

"I'll feed you one more day," he said as he glared at Jazz. "And I'll put cream on you one more day. Then you are off to the pound!"

Jazz struggled as Marshall held him on his lap and rubbed the cold cream over his dry, pink skin. When he was just about done, Jazz lifted his head and with all of his might bit Marshall's forearm. Tiny blood spots instantly oozed from the teeth marks as Marshall yelped out in pain. Within seconds Marshall was dialing 411 and swearing profoundly.

"I need a number to the pound!" he demanded to the computer-generated voice.

"What city or province?" the voice recognition system requested.

"Calgary! Alberta!"

"Thank-you," the recorded voice replied after a pause. "Would you like a business or a residential number?"

"Business!" Marshall shouted. "The pound!" he added quickly as his face reddened in frustration.

Again, the recorded voice paused. "I'm sorry, but I didn't hear you. Did you want a business or a residential number?"

"I want the number to the damn pound!" Marshall shouted again.

After another brief silence, the recorded voice returned. "I think you said you want the number to Goddard's Parking. Is this right?"

"No!" Marshall exploded. "That is not right. This is insane!"

After another moment of silence, the recorded voice prompted Marshall to be patient. "Please wait for an operator to assist you."

The instant he heard a live operator he raged into the phone again. "I need a number to the pound!" he demanded angrily.

"I'm sorry sir?"

Marshall's eyes fell to Jazz, who was hovering in hallway that led to the foyer. Steel blue eyes glared back at him in defiance as Marshall's own glazed over in rage. "I need the number to the dog pound. Cat pound. I need someone to get a damn cat out of my house!" he demanded.

"What is the name of the business that you are looking for?" the female operator asked very curtly.

Marshall's eyes went wild as he slammed down the phone.

Except for Marshall's conviction that Jazz had to go and the ensuing anger that came with this, the rest of the morning went almost exactly as it had the following evening. After drinking a full pot of coffee, Marshall returned to the storage room to continue the search.

However, after going through at least two dozen more boxes, he came up empty-handed - again. Hungry and at odds, he devoured a ham and cheese sandwich and then stretched out on the sofa in parlor in fatigue, falling asleep within minutes. At just before six o'clock his telephone rang for the second time that day, pulling him out of a deep sleep.

This time it was Tony.

"You sleeping?"

"Hell, no," Marshall grumbled. "Reading," he added, instantly wondered why he would lie about such a thing.

"What are you reading?"

"Some book I found in the basement."

Tony knew Marshall Stein better than almost anyone, and was well aware that Marshall was extremely well read and picky with his choice of readings. Marshall would never waste a moment with "some book."

"Sure," Tony said in chagrin. "But I'd put the book down for a moment. She just called me again. Expect a call."

Marshall's eyes opened wide in surprise. "Thanks Morretti," he said as he looked around the room for his cell phone. It was sitting on the end table, exactly where he had left it the day he had bought it, connected to its charger.

"Are you finding your way back to us, my friend?" Tony replied, aware that Marshall had not called him "Morretti" in a long, long time.

Marshall waited with bated breath for the next few hours. Several times he checked his phone for new messages - or to see if he had missed a call. And several times his eyes roamed to the Tarkay painting on the wall behind Sarah's piano and he would remember what was behind it, in the safe. It had been out of sign for almost nine years, but it was never out of mind

. . .

"What do you mean, you are going to pack your things? We still have two more nights together." What the hell was she talking about? Marshall thought.

"Marshall," she sighed as she twirled a strand of honey hair around her finger.

"Don't tell me that you were called on another assignment?" Marshall could hardly believe this. How he had planned for this weekend to be perfect! Only for her to get called for another assignment? "Just quit your job!" he insisted.

"Oh, Marshall..." she said softly as tears filled her eyes.

Marshall leaned towards and gently caressed her shoulder. "You can't leave today," he whispered. "I..." he stopped and cleared his throat. "I love you. You make me feel alive."

"Oh, Marshall!" she exclaimed as she placed her hand firmly on top of his. "Marshall, something quite beautiful did happen today!" Her dewy eyes turned bright. "I bumped into someone today, Marshall. I met him a long time ago. It has been years since I have seen him...Marshall, he isn't married. He's free to travel. And he is a writer, like me! It's quite remarkable. I almost knocked him over in Macy's as I was hurrying back to meet you here."

Marshall's muscular body sagged with each word, and his face had begun to feel hotter by the moment. He wiped his brow and then looked down to her hands. Both of her soft, smooth hands were resting on his, preventing him from touching her.

"I think I am going to marry him Marshall," she continued so matter-of-factly, Marshall's jaw dropped.

"He is tall and dark and handsome, just like you," she continued. "And he is single. He doesn't have a perfect family or wife, as you do," she added in a whisper. "I told myself the moment he spoke that if he was still single I would learn to love him almost as much as I love you."

Marshall closed his eyes tightly, and dropped his chin to his chest. "I love you too," he wanted to say again, but he couldn't find the strength to speak.

He felt her pull herself up from the bed. He opened his eyes and watched her move toward the window. Dusk hovered outside, and the room suddenly felt cold and very dark. He shivered as he searched her profile for something to help him understand what he needed to say to assure her that he wanted her and that she should stay.

"I'm leaving Marshall," she finally hushed. "I'm packing my bags and leaving. I love you, Marshall, oh I do!" she cried out softly. "Sometimes, I could hardly believe that we met... and I know that we were made for one another."

Then she turned to face him, and her stature had turned defiant. "But I never thought it was for forever. And you never thought it was forever. And God forbid, I never thought that I would destroy a marriage! Or a perfect family! I couldn't live with myself if I did that! Not after what I lived through. Not after everything that I said I wouldn't be!"

"This is crazy." Marshall felt nauseous.

Her next words came out in a husky, dark whisper. "You don't want *me*, Marshall! You want the fantasy of what we had in these past three months. Go back to your wife, Marshall. She sounds like a remarkable, strong, beautiful woman that deserves so much more than this!"

Marshall remained silent as she began to pack her suitcase. Then he watched from the reflection of the mirror as she showered and dressed, combed her long beautiful hair and then put on blush and lipstick. By the time she had slung her purse over her shoulders and slipped on her shoes, Marshall's disbelief and despair had turned to a numb anger.

"I wouldn't be surprised if he has more money than me," he said thickly from the bed.

She moved to the foot of the bed. "I told you I never wanted anything from you," she replied quietly. "I never wanted your money. I certainly don't want his." Suddenly, she chuckled. "I don't even know if he has any money. For all I know he is a poor journalist."

Marshall sneered. "Do you know his name?"

"Do I know his name!?"

"This is ridiculous."

"This is life, Marshall," she said very sadly. Then she nodded, as if she had just made a decision. "And in about twenty minutes, I am meeting him for dinner. He covers political stories and stories of war and starvation. And, well, I can't imagine that we won't find something quite spectacular to talk about."

Then she walked to the side of the bed, leaning over and fondly rubbed Marshall's forehead. "Take care of yourself Spunk," she said, fondly kissing his on the lips. Then she rolled her suitcase towards the door.

"Do you know his name!" Marshall demanded again, this time with little fire left in his voice.

"His *name*?" she said huskily. "His name is Charles."

And then she was gone.

. . .

Chapter Nine

Unlike Marshall Stein, Katy welcomed the chant-like song from the river. She embraced its tune, relished its message. She didn't understand the words, and most times they were barely audible as they travelled from the river's bridge to her apartment windows. However, she knew it was beckoning resolve - and it touched a place inside of her that needed rekindling. It reminded her of the innocence of the early morning's sunrise. A mountain waterfall the color of white pop. The first smell of spring's arrival, that delicious scent that awakens your senses and makes you want to inhale repeatedly.

She knew the exact place the song was coming from. One night, a few weeks earlier, she had set her bike down in thick bush just off the pathway and walked around the bridge's old concrete walls to sit by the river. As her sneakers pushed through the foliage, she tripped over the corner of a mattress. As she tumbled onto a sleeping bag and bright red blanket, the smell of old urine instantly filled her nostrils, and she put her hand to her mouth. She struggled to find her feet, and then her eyes fell to the dirty mattress, oozing cotton batten, to a pile of faded magazines that filled a makeshift, cardboard box table. To the long, jagged concrete ledge and the neat collection of kitchen; a rusted cast iron pot, a can filled with utensils, seven or eight cans of food and several faded cereal boxes. Beside this, hanging from a jutting piece of concrete, was a blue dish rag. Directly below, on the ground, lay a porcelain washbasin. It was chipped and rusted, but the water it held looked crystal-clear, as if it had just been poured from the taps.

As she turned to leave, she caught a splash of yellow brightly painting the river's landscape. As she shaded her eyes from the evening sun her pupils widened in amusement. It was a large, stuffed Winnie the Pooh, and her lips turned up in a soft smile. The stuffed animal sat on a green faded lawn chair just feet from the river, positioned perfectly for a view of the flowing water below. It was *almost* the same view that Katy had from her balcony, she realized, and she looked up and over the concrete walls to the place that had become her home. At that moment she realized how close she could be to ending up here if she didn't get her act together, and for a brief second was overwhelmingly thankful that she was where she was.

When she had returned to Calgary after being fired and the warehouse fire, only two days later, she had less than five thousand dollars to her name. Student loans and bad investments had left her broke. Thus, to survive, she began to sell what she had left. Five suitcases of designer clothes were the first to go. Then one of her laptops, a portable laser printer, a digital camera... Eventually, she had no choice but to sell the one carat Princess diamond that Brad had given her when he proposed. She kissed it, as Brad had often done, before passing it across the counter to the goldsmith.

Sometimes, she could still *almost* feel Brad's breath on her neck. When sleep wouldn't come, she would sit on her balcony and beg the river to take away her pain, and to move her to a different place. Sometimes, when it wasn't too painful, she would pretend that he was sitting beside her, holding her hand, or brushing the hair away from her face with that tenderness that she used to embrace.

She thought of him then as her eyes roamed from her apartment back to the place that she stood and the dewy river that went on and on forever. She closed her eyes for a moment and took a small breath. Then, as she turned to leave, a child spoke.

“Do you live here?”

Katy’s eyes instantly found a little girl with a messy mop of golden hair that fell almost to her waist.

“Is this your house?” the sweet voice questioned as her thin legs pushed through the grass, towards Katy.

“My house?” Katy repeated as the child bravely neared. “No. No.” she answered slowly, noticing that the child was holding something in her hands.

“Well then,” the little girl continued quite confidently. “I’m here almost every day, and I still haven’t met the neighbor.”

Katy found the child’s choice of words odd. “The neighbor?” she repeated. “Do you live nearby?” she asked, looking behind the child, then down both sides of the riv-erbank for others.

The child’s eyes darkened with suspicion. “I live down there.” A small, slender fin-ger had lifted and was pointing somewhere towards the southeast. “But whoever *does* live here is quite tidy,” she continued as she stopped in the grass.

“Tidy?” Katy repeated in amusement as she found herself looking back, towards the vagrant’s home. “Yes, I suppose he is tidy.”

“Oh, it isn’t a he!” the little girl exclaimed. “It’s a lady!”

“How do you know it’s a lady?” Katy asked.

“Well,” the child began in a hush, “one day, after school – I come by this way al-most every day after school – she was sleeping. Her shoes were side by side next to the mattress. I couldn’t see her face, but I saw her feet. They were little feet.

Lady's feet. About your size!" she added as she looked down to Katy's running shoes.

Katy smiled as she kneeled down to meet the child's eyes; they were beautiful greens framed in thick, black lashes, a stunning contrast to the honey-colored hair. "Are you here by yourself?"

The child's eyes flickered before replying. "No," she said. "My mother is up there, on the bridge. She's waiting for me. She doesn't like it down here."

Katy glanced towards the empty bridge. Sensing that the child was lying, she began slowly. "Well," she said, "I hope that your mother knows that it isn't safe for little girls to play near the river by themselves, especially at night."

The child shuffled uncomfortably as her eyes dropped to the ground. Katy's own eyes traveled from untied white sneakers, up the thin body and the long, unkempt golden hair, then back down to a black and blue knee. "That's quite the bruise you have there. What happened to your knee?"

The child lifted her right leg. "Oh that! Its from volleyball. At my school."

"Really? Are you a good player?"

"No, I am always the last to be picked," she sighed and frowned. "I think because I am the shortest one on the team. But my teacher says when I hit the ball, I hit it the hardest." Her eyes lit up with tiny pride with these last words.

"Like me," Katy offered kindly. "I wasn't very good in sports, but I always tried my very best."

"Yes, that is what my Auntie tells me to do," the child sighed again.

"You know," Katy continued, instinctively concerned for the child's safety, "you have to be careful around here, especially late at night. You shouldn't be here alone. And you really shouldn't talk to strangers."

"You're a stranger," the child retorted.

"Yes, yes I am," Katy replied. "But my name is Katy and you can tell your mother that I live over there, in that brown apartment building." She pointed to her apartment complex over the bridge.

Silent, the child followed Katy's hand. "Do you have a balcony?"

"Yes."

"Then you can you see the woman from your balcony?"

"No. I can't see this side of the bridge from my balcony."

"Oh," the child murmured. "What number do you live in?"

"Number?" Katy asked. "Oh, apartment 222," she said quickly as she realized what the child was asking.

"222!" the child squealed in delight.

Katy nodded. "Yes. I can't see this side of the bridge, but sometimes late at night, or early in the morning, I hear the music from the river."

"What kind of music?"

"She sings. She has a very strong, beautiful voice."

"She does?" The stunning opals filled with curiosity. "What does she sing?"

"Well," Katy began slowly, not quite sure how to answer this question.

"Does she sing any songs from Harry Potter? Or Lion King?"

"Oh, I don't think so," Katy replied quickly, instantly hoping she wasn't luring the child to return for the song. "She sounds very pretty, but I don't think she sings songs that you would know."

The child's eyes shifted then, as if in recollection. "I was going to bring her something to eat tonight," she said sweetly, holding up a doll. "I don't think she has very much food… but I couldn't find anything that I thought she might like. So I brought Sally," she added, holding up a scraggly, red-haired rag doll.

By the looks of the child's thin, tight clothes and unkempt hair, it was obvious to Katy that she was neglected. Her orange cotton shorts were faded and frayed, and her white T-shirt was dirty and at least a size too small, enhancing the child's thin, bony shoulders.

"What's your name?" Katy asked, instantly feeling a great deal of compassion for the tiny package before her.

The child moved toward the cement ledge, to the pots and pans and boxes and cans of food. Katy watched as she stood on the tips of her toes and carefully positioned Sally on the concrete ledge, beside a faded box of cereal. "There!" she exclaimed proudly and put her hands on her hips. "She'll keep the lady company."

"She certainly will," Katy replied, suspecting the child had few dolls, then added, "Maybe Sally needs to be with you. I think that Winnie the Pooh keeps her company, don't you?"

"Oh, no!" the child retorted. "Winnie the Pooh only likes kids. He guards the fort. He doesn't keep her company! That's what Sally is for."

Darkness was soon coming, Katy thought. She asked the child if she could walk her to her mother. The child's eyes grew suspicious with this question. Katy thought that she would give a great deal to know what the young girl was thinking.

"No. I'll get in trouble. I'm not supposed to talk to strangers," the child replied very quietly, and then she turned to leave.

Katy remembered that she had put a cranberry granola bar in her shorts pocket. She pulled it out and took a few steps toward the child. "I can't eat this. Maybe you want it."

The child hesitated, but only briefly. Then her fingers grabbed the package from Katy's hand. She turned over the wrapper, once, and then again. "Oatmeal?" she asked, and faintly wrinkled her nose.

"Uh, yes. I think so. It's a granola bar."

The child hesitated again. "Maybe the lady would like it," she finally replied, nodding slightly toward the ledge.

Katy sensed the child's hunger. "I'll bring her another one tomorrow. It's really good and its not only oatmeal," she added, sensing the child's dislike. "It also has lots of fruit chunks."

"Well, okay," the child said, and then her small hands clumsily stuffed the granola bar in her shorts pocket. "Okay," she said, "I'll take it to school for lunch. I need all the energy I can get! It's a big day!"

"Why is it a big day?"

"I'm auditioning for the final melody in the band's last concert. And I need all the strength I can find."

"What do you play?"

"The piano!" the child cooed proudly. "I can't practice very much. My Auntie - I mean my mom," she corrected herself quickly, "doesn't have a piano. So I practice at school, when my teacher lets me."

"What song will you play?"

"Circle of Life. It's from Lion King. It's my favorite," she added as her face became very animated. "My Aunt Lynette said that maybe next year she will buy me a piano."

Aunt Lynette was the child's caregiver, Katy surmised then. And from the sight of the child, she also suspected that if this were the case, a year would do little to gift the child with a piano. She wondered if her Aunt had a job. Or if they had food in the fridge. Or if there was someone at home to tuck her into bed. She thought of prying, just a little bit further, but it was apparent that this child was older than her years and she didn't want to scare her away. Instead, she wished her good luck with her audition.

"Thanks! I'll need it!" the little girl replied with a great deal of enthusiasm as she turned again to leave.

"Do you remember where I live?" Katy asked.

"That's easy!" the child said proudly. "Apartment 222 is where my father left me." Then turning, she disappeared through the grass and trees and around the concrete walls of the bridge.

As Katy lifted her bike to the third floor landing, she heard Wanda, the skinny, platinum blonde that lived directly below her, shouting at the top of her lungs.

"The next time you go through my lingerie drawers, I'll call the police!"

"Sure you will!" Norm retorted back from somewhere below. "Bet they would like to see you!"

From somewhere below, a cat whistle echoed down the hallways and into the apartment walls. Everyone in the building knew that Wanda was a prostitute. They weren't whispers in the hallways about their neighbor; the apartment block didn't nurture *that* kind of gossip. It was the comings and goings of men in all shapes and sizes that spoke the truth; Katy had passed them several times since Wanda had moved in. Once, she even spotted Norm coming out of Wanda's apartment, doing up the zipper on his pants. She had sometimes wondered if Wanda paid her rent by serving Norm. She cringed at this very thought as she unlocked her apartment door.

She showered and dried herself off in the middle of the tiny kitchen, beside the sink, beside the tub. Then her calloused fingers rubbed cold cream on her neck and arms, and then her breasts. Her fingers caressed down further, to her thighs, and then her legs, and when they moved to her blistered feet, the old pipes in the walls squeaked and knocked about in a tiresome whine, and her eyes fell to the burn.

It looked like a Jackson Pollack painting she thought. Except its swirls of purplish-red were raw-like and ugly, unlike the artist's creations. It had healed long ago, but it would always look like an open wound - it would always remind her of where she had been - and what she had lost. She closed her eyes and prayed to no one in particular that she would move beyond this place. Beyond these four rotting walls of existence - to a world that she could embrace again.

She threw on a camisole and a pair of sweats, then wrapped a shawl around her shoulders. Moments later she stood on her balcony and peered south, past the Poplars and brush, towards the bridge. She thought of the little girl she had met that evening and hoped that she was asleep in a safe and warm bed. Then, oddly, her thoughts moved to Rory's four kids.

She felt guilty for all of her lies to the odd but interesting father of four. Every word she had spoken had been a lie! When had she become so - so *what*? she thought in a frown. Then she lifted her eyes to the sky and it's half-made moon and she remembered a day long past.

. . .

"You have to look up Katrina, beyond the sky."

Katy leaned into her father to feel his warmth. She lifted her head again as her dark brown eyes filled with confusion. "But all I see is the sky, Papa."

"Yes," Si Fields said patiently as he wrapped his arms around his daughter and pulled her into him. "But look again. You'll also see white balls of fluff."

Katy looked past the vast blueness that seemed to go on forever and ever and ever, finally squealing when she saw what he saw. "I see the fluffy white balls, Papa! I see them!" she squealed in delight.

"Those are the clouds. And sometimes, if you know exactly where to look, beyond the blue and deep into the white, you'll find more than what is there."

"What do you mean?" Katy asked innocently.

"Katrina, if you look hard enough, where ever you might look, you just might find magic."

. . .

"Magic!" Katy whispered sarcastically remembering her father's words from that buttery summer afternoon. Si Fields had always had a way of weaving fabricated hopes into her heart, she thought. No wonder she was such a mess!

Suddenly, the night's breeze turned from teasing to tenacious. As a gust of wind blew across the river's top, she shivered. She curled up in the lawn chair, and her chaffed hands pulled the shawl closer to her neck. As she stared past the rusting balcony railings, Si Fields face emerged again.

"What would you do, Si?" Katy demanded out loud. "What, exactly, would the pundit of words and hope do at a time like this? And how exactly, would you tell the truth, the absolute truth, so help you God?"

Chapter Ten

The following morning, Katy awoke to a sky the color of galvanized steel, and winds that angrily twisted the tree branches to and fro. As she cycled to the Estates, she thought that the gusts were strong enough to blow off children's hats, and make dogs bow their heads to shelter from its force. Pedaling against nature's force almost the entire way, she arrived almost fifteen minutes late, but it didn't matter. Just as she parked her bike it started to rain heavily, and Randy sent the entire crew home for the day.

Once at home, and dry and warm, Katy welcomed the storm, and the thunder and lightning entertained her into the early afternoon. The rumbling of the sky, followed by strings of light that danced across the darkness above took her mind off the present as she listened and watched in anticipation for its next performance. When the storm finally subsided, she turned on her computer and logged into her email account, instantly swearing under her breath as she read her inbox. Except for junk mail she had no new messages - and again, no word from Si. She had been trying to connect with him for months. And with his telephone disconnected, or his number changed, she wasn't sure, she had resorted to sending him emails.

The last message that she had sent him had read "Urgent" in the subject line. "Dad, I need to speak to you," she had begun.

Katy still relived her father's deception, but she needed resolve. She simply needed to connect with him - and as instinct kept repeatedly telling her that there had to be a valid explanation to what he had done - she knew that she needed to work - and work hard - at forgiving him.

Katy also sometimes still relived the massive warehouse explosion, but time had pushed these memories into her subconscious, for the most part, and they appeared mostly in her sleep. Screams that pulled her out of a sleep and the safety of Brad's loving arms. Fear pushing her adrenaline. Adrenaline pushing her fear. Angry blue and orange flames in the middle of the night. Dancing and taunting as the fire spread. Pleas for help. Begging for Brad...

. . .

The blaze of the Chelsea loft warehouse woke up the entire neighborhood and brought dozens of NYC's finest to battle the fire. It was one of the coldest nights of the winter, and as firefighters sprayed the old turn-of-the-century building, the water froze almost instantly and the aftermath was contrasting. Almost instantly the building was coated with a wonderland of ice. This, amidst the angry flames inside was a picture of destruction and beauty wrapped up in one. Some stood in awe, shivering in the cold, helpless and entrapped with the tragedy before them. Others cried for help. Some begged for restitution and the rescue of loved ones and pets.

Katy immediately began to scream Brad's name. He had been right behind her on the emergency stairs as they had tried to flee to safety with the others. As another explosion erupted, the ceilings started to fall just as her bare feet felt the cold sidewalk of Chelsea. Instantly, she realized that Brad was not right beside her as he should have been and she shrieked his name again and again.

"Brad! Brad! Brad!" she cried as the lights from the emergency vehicles shone forbiddingly through the falling snow.

One last fierce explosion destroyed what was remaining of the warehouse, and pieces of burning debris flew in all directions, falling from the sky and onto the street. The impact of the burning cinder that landed on Katy's barefoot threw her off balance. Collapsing to the sidewalk in pain she screamed Brad's name again.

. . .

Katy opened the patio doors and took a deep breath. She loved the smell of the river when it rained. It reminded her of newly cut green grass. Freshly pressed laundry. Softness opposed to darkness.

Her eyes fell to the pregnant river, overflowing from the day's storm as it traveled south and then the heavy leaves of the poplars and the soggy embankment of sand and rocks, and she inhaled again. She had planned on continuing with her manuscript, but it was such a perfect night for a walk. She quickly pulled on some pants and a hoodie and threw on a pair of sneakers. Just as she opened the front door she had a thought. She grabbed a package of cookies and a banana from the kitchen counter and headed toward the river.

As she neared the bridge's underground, her eyes instantly spotted the long mane of honey-gold hair. Apparently oblivious to her arrival, the little girl was crouched down near the river, beside Winnie the Pooh. Her hands were tying a bright, red raincoat around the bear's neck.

"There," Katy heard her say. "Now you won't get too wet."

Katy hesitated. She didn't want to alarm the child - or her scare her away.

"You should know better than to go outside without the right clothes," the child reprimanded gently.

Katy frowned. Instinctively she thought that she might find the child here. But what on earth was such a young thing doing out here so late - and all by herself? She looked back towards the mattress and the concrete ledge, then past these to both sides of the embankment, then up towards the bridge. There was no one else within sight, and Katy shook her head in dismay as she confirmed that the child was most certainly alone once again.

As she stepped through the wet grass, toward the river, she tripped on a log. "Ouch!" she exclaimed softly. When she lifted her eyes she found the child staring back at her.

"Hi," she said quietly.

The child hesitated. "Hi," she finally muttered.

"Remember me?"

Dark opals flickered in recognition. "Apartment 222," the child whispered shyly.

Katy moved towards the child. "That's a very nice thing for you to do for Winnie the Pooh."

Innocent eyes found Katy's. "I didn't want his fur to get too wet. In case it rains again tonight."

"I wonder if he is hungry," Katy said, pulling out the cookies and banana from her pocket.

"Oh, I think he is!" the child exclaimed as she licked her bottom lip. "He doesn't like those bars you gave me very much 'cause he doesn't like oatmeal. But he likes bananas!" she added in a grin as Katy handed her the snacks, "'And they're the same color as his fur!"

"I bet he wouldn't mind sharing those with you," Katy said as the child tucked the banana under her arm and then struggled to open the package of cookies.

"Let me open that for you…"

“I can do it,” the child replied quickly, and her long slender fingers broke open the plastic. Katy watched as she broke off a small piece and put it up to Winnie the Pooh’s mouth. “Hmm,” she cooed. “Chocolate, I think.” Then she quickly popped the piece of cookie into her mouth.

“Hmm,” she cooed again with a grin. “It is chocolate! My favorite!”

Katy studied the small pointy face and uncombed hair. “Is your mother up there? On the bridge?” she asked.

Black lashes flickered for a moment. “No,” the child replied quietly. “She’s working tonight. Until ten. But she said it was okay for me to bring Winnie the Pooh the raincoat. It came in a box of other clothes. Auntie said they were from the rich people. Old clothes that they didn’t need anymore. But most of them were for babies, even though they knew that I wasn’t a baby anymore.”

Katy’s eyes fell to white running shoes, the untied laces, the dirty white-gray socks. “I have an idea,” she began gently. “I have to go and visit a friend, just over there.” She pointed across the river in the same direction that the child had told her she lived. “Let’s walk together.”

The child hesitated. Then she looked down to the cookies in her hand. “Okay,” she said with a shrug. As she repositioned Winnie the Pooh back in his chair, she added in a grown-up voice as she kissed him on the forehead, “Now you behave and we will see you very soon.”

As they crossed the bridge and neared Katy’s apartment complex the child devoured the rest of the cookies. “Which one is your balcony?” she asked with a mouthful.

“It’s that one,” Katy answered as she pointed. “The one on this side. Second from the bottom.”

“Do you still hear the lady sing?”

“Sometimes.”

"What songs does she sing?"

"Oh, I'm not sure. But she's very good."

"I would like to hear her sing sometime."

Katy instantly grew alarmed. "She never sings when there are other people around," she lied cautiously, feeling an urging need to keep the child safe. "And sometimes, the police come and get her. I often hear the sirens from my apartment. They stop on this bridge and take her away."

"Why?" the child exclaimed as her eyes widened.

"Because she isn't supposed to live under the bridge," Katy explained patiently. "It's against the law. And the neighbors probably complain because she makes a lot of noise. If anyone was with her when they came, well! I suspect that the police would take them away too!"

Certain that she had put the fear of God in the child, and feeling somewhat guilty for doing this, Katy stayed just a step behind her for the next block to ensure that she would lead - she wanted to know where she lived. Katy continued to follow as the child turned south and they began to walk up a hill in silence.

"Your shoe laces have come untied," Katy finally offered. "Would you like me to tie them for you?"

The child stopped in her tracks and lifted one small foot toward the sky. "It's okay," she said. "I'm just about home. Silly things don't stay tied!" she added dramatically. "Aunt Lynette says that one day I'm going to trip over my own two feet!"

"Your Aunt Lynette takes care of you?"

"Yes, until my father comes back."

"Where is your father?"

"He went to work. In Abganston."

“Abganston?” Katy repeated, wrinkling her brow.

“You know, Abganston, where the President made the soldiers go.”

“Afghanistan!” Katy exclaimed. “Was your father in the army?”

“I don’t think so. He wrote stories.”

"Your father is a writer!" Katy exclaimed again. “Now that’s an interesting job.”

“Yes. My Auntie says that he is one of the very best.”

“Where does your Aunt Lynette work?”

The child’s eyes flirted up to Katy in suspicion. “Oh, she has a very important job too!” she said quickly. Too quickly. “She’s works very hard.”

Katy was positive that the child was fabricating the story and waited patiently for the rest of the lie to unfold. Instead, as she suspected might happen, too many questions bred another stretch of silence.

“Your father and Aunt Lynette are very lucky to have important jobs,” she offered in kindness.

“Where do you work?”

“I work at a company that builds houses. I help to keep the trees healthy and alive. I’m a landscaper.”

“That sounds like a very important job too,” the child lit up.

Katy smiled inwardly. “I suppose it is.”

They had reached the entrance to a driveway that led to a long row of fading brown town homes and the child stopped. “I am home,” she said.

Katy's eyes roamed from the driveway to peeling fences, neglected lawns and old weathered doors. "Can I walk you to your door?"

"No." the child replied and turned to leave.

Katy wished that she had more time with the child. She was so little and helpless, yet so grown up. "It was nice talking to you," she offered. "And thanks for the company. I often take a walk by myself. It was great have someone to walk with. Maybe," she continued, "I can have your telephone number." Something told her not to let the child go, just yet. "Then the next time I go for a walk by the river, you can join me. With your aunt's permission, of course!"

Dark opals narrowed in suspicion. "We don't have a phone. And besides, I'm not supposed to talk to strangers."

"I understand," Katy replied, nodding in agreement. "I completely understand. But if you want to tell your aunt where I live, maybe you can come and visit?"

A glimmer of hope filled the child's eyes briefly, but was quickly replaced with a look of confusion - or fear - Katy wasn't sure. She suspected that she had drilled the child enough for one night - but she desperately wanted some answers. "What's your name?" she asked softly. "It would be good to know your name, in case you and I see one another again."

"Zig," the child hushed shyly.

"Zig! What a nice name! Do you remember my name?" Katy asked.

The child thought for a moment. Then she shook her head.

"My name is Katy."

Zig hesitated for a moment. "Well, by Katy," she finally said, and waving goodbye, skipped across the parking lot and its collection of older vehicles. Katy watched until the honey-gold hair disappeared behind the tired vehicles and weathered doors.

. . .

It rained hard again that evening and into the early morning. The day was unusually wet and cold for June, the Estates felt dreary and dismal, and Katy was in a funk. Rory was uncharacteristically distant and cold - he had hardly acknowledged her that morning, and had dropped her off at the far edge of the southwest quadrant without saying a word.

At just before noon, he picked her up for their lunch break with the same icy attitude, only to drop her off at the old log cabin that the crew used for their breaks and sped away in the truck.

Katy sighed. She was tired and damp. And she felt confused and guilty. She knew that she owed Rory an explanation. She owed him the truth. But what would this look like? And how much information did she need to share to validate herself?

As she started climbing the muddy pathway that led to the cabin a horn honked, and then honked again and again. She turned to find a black BMW headed in her speeding in her direction and she stopped and waited.

Moment later Tony Morretti and another fellow got out of the car. "Randy said you were in the southeast quadrant," Tony began in a tone thick with impatience. "We've been looking for you."

Katy swung her duffle bag over her shoulder. "We just came from there. Rory just dropped me off for lunch."

"How could we have missed you? We would have passed you on the same road," Tony's hand waved impatiently toward the road that they had just travelled.

"We sometimes take the side roads," Katy explained.

"Sure," Tony replied thickly, as if to say it didn't matter which road they took. "More importantly, this is Marshall Stein, the 'Stein' of Stein Morretti. We need to ask you a couple of questions."

Chapter Eleven

Marshall arrived unannounced and unexpected at Rocky Mountain Estates that morning. Tony's secretary had confirmed with him half an hour prior that Tony was on the site - but Tony wouldn't answer his land line or he cell phone and Marshall put two and two together. The moment he pulled up to the Stein Morretti offices and spotted Tony's BMW, he knew that his premonition was probably right. Over the years, when he wasn't able to get a hold of Tony, for Tony was almost always accessible, it meant that he was either dealing with deadlines or a pressing issue of the day.

However, Marshall wasn't concerned about Tony's latest agenda, or any ensuing problems or deadlines at the Estates. The fact was that Thomas' latest call that very morning had brought the mystery of the missing child and her mother a little closer to a head, and Marshall was ecstatic. Thomas had found proof that the child existed, and one that was his own flesh and blood. Marshall simply needed to talk to someone. He needed his friend.

Tony looked shocked to see Marshall standing at the door to the large planning room. “Marshall?” he said in disbelief as he looked up from dozens of site plans strewn across the boardroom table.

“Have a minute?”

Tony’s eyes were heavy with fatigue, a sign to Marshall that the workaholic was again going beyond the status quo. However, the moment Tony opened his mouth to answer, Marshall sensed that Tony’s fatigue was from more than just a few hard days work or sleepless nights.

“I have trouble,” Tony hushed grimly.

Marshall shook his head selfishly, but honestly. “I don’t have the energy. I’m retired. And I‘m not here on business.”

Tony stood up from the table. “I’m talking potentially catastrophic trouble,” he said gravely, and grabbed Marshall’s arm and led him to his office.

Tony closed his office door and began pacing between his desk and the window. Suddenly unsettled, Marshall’s eyes fell to the landscape of the development outside. He briefly mused at the fleet of vehicles and the construction in the distance. It looked familiar, like the back of his hand, and for a moment he reminisced. Flashes of several other developments that Tony and he had created over the years resurfaced, as if in a movie... It was the first time that Marshall felt a pang of remorse - or perhaps melancholy about stepping down.

“This whole thing could come crashing down on me within days,” Tony exploded.

Tony's words instantly pulled Marshall back to the room. Except for when he was in his sales mode, forever positive Tony never embellished a thing. The comment “This whole thing could come crashing down on me within days,” was as uncharacteristic a comment as Tony could have made. Something serious must have happened, Marshall surmised.

“What’s going on?”

Tony quickly explained the signs of death oozing from the firs.

Marshall squinted his eyes in thought. “Too much fertilizer?”

Tony’s eyes were dark and brooding. “Fertilizer? Shit no! Looks like it’s coming from the dirt!"

“The dirt? Are you talking an environmental problem?” Marshall asked. As he spoke, he thought how absurdly ridiculous his question. Developers had to comply with municipal and provincial guidelines, and conduct environmental testing for contaminants, prior to obtaining permits or beginning any construction. Stein Morretti had always gone the extra mile and obtained the most trustworthy testing from the most respected companies in the industry. They had also been one of the most aggressive in the country at implementing internal environmental policies and procedures and executing environmentally friendly and energy efficient developments. Most in the industry recognized Stein Morretti as leading edge when it came to any building or operational component that touched the environment.

Tony fell into his leather chair. “Environmental problem? Yeah, maybe,” he replied as he pulled off his glasses and rubbed his eyes.

Instantly, Marshall had a suspicion. “You didn’t take any short cuts, did you?”

Tony avoided Marshall’s eyes, and silently shuffled a few folders across his desk.

“Tell me, my friend, that you didn’t take any shortcuts?” Marshall asked quietly.

Tony looked up to Marshall and laughed. It was a high-pitched nervous sound that seemed to go on forever, turning his face and neck the color of the Stein Morretti fleet of vehicles.

For the first time since his retirement Marshall was more concerned for someone else then he was for himself. His gut told him something was seriously wrong. "Tony, what's going on?"

Tony looked at Marshall through tired, bloodshot eyes. "Sit down," he said hoarsely.

Marshall had been instrumental in acquiring the dozens of pockets of properties on the once sprawling countryside. He had assertively and successfully convinced every owner that the time was right to sell, the price was right, and that Stein Morretti had a master plan that would benefit everyone. However, Marshall had sold out of the business just as the master vision was approved and since then, had no idea of how things were going.

Tony gravely brought Marshall up-to-date. By the time he was finished, Marshall's face was almost as contorted with stress as Tony's. Tony had breached the cardinal rule and turned a blind eye on one of the most important aspects in planning a community. Once the first signs of environmental contamination had surfaced, Tony had made a move that could cost him everything that he had worked for.

"You paid Greenstay Environmental to forge the final environmental assessments?" Marshall whispered in disbelief.

Tony stared at Marshall in defiance. "Greenstay was absolutely positive that the problem wasn't that deep," he replied, shrugging his shoulders. "Nothing even potentially health threatening. Just a few chemicals in the dirt, primarily concentrated in the northwest quadrant. I couldn't afford to stall for another year while we proved this to the city."

"Northwest quadrant," Marshall repeated. That was the Billingsgate Ranch for thirty years."

Tony was shaking his head. "Apparently prior to Billingsgate an oil and gas company owned the land. They dumped their shit there for almost a decade."

Marshall looked shocked. "You knew this?"

"Everyone knew this Marshall! But Greenstay was emphatic that it was insignificant. They told me that time would sink the chemicals deeper into the soil, dispersing, until eventually, there would be no trace."

"Looks to me like they were wrong!" Marshall boomed.

"I don't need you to berate me now!" Tony shouted. "With everything that I've heard and read in the past twenty-four hours since she gave me the news - and believe me - my eyes have been glued to the internet - then I've got to clean it up. But this could cost me millions! Son-of-a-bitch!"

"Well," Marshall stood up. "Let's go see for ourselves. Perhaps there is an easier answer than throwing a couple of million dollars out the door. Let's go see what we can do."

Tony called Randy from his cell phone as they left the offices, instructing him to find *them* and *Katy* immediately. Both men were silent as he steered his BMW to the northeast quadrant.

Marshall was familiar with the land. He had probably walked it a hundred times, and his gaze was intent as they travelled across the Estates, surprised at how quickly the community was being developed. A few times, he turned to ask Tony a question. However, each time he did he saw that Tony's face was twisted with stress and he would change his mind.

As they neared the turn to the northeast quadrant, Tony turned to Marshall.

"What did you need to talk about?"

The question took Marshall by surprise.

"It can wait," Marshall replied quietly, but he remembered Thomas Sinclair's words vividly.

Chapter Twelve

As the "Stein" of Stein Morretti held out his hand, two things immediately struck Katy. He was tall, lean and handsome, with deep set green eyes. He also looked intensely unhappy. She knew that look. She felt how he looked.

"Hi," she replied timidly as she pulled off her right glove to shake his hand.

Marshall shook her hand then buried both of his own deep in his pant pockets. "So you discovered the signs of the poisoning a couple days back." It was a statement more than a question.

Katy was mesmerized by Marshall dark solemn eyes that were framed with thick, long lashes. "Yes," she nodded. "I manage the firs. I work on each quadrant on a rotating basis every morning."

"Why don't you just get into the nitty-gritty?" Tony interrupted.

Given the impatience in Tony's tone Katy very quickly summarized what she had explained to Tony and Randy a few days prior.

"Are you are sure the poisoning is across all four quadrants and not contained to just one or two of them?" Marshall asked.

"Yes," Katy answered, nodding.

Marshall turned to Tony. "Then it's likely not stemming from the Billingsgate land," he offered quietly.

Tony looked relieved for a moment. "Probably not," he said, "but I'll still need to do some tests."

Katy continued, explaining what she had found on the internet, confirming her fears.

"What does that mean, exactly?" Tony asked.

Tony's face and demeanor made Katy uncomfortable. He looked jittery and over-the-top stressed. "It means," she began, choosing her words very carefully, "that it is possible that someone has poisoned the tree wells. 2,4-D - Dichlorophenoxyacetic acid maybe. Or perhaps Tebuthiuron. And most of the firs are showing the same signs. It can probably be cleaned up. Remediated," she quickly added, "but yes, you should have a soil test done to analyze the samples to determine the contaminants and toxicities." She didn't have it in her to tell them that it was possible that it could leach to groundwater - and the potential implications of this.

Tony and Marshall quickly shared a knowing and concerned look as they both processed the potential magnitude of the problem. The cost of remediating the lands would be exorbitant, but there was much, much more to be concerned about. The city was small. Word traveled quickly. If news like this, even hypothetical news, reached the media, the city, builders and existing homeowners would be up in arms. Katy didn't have to tell them that a problem like this could lead to unwanted problems, potential health concerns and perhaps even lawsuits.

"This could bastardize sales, when the news gets out," Tony muttered helplessly.

"One step at a time," Marshall replied evenly and turned back to Katy. "I understand that you are a horticulturalist?"

Katy hesitated, and then lifted her chin slightly. "No," she replied, looking him straight in the eye, "I have a Masters in Communication and an undergraduate degree in Environmental Planning and Horticulture."

"This education makes you an expert in poisoned dirt?"

Under normal circumstances, Katy would have thought Marshall's comment was meant to insinuate that she wasn't qualified to make a prognosis. However, this wasn't the case. She saw something else in his eyes that brought her to another conclusion. The Stein of Stein Morretti was wisely prodding her. "I was also a Director and Publicist with an environmental company," she added, "and I've been exposed to several environmental issues over the years."

Marshall's green eyes brightened slightly, and Katy caught it. She thought that it was because she had impressed him, but his next words proved that this was not necessarily the case.

"So what the heck are you doing wasting you time here?" he retorted gruffly.

Katy was taken aback with Marshall's brazen question, and her eyes showed it. She looked defiantly into the handsome man's eyes. "It's not a waste of time, Mr. Stein," she said very calmly, lifting her chin slightly again. "Career change. I needed some fresh air."

Marshall studied Katy for a moment, his eyes fixated on the attractive and interesting woman before him. Then, in a tone that oozed that he wasn't convinced, he mumbled "Sure." Just "Sure."

Without another word, the two men got into Tony's BMW and its tires kicked up dirt as they disappeared across the Estates.

At just before one that afternoon, Rory found Katy at a picnic table in the staff cabin finishing the last of her lunch and reading a book. "Ready to go?" he asked.

"Sure," she replied. She closed the novel, threw it in her duffle bag and followed him out the door.

"Where to?" she asked as she jumped into the Chevy, hoping his mood had changed.

"I need to pick some stuff up," Rory replied bluntly. An annoyed expression twisted his face.

Both were silent as Rory steered the red Chevy to Stein Morretti's offices. He parked at the loading dock and shut off the engine. "Back in a minute," he said coldly as he slammed the door.

Katy quickly rolled down the window. "Can I help?" she shouted out, but Rory ignored her offer. About twenty minutes later she spotted him pushing a trolley full of poles.

"You could have told me you needed some help," she said as she jumped out to help him.

"I didn't need no help," Rory replied as he opened the tailgate of the five-ton.

"For God sakes, let me give you a hand," Katy replied.

"Grab one end," Rory grumbled, "and I'll maneuver it to the edge."

"What are these for?"

Silently they stacked several metal poles and rolled up banners into the back of the Chevy.

As Rory steered onto the back dirt road, Katy shifted in her seat. She owed him an explanation. She owed him something.

“I owe you an explanation,” she said suddenly.

“Forget ‘bout it,” Rory mumbled and pushed on the gas pedal. "You don't owe me nothing."

Katy closed her window and turned back to Rory. “I wasn’t purposely lying to you. The other day.”

“I said forget ‘bout it. I got better things to do then think about what makes you tick.”

Her eyes widened at his blatant coldness as the engine whined in complaint, for Rory had pushed hard on the pedal again. She bit her lip, contemplating where to begin.

“I’m really not sure what I will do for work,” she started humbly as she turned toward Rory. His ruggedly tanned face remained stoic and his eyes were glued to the road. “I...” she hesitated, “I mean in the winter. I was thinking that I might bartend, because I need to work and the only thing I know how to do well I can’t do anymore.”

She had watched Rory carefully as she spoke, anxious for a reaction - or acceptance. Rory’s face flinched slightly, she caught it, but his eyes remained on the road in front of him.

She continued with the truth. “I have seven years of expensive education behind me.” She chuckled then, and a sarcastic little sound popped out of her throat. “But it means nothing now. No need to go into details, but I was fired from my job about a year and a half ago.”

Rory squinted. “Fired, huh. Why?”

Katy felt almost desperate to justify her credibility and to tell Rory the truth. She took a deep breath. “I was a publicist for an environmental company. One of our clients, an international oil and gas company, discovered that one of their departments had been dumping chemicals illegally. For years. Only a few people had the real scoop. I was one of them. We were diligently trying to figure out how much damage had been done and if there were any health issues - and how to remediate the land. That year my father released a fictional book that told the story. There were way too many similarities. Uncanny similarities. After the Wall Street Journal published a review on the book, everything exploded. The company's stock plummeted, everyone pointed the finger at me for releasing confidential information to my father, and I was fired that day."

"Whoa!" Rory exclaimed as he glanced toward Katy. "Who's your dad?"

Katy hesitated. The man beside her didn't appear to be well read. He wouldn't know that Si Fields had twenty-nine New York bestsellers under his belt. "Si Fields," she answered quietly.

"You *kidding* me!" Rory exclaimed again. "My wife is one of his biggest fans. She's read every one of his books! Wasn't a movie made on his last book? I think I watched it! What was it? Tormented…tormented..."

"Tormented Skies. But Purple Waters was his last book," she added and then paused as she struggled to find strength in her voice. She didn't want to sound like she was feeling sorry for herself - or vulnerable. "You know," she finally continued, "it has been a good experience working here. Sure, I have blisters on my feet. War wounds, I'll tell my grandkids, from my days as a landscaper," she added in a chuckle. "It's just like the burn on my foot. It will always be there, a memory of the roads I've traveled."

"What happened to your foot?"

She closed her eyes for a brief moment. "Warehouse fire," she answered in a whisper. "My fiancé had a loft. There was a gas leak and the whole building exploded. I was one of the lucky ones, I suppose. I escaped."

The cabin was silent for several seconds before Rory turned to Katy. His face had softened and his voice was full of compassion. "So a bit of a tough go for you recently, wouldn't you say?" he said with a gentle smile.

Katy took a deep breath and realized that just talking about it had lifted a tiny bit of the burden. “Yeah, it has been a bit of a tough go, sure, but I am fine. Some days I feel like I’m sailing across the ocean, not sure where the next island might be,” she added, “but I’m okay. The fresh air and exercise here has really done me a world of good.”

They had reached the main entrance to the Estates. Two of the crew members were waiting for them with a five-ton truck and a picker and the team instantly got to work. When they finished three hours later, they stood back and inspected their work. Two rows of colorful new banners lined the stone and iron entrance, bragging Rocky Mountain Estates as *the* place to live. Then Rory surprised Katy. He invited her for a drink.

“C’mon,” he insisted. “It was my birthday yesterday and all I had was birthday cake. I need a beer. Besides, wife is hosting some toy party tonight. It’s like a multi-level marketing company, or something like that, so she won’t miss me.”

Twenty minutes later the two sat at the end of the bar in Penguin’s Pub, a couple of miles down the road. The small neighborhood lounge was packed with construction workers and suits, many who frequented the pub as a pit stop on their way home from work. The atmosphere was alive and buzzing with conversation, and for the first time in a long time, Katy embraced the new environment. The change of scenery from the four walls of her apartment felt refreshing and her conversation with Rory earlier that day had made her feel a little more at ease. She responded to Rory’s questions and unconsciously embraced his obvious interest in her. It was the first time she had told her story and found herself living outside of her shoes. The wounds didn’t ache as if they’d just happened yesterday - and she almost felt as if she was telling someone else’s story.

“I was a woman on a mission back then. Everything that I touched turned to gold. It was a dream job for me. I’d aspired for years, twelve or fifteen at least, to work on Wall Street. I came in on a sail and left with my tail between my legs.”

“Pretty hard to swallow your pride, isn’t it?”

Katy's eyes found his dark brown pupils. "Yeah, but I still feel like I have unfinished business. I might have been able to make amends, get to the truth, had it not been for the fire. But after that, well, it was time for me to leave."

"What about the fire? You lost your fiancé?"

Katy nodded silently. She looked towards the bar and the faceless strangers around it. She thought of Brad and the others that had filled that night, and the many nights to follow. In that instant her wall went up - again. Enough information for one day, she thought. She had already shared much more then she had intended. She wouldn't tell Rory about Brad, or how he had disappeared under the flames. Or how she used to sit on her sofa and hope that he would walk in the door, the whole while remembering the night and the smell in the air and the shrill ringing of sirens.

"I did," she finally replied, avoiding Rory's eyes, and then changed the subject. "How about another beer?" she suggested. She pulled off her cap and brushed a strand of hair away from her eyes. "I'll buy, but it's your turn to talk," she prodded. "Tell me about your family," she added with a smile.

Rory's eyes were filled with compassion, softening his oddly crooked and rugged features. "Don't know what to say. Sorry for you, Katy."

"It's okay," Katy smiled again. "I wasn't looking for sympathy. But it really did feel good to talk, but I would like to hear about your family!"

"My wife taught me that talk'n is sometimes the only thing that makes the world seem okay."

"Your wife sounds like a smart woman."

"Oh she is that alright!" Rory mused, then waved down the waitress. "You sure you want to hear about my family. My wife says I talk too much sometimes," he added sheepishly. "'sides, my story is not nearly as interesting as yours."

"I'm sure it is," Katy insisted.

Rory bragged about his children, pulling out his wallet to show Katy his family. He talked about how he loved being a dad and how fast his children seemed to grow. He spoke with genuine softness on his face when he talked about his wife and how she was the strong one and the glue of the Spradlum household. “She’s my rock,” he admitted humbly. “Don’t know what I would do without her.”

As they were almost finished their second beers, Rory remembered something. “Did you tell me that your father wanted you to be a writer?”

“Wanted!” Katy chuckled. “That’s hardly the right word. From the time I learned the alphabet, my father insisted that I *would* be a writer.”

“Can you write?”

Katy took a sip of her beer and frowned. “Odd, but I rebelled in the beginning. I always had other plans. But the older I got the more I wanted to write. Now I’m trying to do something with the words in my head. I’ve spent the better part of my time back in Canada hiding behind my computer and writing my first novel. But I’ve got writer’s block. I’m not in the same league as old Si.”

“Think there’s a story at Rocky Mountain?”

Katy grimaced, knowing that Rory was referring to the firs. “I don’t know. I am relatively sure that it is herbicide like 2,4-D or Tebuthiuron. Probably 2,4-D. It has to be intentional. They need to get a soil test done.”

“I’ve already been advised that mum is the word.”

“Absolutely. Until the problem is identified, Stein Morretti needs to keep this under wraps. It could create a lot of problems for them and cost a whole lot of money.”

Rory grinned mischievously then. “Isn’t this right up your alley? Wouldn’t this be a story for you to bite into tooth and nail?”

“Don’t worry,” Katy smiled mischievously. “I need my job.”

Then she told Rory that she had met Marshall Stein that very afternoon.

“Yeah, I saw that they called in the big guy. They were behind closed doors when I went into the offices this morning. Thought he had retired,” Rory mused, adding, “your discovery must have really made the shit hit the fan. Don’t know if you know, but word is that Stein was the founder and biggest shareholder of Stein Morretti. Until he lost his son and then his wife within a matter of months.”

“That was it!” Katy gasped. “I saw it in his eyes! He looked lost - or depressed.”

“Apparently, now he lives like a hermit in some mansion downtown. He sold his share of the business a couple of years ago, just after his wife passed away.”

“How very tragic.” Katy shook her head.

“Yeah. And apparently now he has other problems.”

Katy thought that Rory was referring to the firs. Instead, he continued with the gossip he had overheard in Stein Morretti’s offices. “Word is that now he has hired a private detective to find his missing grandchild.”

“Missing?”

“I only got the tail end of the conversation but sounds like the kid, a little girl, was left with Marshall’s son before he left to take a stint overseas.”

“Where’s the mother?”

“D’ know.”

“The instant I saw him I could tell that he was living with something... awful. I can’t imagine.”

Rory shook his head. “One tragedy after another. Apparently, Marshall’s son passed away only months before his wife,” he said grimly. “And word is that Marshall is an orphan and didn’t even know he had a grandchild until recently.”

“Wow,” Katy exclaimed under her breath.

"Man," Rory continued, shaking his head in disbelief. "Can't comprehend what it would like be searching for a child that is your own flesh and blood."

Chapter Thirteen

She hardly looked her age. It wasn't until one looked into her green eyes, and their dark brown irises, and held this sight for a few seconds, that one saw that the toughness and wisdom that stretched beyond the child's short eight years of life.

Zig Orman, baptized Zigourney Jessica Stein, was a poor kid from the low-income housing projects two blocks southeast of Marshall Stein's home and a few blocks and a river's skip away from Katy Fields' apartment.

Every day after school, Zig would take the same route home, across 4th Street to 26th Avenue and then towards Mission Bridge. Often she would stop for a moment and her eyes would fixate on "A Gift to My Family. She would think how pretty it was and wonder who lived there, or if she would ever live in a house where she had her very own bedroom, and a piano and a puppy.

Then she would wonder if Charlie would ever return, and her thin chest would fill with an emptiness that was all too familiar.

Zig had stories of abandonment and hunger that she shared with no one. A mother who disappeared when she was less than a year old. A father who left for work one day and never returned. And an aunt who worked part-time, when she was able to keep her job, or when men, booze or prostitution didn't consume her life. Often Zig would sit alone in the evenings in their small, one-bedroom townhouse and make due with what she had as she waited for her Auntie to come home. Often, she would fall asleep on the sofa long before the woman returned.

This particular morning she awoke before her Auntie, as she often did, and her eyes instantly fell to his black leather jacket and boots, and she knew what this meant. The old boyfriend had been allowed back for a sleepover, even though her Auntie had promised her that this would never happen again.

Zig remembered how the bedroom door would remain closed, sometimes for days at a time. Then she wrinkled her nose as she recalled his terrible smell. It started at the front door, where his things now lay, and filtered down the hallway, always more pungent near Auntie's bedroom. Zig also remembered some of the other times that *he* slept over. The long nights of loud music. The kitchen counter covered in beer bottles and other bottles with large "Alberta Vodka" on their labels. Cigarette smoke lingering in every corner. And the frequent fights between Auntie and the boyfriend that often resulted in the neighbors banging on the walls and threatening to call the police.

Zig shrugged her thin shoulders as a tiny morsel of thankfulness filled her. At least it wasn't the *other* boyfriend that had come to visit, she thought. The huge man with the tattoos covering his neck and both arms. The one that used to sit on the edge of her sofa in the middle of the night and watch her sleep.

"God forbid," she muttered under her breath in a grownup-like voice.

Then she began to dress for school: the same jeans and T-shirt as the day before and a thick pair of wool socks, even though it was another hot day. Then she put on a white pair of sneakers at least a size too big - the only shoes that didn't hurt her feet. Then she made herself a bowl of instant oatmeal, adding water instead of milk, for there was no milk. Other than a stale loaf of bread, a rotten head of lettuce and a few condiments, the fridge was empty. As she swallowed the last of her ghastly breakfast, for she hated oatmeal, she heard noises coming from her Auntie's bedroom. She closed her eyes tightly to block out the sounds.

Moments later, she pulled a faded baby blue duffle bag around her shoulders, grabbed her lunch, the cranberry granola bar that the woman on the river had given her the night before. Then she shut the door quietly and headed off to school.

At noon sharp, the lunch bell rang across the PA system, and Zig disappeared to the washroom. Auntie Lynette constantly warned Zig to "never, ever, wait in the food line" and to "never, ever hold out your hand hungry." For if she did this, she would threaten, the social workers would find her and the government people would take her away - and she would never see Charlie again.

Thus, as the other children sat in circles of the gymnasium floor and gobbled up their sandwiches and thirstily drank their boxed juices, Zig often hid behind the closed door of a washroom cubicle on the edge of a toilet, picking away at whatever little she had for a lunch. When the hallways filled with footsteps and giggles, and she was certain that most had finished their lunches, she would inconspicuously follow the children to the school playground.

Most lunch hours she found solitude in the poplars that stretched high on the hillside behind the school yard. Often she would draw in her scrapbook, usually colorful pictures of Charlie holding her hand, and puppies and blue-skies and flowers splashing hope and happiness across the page - hopes that Zig just needed to hang onto. However, on this very day she held a newfound hope. Soon, she would be trying out for the final school concert - and this was her chance to play the closing melody on the school's beautiful piano.

She could hardly contain her excitement as she climbed the short, steep hill toward the large, comforting trees. Falling to the grass, she instantly closed her eyes and began to practice. She hummed a tune as her long, slender fingers moved over the imaginary keyboard. Then she did it again - and then again - until the school bell rang. Then she picked herself up, and with butterflies teasing her stomach wall - from excitement or hunger, she wasn't quite sure - and her small feet hurried towards the large brick school. As she neared the back doors, she clasped her hands together tightly and silently begged that the next hour would bring magic.

As Zig sauntered home from school that afternoon her long, blonde hair - unkempt and knotted - for she had forgotten to brush it that morning, swung like thick, teased honey around her large green eyes. She took the same route as always, across 4th Street toward 26th Avenue and then towards Mission Bridge, however, this day, instead of stopping at "A Gift to My Family" and daydreaming about the possibilities, she mindlessly began her descent down the bridge and toward the river. She was hungry, but she doubted that there would be anything in the fridge or that Auntie would be home. She sighed with this thought, a heavy, windy sound for such a small child and her eyes fell to her white Nike running shoes. She stopped and wiggled her toes under the thick wool socks. Still too big, she thought and frowned in frustration. Her Auntie had told her that her feet would grow quickly and that soon they would fit. She wondered how long it would take for this to happen. Then, for the hundredth time that afternoon, she wondered again how she would tell her Auntie, if she asked, that she hadn't won the part in the concert.

As Zig neared the bridges' underground, three yellow butterflies landed on a wild rose bush and she stopped and held her breath. They fluttered around the bursts of pink wild flowers for a moment and then frolicked around her legs and torso in a playful dance. A mirthful smile filled Zig's thin, drawn face - and for a brief second she looked her age. Then, as they took flight across the river, Zig watched, until they disappeared somewhere in the distance.

Then her eyes fell to Winnie the Pooh and she nodded in satisfaction - he was safe and exactly where she had left him the night before. She tippy-toed toward the concrete wall and the home that she had discovered, then stopped about twenty feet from the mattress and looked in all directions to ensure that no one was home. Then her eyes sparkled as she noticed that someone had placed a small bouquet of flowers in a pickle jar on the concrete ledge, the same ledge that held pots and pans and cereal boxes and cans of food, arranged side by side in perfect order. She was caught by the neatness and simplicity of the kitchen. It was so clean and tidy, she thought. It was so unlike their kitchen! Suddenly, her face lit up with an idea, and after kissing Winnie the Pooh goodbye, she turned to leave. As her small feet, clad in the oversized white Nike running shoes still with a $2.99 sales sticker from the Salvation Army, quickly began the journey home she filled with a tingle of excitement, and the disappointment from the day felt less heavy. She had thought of sometime to do to keep herself busy.

Zig spent hours that evening painstakingly reorganizing her Auntie's kitchen, snacking on cornflakes and crackers, a piece of bread and jam, and a few peppermint candies that she had discovered in the bottom of one drawer. She organized the sparse cupboards, carefully arranging the few odds and sods of dishes and non-perishables that they held. She pounded nails across one wall and hung four old pots and pans side by side, then a dishtowel, and then a dishrag. She put a red plastic vase that she discovered under the kitchen sink in the center of the small kitchen table, and although she had no flowers to fill it, she stood back for a moment and imagined what it might look like if she did. Then, finally, she did what Auntie had always said she wanted to do, but had never gotten around to. It was a bit of a struggle for the small child, but after numerous pushes and pulls and pulls and pushes, she managed to move the apartment size fridge tight against the corner wall. Auntie had been right. It made their tiny kitchen look much bigger.

At just before midnight, Lynette returned from wherever she had been and Zig greeted her at the door. She immediately took the purse out of the woman's hands.

"Where is he?" she asked in apprehension as she looked past her Auntie and into the hallway.

"He found a job," Lynette replied vaguely.

"Is he coming back tonight?" Zig's words were barely a whisper.

"No. I told you, he found a job..." her voice trailed off.

Lynette's explanation seemed to satisfy the child, for she bobbed her small head up and down quickly, as if in approval. "Okay, close your eyes, Auntie," she continued excitedly. “Close your eyes, Auntie. I have a surprise for you.” Then she took the woman’s hand.

Lynette smiled wanly as her bloodshot eyes fell to the spotless kitchen. She leaned down and hugged Zig. She kissed her forehead, pulled a strand of honey-colored hair away from her forehead and then mumbled something about needing a bath.

Zig found her almost an hour later. She had fallen asleep in the bathtub, a half-empty bottle of Alberta Vodka on its edge.

“Auntie, you must go to bed,” Zig insisted as she poked the woman’s arm.

“How did your recital go?” Lynette asked as she looked up to Zig with tired, stoned eyes. “Did you make it?”

“No, Auntie.”

“I’m sorry.”

“It’s okay, Auntie,” Zig said as she reached for the woman’s hands and helped her out of tub. “Come to bed, Auntie. It’s time for bed.”

Zig tucked her in. She plumped up the pillow. She made sure that the large cotton blanket was tightly wrapped around Lynette’s feet and sides. Then she very gently brushed Lynette’s damp hair away from her cheeks and then her temples and tenderly kissed her on the forehead before shutting off the light and closing the bedroom door.

Then she returned to the kitchen. She knelt down and carefully pulled out a white envelope from under the fridge. She had discovered it that very evening, when she had moved the fridge. It was addressed to Lynette Orman, at their old address in Vancouver. They hadn’t lived there in over a year and Zig only vaguely remembered the place, but she had memorized the house number. “Remember number 222, Zig. In case you ever get lost coming home from school,” her Auntie had told her repeatedly. Zig couldn’t imagine getting lost, and the number 222 was embedded in her memory forever.

She ran her long, slender fingers over the handwriting on the envelope. Then she pulled out a photograph and held it up to the light. He looked so handsome and strong, she thought with a tender and proud smile. Then she pulled out a letter and unfolded it. She'd read it several times that evening. She began to read it again.

Dear Lynette;

You know how I hesitated with this assignment. It is both dangerous and complex, but more so, it is very difficult for me to leave Zig behind. As you know, Afghanistan is no place for a six-year old. Knowing that she will be warm and safe in your hands gives me a great deal of comfort and I am at ease that I have made the right decision and relieved that I was able to entrust you with the little package of wealth that we call Zig.

I hope to be gone for only three weeks, maybe four. It will be impossible for you to reach me, but I promise to call if I am able. Please tell Zig this and give her this photo to put under her pillow; it will remind her that I am coming home soon and that I love her.

I am so proud of you, Lynette – almost a year "clean". Your world is just beginning. I do know that you will make it – you are determined like your sister used to be. Don't I know this! I respect how you have met your challenges and that you have realigned your life to a better place. Drugs and booze are the crutches of the weak, and I know you are much stronger than that. This next chapter of your life, this next journey, is going to be a remarkable one! I can feel it. When I return we will celebrate your anniversary!

In the event that you need anything, please call Sarah. You know well that I do not speak to my father and that he has no idea about Zig, but I can assure you that Sarah will be there if you if you need her. She's in Calgary, Alberta, but it is only a phone call away. Below is her phone number and address. Remember that she will be there for you in the event you need anything!

Also, enclosed is three thousand dollars. It is a small gift that will help you get back on your feet. You can buy some clothes for your new job, and some clothes for Zig for school. Perhaps something for your new apartment, and please, warm and comfortable bedding for Zig while she is with you. And embrace the time that you and Zig spend together as family.

Love you always,

Charlie

Zig read the letter three more times that evening. Each time she got to the words, "Love you always, Charlie," she would run her fingers over the neat print. Then she would hold the photograph up very close to her eyes. He looked so nice and important, she thought, and he had such a big and handsome smile. Not at all like the boyfriends that her Auntie had for sleepovers.

At just before midnight, Zig carefully tucked the envelope under her pillow, just as her father had suggested. Then with hopeful and dreamy eyes, she wrapped the blankets around her shoulders and curled into a fetal position. Just seconds before she fell asleep she silently vowed that she would find Charlie.

Chapter Fourteen

Zig was nearing her sixth birthday when Charlie dropped her off with a suitcase to leave for Afghanistan. Within days of Charlie's departure, she began to ask where her father went, and even more frequently, when he was coming back. In the beginning, Lynette's answers were always the same, and always offered with the greatest of sincerity. He was working. He would be home very soon. And he loved her very much.

Lynette did her best to create a healthy environment for her niece. She had promised Charlie this and absolutely nothing would get in the way. She couldn't possibly disappoint the only man that she had ever respected - a man who had been instrumental in pulling her out of the trenches and allowing her to turn a new leaf.

However, three weeks passed, and then four, and then five, and as weeks turned into months and no word from Charlie, Lynette breathed a sickly premonition that something terrible had happened.

At the six month mark, Lynette fell back to the bottle. At first, her drinking was sporadic, but eventually a night out with old friends here and there began to affect her part-time position as a cashier so that she could be home for Zig after school. She more frequently called in sick, or would show up at work late and obviously hung over - until eventually she lost the first real job that she had ever had.

By this time, any hopes that Lynette may have held of building a new life, a clean life, had all but dissipated - as had any hopes that Charlie would ever return. She had long spent the money that Charlie had left her, and with no income or savings, she returned to the streets.

As Zig was left alone more frequently, she silently questioned *if* her father would return opposed *to* when. Sometimes, when she was in desperate need of comforting, she would crawl onto Lynette's lap and wrap her arms around her neck and ask these very questions. When Lynette was high on cheap vodka or Black Label beer, her anger at both the world and Charlie for leaving her with such a responsibility would erupt. Sometimes she would reply that maybe Charlie was dead - as her mother was dead. Sometimes she would say that Charlie must have found a new girlfriend. Once, Lynette even exploded that Charlie was never coming back.

When Lynette sobered, and hadn't been so drunk that she couldn't remember these conversations, she would fill with guilt. Although she had a dysfunctional childhood, she was very cognizant of the negative effects that her words were having on the child - and would try and make amends. She would hold Zig very tightly. She would caress her arms and pull her hair away from her face and kiss her forehead. She would very gently tell the child that she'd been in a bad mood. And that she didn't think that Charlie had left for a new girlfriend. And that her mother wasn't dead. And she would do and say everything that she was emotionally capable of doing and saying to reassure her niece that Charlie would probably be home very, very soon. As soon as he possibly could. And that he loved her very much.

However, the damage was manifesting, and regardless of Lynette's attempt to undo the negative and instill some positive, Zig progressively became more withdrawn, and her feelings of abandonment escalated. As her grades began to drop her demeanor imploded, and her classroom teacher called social services to express her concern. Soon after, a young, male social worker paid Lynette and Zig a visit. However, whatever it was that Lynette said or did was convincing and compelling. Rather than apprehend the "orphan", as he should have done, he left Lynette with pamphlets to free family counseling and food banks, and Zig fell through the cracks.

By this point, Lynette was poisoned with resentment, but towards whom, she wasn't sure. She couldn't feel angry towards Charlie. Charlie had been so good and kind to her. Nor could she point blame to Zig's mother for just disappearing one day. Hadn't she long known that her own sister had caught the "curse"? Just like their mother. Just like her grandmother. If Lynette felt any strong emotions about her sister, it was only genuine concern. For didn't she know first hand that the curse was the devil himself?

One evening, after several hours in a seedy pub in a seedier motel on the south-east edge of Vancouver, Lynette returned home much later than she had planned. She found Zig under her bed blankets, crying a river, hiccuping and convulsing from the strong tears she had already long shed. Drunk and completely overwhelmed with the package of despair in her arms, Lynette tucked Zig in, kissed her on the forehead and promised in a slur that she'd be right back. She found the letter from Charlie and then searched her jackets and drawers for any spare change and then headed out the door. She swaggered a block west and then another block south until her eyes spotted the telephone booth. Moments later her fingers were dialing the number that Charlie had written at the bottom of his letter.

"Hello!" A sleepy male voice answered on the second ring. He sounded annoyed.

Lynette was surprised to hear a man's voice, and one so irritated and unfriendly. She hesitated. "I need to talk to Sarah," she finally replied, trying very hard to sound sober.

"Do you know what time it is? Who is this?" the voice demanded.

Lynette had no idea that it was almost midnight, nor did she know what to say.

“Whom, exactly, is looking for Sarah?”

Suddenly Lynette realized that it must be Charlie’s father. The icon of a monster that Charlie had told her about. She hung up the receiver before uttering another word.

One week later Lynette met a fellow by the name of Frank at the same seedy pub in the same seedy motel. Frank instantly lusted over Lynette. Eager to get into her pants, he also teased her with greener pastures. He was driving to Calgary, Alberta the very next day and bragged that he had connections that would help him land a great job and a greater paycheck at the Calgary International Airport.

Calgary! Lynette thought. She immediately saw this as her ticket to a solution. If Charlie wasn’t coming back then she would find Sarah. She would drop Zig off at Sarah’s door and hug her goodbye. She would probably cry, for she’d grown very attached to the child. However, at very least this would give Zig a better life and *she* could get back on her feet and start over again.

Three days later, Lynette placed the second call to the Stein residence in less than a fortnight. She called from a pay phone on the northeast edge of the city, just a few blocks from friends of Franks, where they had holed up. However, Lynette was in for another disappointment. It was the very day of Sarah Stein’s funeral, and whomever it was that had answered the phone told Lynette in a very solemn tone that the woman had passed away.

Lynette dragged Zig from bed to bed for two more months as she clung to the coattails of Frank. As Frank half-heartedly continued to look for work, he also put pressure on Lynette to “get rid of the kid” and drop her off at the nearest government office. He had no use for the child. She was getting in the way.

To Lynette’s credit, if her willpower and strategy were void, her commitment and promise to Charlie were very much intact.

“Never!” she would reply. “I will *never* let *that* happen!”

One day, miraculously, for miracles sometimes did happen - didn't her mother once tell her that? - Lynette left Frank for another fellow named Simon. Simon lived in a downtrodden, albeit furnished, one bedroom townhouse close to the downtown core, and overnight Lynette and Zig had a safe roof over their heads. Simon immediately took to Zig, and for the first time since Charlie had left, someone was able to put a genuine smile on the child's face. He teased her fondly - and daily.

Lynette enrolled Zig in the closest school, which by chance was only a ten minute walk away, down the street, over the bridge and a few blocks west. Then she found a day job as a waitress at a family restaurant and began to clean up her act. She left the streets, and for months, she didn't miss a day of work - and drank only on occasion. Simon was into pot more so then Alberta Vodka, and this curbed her thirst. Sometimes she stayed away from the booze for one or two weeks at a time.

Often, Lynette would think that they had turned a new leaf as she did her best to provide and care for Zig. Not knowing much of a different childhood, she was quite proud of the fact that she was able to take care of the kid, especially under the circumstances. She was also thankful that Zig seemed to be doing okay.

However, contrary to how Lynette perceived her niece's well-being, Zig, now eight years old, was progressively becoming even more withdrawn. She was confused and felt very alone, and except for his stories, the safe memories of her father were fading. She craved the warmth of his hugs and how he made her feel. Thus, the envelope that she had found under the fridge spoke a million hopeful and encouraging words that the child *needed* to hear. They didn't explain why her Auntie would sometimes get drunk and say mean things, or why they hardly had food in the fridge. They didn't explain why Simon just up and left one day - and why her Auntie was disappearing again, returning late into the nights. Nor did they explain why or where her father had disappeared - or when he might be coming home. However, they reinforced that at least she had a father, and one who loved her very much. And although it was unclear to her whom Sarah was, her young mind was able to process that a real, live woman did exist and that she was looking forward to meeting her.

Chapter Fifteen

Thomas's discovery that Christina had been in a mental institution several times since she was eighteen years old had taken the quirky PI mildly by surprise. However, Marshall's shock was profound.

"Schizophrenia, sir," Thomas told Marshall the very day he spoke to the hospital administrator. "It`s ah... not a curable disease. She was diagnosed with it when she was eighteen. In and out since. She had been on a variety of meds since her diagnosis. And wouldn't you know, she always checked in with a different name. Last time was in 2004 under the name of Germaine Brown."

"Germaine Brown!" Marshall exclaimed in a scoff. "She has a multi-personality disorder!"

"Sounds like it, sir. But according to her medical records this isn't the case. Apparently, she is very cognizant of her sickness - and very ashamed. Since she was diagnosed she tried to hide her disease from the world. However, when she is well, when she takes her meds, she is quite functioning."

Thomas' findings disgusted Marshall. He could not get his head around the truth that the woman he had once loved had a serious mental illness. Just as daunting was the fact that she had duped him. If Thomas' information and timelines were correct, Christina had been out of the hospital for only three weeks when they had met!

"That explained her oddness," Marshall voiced quietly, "and how she used to stare off into space sometimes." He had thought that she had been daydreaming. Or how she used to disappear for days at a time. He had thought that she had someone else in her life - for she was a stunning and remarkably beautiful woman. He remembered how she carried her little medicine chest full of "miracle drugs". He had thought that it was nothing other than natural herbs and teas, just as she had told him. God knows what shit was in that chest!

Marshall remembered an afternoon that Christina had stopped in the middle of a conversation and began talking to herself. She had done it with a smile on her face and in that playful, teasing way that he had so adored. He didn't know why, but he had found this endearing.

He had found the bitch's sickness endearing! Marshall thought in disbelief.

"Apparently," Thomas continued, "the doctors experimented with several medications over the years. The meds that she was on when you met seemed to be working," Thomas explained.

"Oh, they were working alright!" Marshall shouted.

Thomas' trail came to another halt with this disturbing news. Then, finally one morning in August, he received an unexpected call from Vancouver from a Mrs.

Lynn Macara, a seventy-six year old woman who still lived in the condo beside the one that Charlie had once owned. Thomas had interviewed her briefly during his trip to Vancouver, and although she vaguely remembered the "kind and good-looking Charlie" and the "sweet little girl" - she couldn't recall anything else. However, three months later her voice was overflowing with excitement as she shared her rekindled memory with Thomas.

At just before ten o'clock that evening, Thomas called Marshall to give him the news.

Just as Marshall answered his phone the air erupted with the forbidding chanting from the river below. "Hang on a minute!" Marshall boomed into the phone. "I can't hear you."

Seconds later the French doors of his parlor banged shut. "Damn noise pollution," Marshall complained moments later into the phone, mostly to himself.

"Pardon me?"

"Ah," Marshall said with annoyance thick in his tone. "Vagrants living on the river. Polluting the air. What did you say? I couldn't hear you, over the noise."

"Mr. Stein, I am sorry to be calling so late. I tried you this morning, but I didn't want to leave a message."

"I've gone back to work for a while," Marshall explained. "Call me on my cell next time - if you have news."

"Oh. Oh, now that is a surprise!" Thomas exclaimed. He had thought that Marshall had retired for good. "Well. Well, then. Like I said, it's a little late to be calling. But we had to visit a friend in the hospital this afternoon, then had tea with a dear old friend and Mrs. Sinclair simply got overtired. I had to tend to her before I called you. Her arthritis is acting up bad this time. "

"Thomas, I'm sorry about Mrs. Sinclair but could you please just get to the point."

"Oh, yes, I'm sorry," Thomas apologized. "I'll be quick. I spoke to Mrs. Macara again this morning. Remember her? She is the woman that lived - still lives - right next door to the condo Charlie had in False Creek. When I originally interviewed her she didn't remember anything relevant, but I left her my card, in the event she did remember something. Well! She called me this morning. She remembers your granddaughter's fifth birthday. She has a grandson almost the same age and he was invited to her birthday party!"

"When?"

"Three years ago."

"That would make her eight years old now," Marshall quickly calculated.

"Yes. That's probably correct."

"If her memory is right, then it is correct!" Marshall retorted.

"That's right, sir," Thomas replied, ignoring Marshall's gruffness. "But she also remembered something else. After Christina disappeared Charlie's kid sister started hanging around."

"Charlie didn't have a kid sister!" Marshall rebuffed.

"Let me speak, please, Mr. Stein!" Thomas replied in exasperation. It wasn't the first time he had lost his cool with his client over the past several weeks.

Thomas continued with Mrs. Lynn Macara's story. "It turns out that it was Christina's kid sister. Mrs. Macara is positive that the sister's name was Lynette, because *her* first name is Lynn. Lynn Macara. She remembers because she found the name Lynette quite odd. Not Lynn, like her name, but *Lynette*."

Marshall winced at Thomas' running of words. "I understand what you are telling me Thomas."

"Mr. Stein. I apologize. I tend to ramble when I get excited." Thomas cleared his throat before continuing. "Sometimes my old memory does wonders," he added in a chuckle. “So you see, I am certain that Lynette was the kid sister Christina was taking care of when I worked on the case last time. She was around eighteen at the time. Remember? That would make her ‘bout twenty-six years old now.”

“How does that do you any good?” Marshall shot back. “You haven’t been able to find the kid sister!”

“That is correct. But as luck would have it I called Vancouver General Hospital again this morning, right after speaking with Mrs. Macara. I spoke with the administrator that did me a favor last time. Remember, she...”

“Get to the point Thomas?”

“Mr. Stein. Please bear with me. I’m getting to that,” Thomas hastily replied. “She found Lynette’s name and address in their old records as Christina’s next of kin. The file was stored in the basement. After so many years that is what they do, they store patients’ files in the basement,” Thomas explained. “That`s why it took them so long to find. I must have asked, oh, well, must be at least three weeks ago now, for any records of anyone that had visited Christina. But Mr. Stein, I hope you are sitting down for I do believe we may have cracked a big one here!”

Marshall didn’t move because he was already sitting down, but admittedly, his heart skipped a tiny beat.

“According to their records,” Thomas continued excitedly, “Lynette visited Christina several times during her last stay. And I have the address that she provided.”

“You have her address?”

“Well, not exactly. They had her Vancouver address, but miraculously, that led me to her address here in Calgary! Don’t ask me how, just luck that I happened to find this. But she is, or at least was, living here! Northeast end of the city!”

An odd taste had crept into Marshall’s mouth. He only vaguely remembered what Thomas had shared with him years ago regarding Christina’s troubled kid sister - he’d hardly paid attention. However, Marshall’s genius mind was like a sieve. He was usually able to quickly process and retain enough high level information to give him a very clear picture, and as he sat clutching the phone to his ear a dismal image emerged. Why had Charlie entrusted his very own child with a woman that had been an addict. It was beyond his comprehension. And if the child was left with Lynette, her life must have had been very, very difficult. "Thomas," he retorted, "you told me to sit down to tell me that you found where my granddaughter was living two years ago? And that she is probably living off the food bank?" Marshall's voice was thick with cynicism. "How the *hell* is this good news?"

Thomas instantly grew very frustrated. His voice oozed annoyance as he spoke again. "Mr. Stein," he sighed, "there is a little bit more that I would like to share with you, if you would please allow me?"

Marshall stood up and looked out the window, silently waiting for Thomas to continue.

"Well," Thomas finally sighed before continuing, "apparently the story goes that Charlie left the child with Lynette before he went overseas. But she had been clean for a year - Mrs. Macara specifically recalls how he helped her through rehab. And she also reinforced that the kid was the apple of Lynette's eye."

Marshall's gaze dropped to the floor. Jazz was sitting inches from Marshall's feet and his bright blue eyes were staring at him intently.

"But no one could lead you to the child?" Marshall asked.

"Well, sir. No."

"Social Services doesn't have an address? Vital Statistics? There has to be some other government department that has her address?"

"Lynette has never been in the system. Or she got lost in the shuffle. No one can has a record of her."

Clutching the phone to his ear, Marshall knelt down on one knee beside Jazz. He squinted to inspect Jazz's skin. The medicated cream had healed the rash and a soft blanket of new fuzz covered Jazz's torso. As Marshall's hand instinctively reached under Jazz's chin to give him a chin rub, Jazz hissed with a vengeance and Marshall jumped. "Shit!" he yelled into the phone.

"Sir?"

"Thomas," Marshall belted into the phone, "you still haven't told me the good news!"

His client's last comment exasperated the PI and his wrinkled lips gasped into the phone.

"Mr. Stein," he began coolly, "the good news is that I found a couple of fresh trails. Something new to go on." Thomas had lost his steam. He didn't want to deal with this difficult client any longer. He was retired. He should be enjoying his golden years with his wife and children and grandchildren. Marshall's mood swings and outright egotistical attitude was simply not worth it.

After a few seconds of silence, Thomas words came out in a loud but raspy and almost indecipherable tone of disbelief.

"Mr. Stein! Not everyone is as fortunate as you. Some people, many people, struggle to put food on the table. Some people, many people, have their addictions! I would have thought that just the fact that the child was the apple of Lynette's eye would give you satisfaction, sir. This alone is good news! At least we now know that wherever the child is, she's in God's loving hands."

Chapter Sixteen

Thomas' once lively and hopeful trail to the missing child almost stopped in its tracks, until another neighbor in Calgary remembered both Lynette and the little girl. Through this lead, Thomas found Frank Bellman, the neighbor's casual drinking buddy, and Lynette's free ride from Vancouver.

Frank was now working as a bartender at a biker's pub in the deep southeast of the city. He openly bragged to Thomas about his affair with Lynette, and how he was the one to persuade her to move east. He also begrudgingly led Thomas to another of Lynette's old boyfriends, whom he referred to as "the prick with no conscience."

Geo Smith met Lynette sometime after Simon, Frank explained with a scoff. "The whore had no scruples. She left me for some pot-smok'n druggie! Then when he left, she fell into the arms of the biggest prick east of the Rocky Mountains."

Geo Smith intimated the frail PI the moment Thomas laid his eyes on him. Standing at no less than six foot four inches and at least two hundred and sixty pounds, Thomas quickly calculated that this fellow was obviously as hardcore to the bone as they get. The tattoos across his arms and neck, most probably spreading to his back and chest, he guessed, painted a vivid picture of violence and sex. And as Geo spoke, he pumped up his colorful muscles as he told Thomas with a greasy smile that sure, he knew Lynette. He knew her intimately, and she was nothing short of a cheap lay. Where she lived, whom she lived with, or what she did for money besides hook now and then, he couldn't answer.

"When was the last time you saw her?" Thomas asked.

"A few months back," Geo smirked and winked. "We had a rocking' night on the town, if you know what I mean old man."

"A rocking' night on the town?" Thomas repeated as he frowned. "Where?"

"Party started here," Geo replied, "here" being the same seedy pub where Frank worked. "Went to her place afterwards. She was holed up in some hole near downtown."

"Downtown where?" Thomas pressed.

"Hell if I remember where the bitch lived!" Geo belted out in a growly laugh. "We partied pretty hard that night. She was as ripped as I was!"

"And the kid?"

"What about the kid?"

"Was she there?"

"Sure wasn't in bed with the two of us!" Geo sneered.

Thomas grimaced.

"Yeah, man. Yeah, she was there. Sleeping like a baby angel on the couch."

"How was she?" Thomas asked.

Geo smirked again. "Lynette's a pretty lame lay."

"I meant the kid!" Thomas exclaimed in embarrassment. "Was the child okay?"

"Damn if I know 'bout the kid!"

Geo's trail to the child died in its tracks with his storybook arms that oozed of the dark and sultry side. Although Thomas pressed him to remember the child's name, or anything even 'trivial' that might lead him to the child, he came up empty-handed.

However, at this point, Thomas had another hunch. He had learned enough about schizophrenia to know that the disease doesn't go away. His sister's daughter had been diagnosed with it a few years back. Thomas concluded that although Christina had checked herself out of the hospital, he'd bet a cup of coffee she would most certainly need to check herself back in. Especially if she hadn't stayed on her medications.

"It's a scary sickness," Thomas told Marshall. "My sister's daughter has had schizophrenia since she was seventeen. It wasn't until they found the right meds - and that took some experimenting I must say - that she was able to function in the world. But a day or a week off of the right medication? Well! Now that can be a very scary situation."

"That explains her disappearing act," Marshall muttered, half to himself.

"Likely, sir. But you never saw the signs?"

Marshall shook his head humbly. "No. She was fully functioning. There was nothing she did that even suggested she was that sick. I mean, she was a bit tipsy, or loose. Maybe a bit eccentric."

Marshall had found Christina's eccentric quirks endearing. He had frequently thought that it was her free spirit talking and breathing. Sometimes he used to wish that he could crawl inside her and feel what she felt.

"Odd behavior can be one of the signs," Thomas voiced knowingly, then added with a thought, "She must have been taking medication?"

"Christ, I can't remember all of the crap that was in her medicine chest!" Marshall retorted.

"Mr. Stein, I know from Linda. Linda is my sister with the kid that's sick," he explained quickly. "Without medication the disease torments the mind. Victims become delusional. They hallucinate. They see other people in their space and hear voices. Not even the strongest of minds can will it away. Clinical treatment is critical. My sister said that only about one in five people recover from the illness, with the right treatment. But just like my niece has attempted, four or five times now, about one in ten people commit suicide." Thomas shuddered. "It is a very sad disease. But regardless, do you recall me telling you that Vancouver General Hospital said that Christina had a controlled case? What I am getting to is that I can almost guarantee that there are no sweat lodges or natural healing medicines on the face of this earth that would replace the medication that her body needed."

Marshall didn't want to talk about Christina's sickness any longer. "What's your next move?" he asked Thomas, changing the subject.

"Leave it with me." Thomas sounded defeated, deflated and tired. The trail was thinning. "Let me get back to you?"

A few days later Thomas called Marshall at Stein Morretti's offices. He sounded nervous and jittery. "Well, sir. I guess then, well..." he began, "hmm... I'm not quite sure where to go from here. You see, my wife and I were thinking of taking a trip to Florida. The doctor says that the air will be good for her arthritis."

'When?"

"Well, a week Sunday. Only gone for ten days, but, hmm, well, I'm not quite sure how to put this."

It might have been the tone in Thomas's voice - or the fact that throughout Marshall's career someone was always holding out their hands for more. Regardless, Marshall knew that Thomas was preparing to ask him for more money. "We have a deal, Thomas," was all he said

"Sir! We most certainly did! I mean do. But my wife is quite frugal. English descent," he added in a nervous chuckle. "And believe it or not, she took it upon herself to keep a record of every hour I've spent on this case," he rambled on quickly. "To-date, and I'll tell you, I was quite surprised myself! I've spent over three hundred hours looking for the child. Plus another seven hundred and sixty-two dollars and forty-two cents in expenses out of my pocket. Long distance. Gas. Parking. Taxi cabs in Vancouver. Adds up. Sure does!"

"We had a deal, Thomas. And more than a fair one, I think. You'll get another twenty-five thousand when you find my grandchild."

"Well, sir. Don't get me wrong. It was a good arrangement! But it's been a very complicated case. You see, Cecilia has calculated that five thousand dollars, less seven hundred in expenses at three hundred hours equates to only fifteen dollars an hour. Mr. Stein, my grandson is making fifteen dollars an hour in his last year of high school, packing bags at the grocery store."

Throughout his life Marshall never readily parted with a nickel, unless he absolutely had to, or unless it was something that he had absolutely wanted. Over the years, he had also learned how to negotiate with the best of them - and seldom didn't get his way. He had succeeded with this by figuring out early what made someone tick, and at that very moment calculated that Thomas Sinclair was as much on a mission to find the child as he was. The hunt was in his blood. And without another cent it would remain in his blood, especially with a twenty-five thousand dollar carrot at the end of the stick.

"We had a deal, Thomas. You think about it on your trip with your wife and let me know."

As Marshall hung up the phone he thought that Christina had probably disappeared into a dark abyss that he would never understand, Lynette had probably disappeared with the bottom feeders and degenerates of society, and, that between the two of them, one child, his grandchild, had literally vanished into thin air.

Then he thought of Sarah.

Then he thought of Charlie.

Then he thought of Christina again and how she was an evil, wicked, heartless woman. To hide such a sickness from him. To tease him like that. To throw his son right back in his face. To abandon a child? Suddenly, this thread of agonizing thought was almost too much to bear for Marshall, and he felt physically sick and emotionally drained. He left Stein Morretti's offices without saying goodbye to anyone, and the moment he reached "A Gift to My Family" he crawled into bed. Jazz was soon to follow.

Thomas' call the very next morning might have put Marshall over the top.

The little man nervously apologized about waking Marshall up.

"I'm awake," he mumbled as he glanced at the clock on the bed table, surprised that he had slept so long. It was eight o'clock in the morning.

Thomas explained in a tone of angst that he and his wife had a very long and serious talk about life. As Marshall pulled himself up and sat on the edge of the bed he envisioned Thomas' thin and drawn face and how it was probably twitching as he spoke. His tone gave *everything* away and Marshall surmised then that Thomas was quitting on him.

Thomas continued about Cecilia's health, and how his doctor had warned him to watch his own health because of his high blood pressure.

Marshall suddenly felt odd and empty. "It`s okay, Thomas," he replied quietly. "Take care of your family. Take care of your wife."

Thomas's watery eyes popped wide open in surprise. He had anticipated an outbreak. Or, at very least, some rude and arrogant comment that would leave him feeling smaller than he already felt. "I most certainly will take care of them, sir! And if you need anything, anything whatsoever, please don't hesitate to call me. I'm sure Cecilia could do without me for a few hours here and there. Perhaps I could work on an hourly rate," he added, and then chuckled. It was too boisterous a sound for the topic of conversation, or for the man himself, and it popped out of his throat and stopped as quickly as it had started. "Of course," he continued, "the rate would need to be increased substantially from fifteen dollars per hour. But then, if the child ever does surface, well, you would save yourself quite a bit of money. And of course, I would suspect that I would have to forfeit the twenty-five thousand dollar reward with this agreement. It's a lot of money in this day and age, sir. A *lot* of money!" Thomas repeated, as if he was reminiscing.

After a long pause, for Marshall was still at a loss for words and Thomas was searching for just the right words, Thomas finally broke the silence. "Mr. Stein," he began in a voice full of compassion and sincerity, "I am genuinely sorry that we didn't find your grandchild. But we need to remember that wherever she is, she's in God's loving hands."

Chapter Seventeen

White cashmere grew thicker and thicker over the poisoned lands of the Estates as fall passed and winter arrived. As the lands filled, almost obsessively, with the wrappings of the season, the walls inside Stein Morretti's offices reeked of havoc as the team struggled to delay the oncoming storm and repercussions of the poisonings.

Greenstay Environmental's forgery of documents on the Billingsgate land two years prior was the least of Stein Morretti's concerns. The new soil tests by an independent, Fourdow Environmental, confirmed that the contamination on this pocket of land was the same as on the rest of the Estates - meaning that the Billingsgate land was not the problem. Meaning the problem intensified. The laboratory tests confirmed that except for the south and a tiny portion of the east quadrants, the trees were toxic with 2,4-D, a lawn care pesticide that is one of the most widely used herbicides in the world and sold under a variety of names. With the right mix-up, Fourdow engineers explained, it is commonly used to kills unwanted trees.

By December, many of the firs that had once proudly wrapped their branches around the Estates now stood as defeating reminders that soon they might be uprooted from the comfort of Mother Nature and taken to the cold machinery of the lumber yard. Many of the older needles were brown and purplish, and new growth from that very spring and summer were mostly curled and dropping - more signs of the poisoning.

However, as dormant as the new community might have appeared, it bustled with a new kind of energy. The positive news was that Fourdow had confirmed that they could in fact remediate the contaminated soil - and possibly even save many of the trees. Still, city and provincial government officials haunted the offices of Stein Morretti with questions and accusations, monitoring the progress like a tenacious and nervous mother hen. The media was relentless. News surfaced almost daily - often hypothesizing whom the culprit was - or the reasoning behind the crime. Anxious homeowners and landowners tied up the phones and pounded on the doors of Stein Morretti's offices as they voiced their confusion, concern and often rage. It appeared that no one wanted to live or develop in a community ridden with poison.

Stein Morretti was dealing with significant and expensive problems. Landowners that had not yet begun construction demanded a refund. Phase Two of the Estates, which had been slated to begin construction that previous fall, was delayed indefinitely. Until the land was poison-free, the inevitable meant construction delays - for months, perhaps years. Both Stein Morretti and Tony personally were at risk of losing millions of dollars.

Tony needed a plan. He also desperately needed cash, and a lot of it. After Marshall's retirement, Tony operated "standalone" for the first time in his career, and frankly, not that well. He had gone over budget on almost every project, and there was little reserve left in the bank. Fourdows' bill, the likelihood of lawsuits, coupled with delayed construction and lost sales meant the inevitable would soon follow.

Without an influx of cash, Stein Morretti would not be able to operate, curtailing both the Company and Tony Morretti into bankruptcy.

At Tony's begging, Marshall temporally and "unofficially" stepped back into his old shoes. He began by helping Tony refinance a builders' loan with the bank - with his personal guarantee on the financing. He didn't completely do this out of the kindness of his heart, or to save his best friend's financial crisis. He protected his investment with an agreement that gave Marshall ownership of several acres of land that weren't contaminated.

Marshall welcomed the challenge as much as he did the distraction. Hi new responsibility diverted his fixation from his missing granddaughter, temporarily, and he often kept himself busy into the late hours of the night. His face, once drawn and gray, looked more vibrant and alive. And although it sometimes held a newfound stress that came with the massive problems at the Estates, it also sometimes showed a glimmer of humor and other emotions that proved that Marshall had returned to a relatively healthy state of mind.

As he forged ahead, Marshall also became increasingly more perplexed. Where, exactly, had the poison come from? he questioned repeatedly. And by whom?

At seven o'clock one evening, two days before the Stein Morretti Christmas party and three days before Christmas Eve, Marshall had just concluded a long, drawn out meeting with Bernie Cummings, the President of Fourdow Environmental. He found Tony in his office, hidden behind his desk and several stacks of documents. A glassful of drink, obviously not his first, was tight in his hand.

"You're still here," Marshall said wearily as he fell into Tony's leather sofa. Lately, Tony had come and gone like the wind, often disappearing early in the afternoons. Some days, he didn't show his face until ten or eleven in the morning.

Tony's tired, bloodshot eyes stared back blankly. "Someone had to finish the financial statements for year end," he replied in that vague, slow, alcohol-induced drawl that comes with several drinks, but not too many.

"The rest of the money will be transferred into the account by noon tomorrow."

"Good. Thanks," Tony replied thickly. "My knight in shining armor has come through again."

Marshall sensed the sarcastic tone, but he ignored it. Just as Tony had seen several glimpses of Marshall's contemptuous ways over the years, Marshall had recently witnessed, on numerous occasion, Tony's blatant bitterness. Occasionally, he even felt contempt coming from his old partner - but tried to shrugged it off as stress. As he leaned back into the soft leather, he realized that Tony's face was puffy and he looked unusually out of sorts. He wondered then if Tony was closing in on a breakdown. Perhaps this was just too much for him to deal with?

"Are you coming to the Christmas party?" Tony asked.

Marshall hesitated.

"Cheryl's confirming the dinner - for the hotel. She was asking this afternoon. You haven't RSVP'd."

"I don't know."

Tony scoffed. "Stein, just make the effort. You have to be there. Just show your face. You know that we've got a lot of stakeholders coming."

Marshall was well aware that the room would be full of influential people and that it was his duty to show his face and his support. He had even taken his dark charcoal gray suit to the cleaners. Sarah would have taken care of the cleaners, Marshall had thought as he was doing this very errand. And Sarah would have laid out his suit and shirt and tie and matching socks, he thought at this very moment.

"Just finished meeting with Bernie," he replied matter-of-factly, changing the subject.

"And? What?" What good news does Fourdow have for us today?"

"They estimate that the north and west quadrants could be clean as early as February. More likely March. The south quadrant won't happen until next fall. Too much crap there."

Marshall had ensured that he had close and daily communication with their team and had been diligent at keeping Tony up-to-date on a regular basis. Tony had already received wind of the delays, through earlier conversations with Marshall, but he still smirked before draining the remaining drink from his glass.

“Hardly what I needed to hear, considering that I’ve got thirty-two sales for the south quadrant right here on my desk.”

“I thought it was thirty-three?”

“Thirty-two. The Wright’s have backed out - thanks to the media. We didn’t have a deposit.”

“Could we have saved the sale?”

Tony shrugged it off. “Who the shit cares?” he spat. “Just means I’ve got one less buyer to contend with.”

“I told you I’d deal with the lot,” Marshall said evenly, but he was frustrated. It had become increasingly apparent that Tony had been letting things slide.

“I’ll deal with them,” Tony replied arrogantly. “You do what you do best.”

“What does that mean?”

Tony leaned over his desk. “What do I tell these people, Stein? What would you tell them?” His face slowly contorted into a rage. “What do we say? Mr. landowner, you just spent four, five hundred thousand on a piece of land that is poisoned to the core of the earth. I know, I know,” Tony held up his hands as his face mocked ridicule. “I know we told you it would be ready to build in November. Our apologies. We were grossly mistaken, but some mother-son-of-a-bitch seemed to have put rat poison into the soil and, well, it’s not exactly the safest damn place to build. But might I interest you in another piece of land? How about one over there, on the north end? You don’t have much of a view of those pristine Rocky Mountains and most of the lots are facing north, but soon they will be as clean as a whistle and you can move in. Come on Mr. Landowner! We’ll even give you a deal. We'll give you a healthy discount on the sale because we certainly won't be able to sell to another stupid unsuspecting mother-f-ing buyer!"

Marshall's eyes had grown brooding throughout Tony's outbreak. He had felt Tony's growing hostility - or concern - over the months, but until now, he had no idea of its magnitude. Nor was he prepared with what was to come next.

Tony's eyes had changed from verging on an alcohol-driven high to mania. He pushed his chair away from his desk in a rage. Then before Marshall knew what had happened, Tony was towering over him. "I am tired of this game, Marshall," he sneered.

"What game?" Marshall asked evenly.

Tony shook his head dramatically, as if in disbelief. Then he sighed as he moved towards his desk and pulled out a fresh bottle of scotch from a drawer. "You're some arrogant son-of-a-bitch," he said grimly as he poured his glass until it was brimming with the rich gold liquid.

Marshall was filling with anger. He clenched his fists and took a deep breath. Now wasn't the time to lose control, he thought. There was too much at stake. He turned his eyes to the world outside. The lights from Stein Morretti's offices cast a yellow hue beyond Tony and the dark panes of glass. As thick white snowflakes free-fell from the sky above, Marshall had a profound thought. Tony was as reckless as the cold white proof of the season. With winter on their doorstep, the real storm was yet to come - and it was inevitable that a winter in Calgary wouldn't come and go without a raging blizzard.

Tony's voice filled the room in a husky drawl. "Stein, you were an absolute genius at assembling the land," he started, in a low, story-like voice. "Not only did you achieve everything that we were after, you did it in record time! But you managed this project in your usual contemptuous ways. And now we have proof that you made one too many enemies this time!"

Marshall's eyes opened in alarm at Tony's last words.

"I should be claiming victory at this stage in life! Sailing in Monaco!" Tony exploded. "Or drinking wine in a villa in France! Basta! After all of this hard work!" He dropped his head to his glass in miserable defeat, then swallowed its contents in one large gulp.

"Look, Tony, you've had a few drinks. We've got better things to do than to..." Marshall began, but the look on Tony's face alarmed him and he paused.

Tony's eyes were black. Brooding. Filled with hatred. "Marshall Stein!" he boomed, shaking his head as he smirked. "I worked with the man for almost thirty years. Thirty f-ing years. I was his partner! I was his friend! And wouldn't you know, I don't remember a soul, not one single individual on the entire planet that ever said to me, "What a great guy that Marshall Stein is?" Basta!" Tony sneered. "If I had a dollar for every time someone we dealt with or one of our employees came running to me with a complaint about you and your bad-ass contemptuous attitude - well! Basta! I'd be a hell of a lot wealthier than I am today!"

"Hold on there for a minute!" Marshall cried out defensively. "Tony, you've had too much to drink. Don't say another word. I'll take you home." Visibly shaken, Marshall pulled himself off the sofa.

Whether from the drink, or his running emotions, Tony had escalated out of control. "Why wouldn't a man that had touched so many lives not have made more friends? Why? And why would I put up with his contemptuous ways? Day after day! Night after night! Deal after deal! It's because of you that this development is infested with poisons! You continued with your bad-ass ways - and then you bolted on me. You deserted me, for Christ sake!"

Marshall felt numb. The two men had shared many a heated moment over their lifetime. Often, their arguments began with Tony begging Marshall to put on the brakes. Or to show his human side. However, never had anything so personal and blatantly insulting been spun into either of their courts. Marshall's hand reached for the door. "Let's go Morretti. I'll drive you home."

"You'll drive me home? Seriously? Until a couple of months ago, you could hardly get out of bed. *You* are going to drive *me* home?" Tony sneered before he broke out into fake laugh. "You *know* that I *know*, Stein."

“What do you know?”

“This problem stems from you, you mother...! Because you are such an blazing asshole!”

Marshall’s face turned red as he clenched his fists. Every ounce of him wanted to retaliate, but he held his composure. For the sake of the project.

For the sake of Tony.

For the sake of the only friend that Marshall had left on the planet.

“You’ve had too much to drink, Morretti,” he repeated gravely. “I’ll drive you home or you can sit in that chair and blame me for the rest of the night. Or for the rest of your life. Your call.”

Tony dropped his head to his chest. Marshall, uncertain what to do, or what to say, looked past Tony and his scotch and the piles of sales agreements on the desk, to the ghost town outside. The wind had shifted, Marshall thought. As his eyes watched the thick, wet flakes fall onto the panes of glass and melt away, he thought of Sarah. Sarah would have suggested that perhaps a Chinook was coming.

“The wind has shifted, Marshall. Perhaps tomorrow a Chinook will bring us sunshine again,” she would have said.

“Come on, my friend,” Marshall held out his hand. “Let’s go, my friend.”

On the drive home, Tony curled up like a child against the passenger door. He was so still and so silent that Marshall thought that he had fallen into a drunken slumber. When they reached the street that led to Morretti‘s sprawling estate, Marshall called Tony’s wife Vivian and asked her to meet him at the door.

“Is he bad again?” she asked anxiously.

“I suppose. It’s been another tough day. Just put him to bed.”

As Marshall pulled his Lexus into the winding driveway, Tony mumbled something.

“What did you say?”

“You are a son-of-a-bitch,” Tony repeated in a slur.

Marshall noticed that Vivian was standing outside in a light housecoat. “Tony! You have to go. Vivian is standing outside barely dressed and she must be very cold. Tony, Vivian is waiting for you!” Marshall prodded.

“Vivian knows,” Tony drawled.

“What does Vivian know?”

"She can’t stand the sight of you. D’ya know that Stein?”

Marshall flinched as his eyes lifted again to the petite silhouette in the doorway.

Suddenly Tony began to laugh hysterically. “She k-n-o-w-s, Stein!” he said finally, catching his breath. And she isn’t surprised at what’s happened,” he slurred. “D'ya you know what she said, Stein? D’ya know?” he struggled to open the door.

“What does she know Tony? Tell me. What does Vivian know?”

As the passenger door swung open Tony spilled onto the driveway. He pulled himself up and his tall, lean body teetered toward the winding rock stairs before he bellowed out his next words.

“She said,” he paused as he struggled to find his next step in the dark, “she - she said, ‘Stein has made so many enemies in his life that she’s surprised that this hadn’t happened sooner.’ And Marshall, I never told her a damn thing!”

Chapter Eighteen

Marshall's face was painfully white and drawn as he drove home from Tony's that evening. He'd never had such a cold and accusing finger pointed in his direction, and he felt shaky and cold, verging on numb. He felt empty, verging on hollow.

As he entered the foyer he found Jazz curled up in the corner by the door, and for some reason this sight brought tears to Marshall's eyes. He leaned down and gently patted the swirls of cream and chocolate beneath his feet.

"Hello, Jazzman," he mumbled gruffly.

Until that evening, the months at the Estates had been a blessing in disguise for Marshall. The challenging and busy days diverted his mind from the darkness that had manifested within the walls of "A Gift to My Family" for so long. And although his obsession with finding his missing grandchild was *always* at the forefront, the obstacles and delays had somehow become easier to bear. The day that Thomas had called to resign, Marshall had accepted that he would find his granddaughter when she needed to find him. Until then, he could only assume that Christina's sister was, in fact, providing the essentials for the child. And the child *was* "in god's loving hands", as Thomas had suggested on more than one occasion.

Marshall hardly noticed the annoying song from the river that evening. He barely grimaced as it rose to the chant-like climax that he hated most. He had other things on his mind. He thought of Tony's hurtful words and his tired eyes and his swollen face. He thought of the brown and purple firs on the Estates, the abandoned land and the white blanket of snow that covered what was once a dream. He thought of the faceless stranger that lurked in the distance, laughing at the demise he had created with the poison.

Then he thought of the child, and both hope and helplessness instantly consumed him. She was out there somewhere - he was certain of this. And she was the only living being on the planet that was his own flesh and blood. How could he not continue to look for her? He would look for her until his death, he concluded and dialed Thomas Sinclair's telephone number.

A tired and fragile sounding Mrs. Sinclair answered the phone.

"Hello, Mrs. Sinclair. It's Marshall Stein. How are you?"

"Oh, Mr. Stein!" the frail voice exclaimed. "Thank you. I am as best as I can be under the circumstances. And how are you?"

"I'm fine. Fine."

"You must have found the child? Yes?"

Marshall closed his eyes and swallowed. Tony's bludgeoning that very evening had left him raw and vulnerable. “No, I haven't. I'm sorry to be calling so late. But it's important. Could I speak to Thomas for a moment?”

“Oh, Mr. Stein!” the woman blurted out in a tiny, pitifully hollow voice. “Thomas is in Peter Lougheed hospital. I thought you knew!”

“Knew?”

“Oh my!” she continued, “Thomas had a stroke yesterday.”

Marshall closed his eyes.

“He is okay. There is no apparent lasting damage. And the doctors told me this afternoon that he might be able come home soon. Maybe even in time for Christmas. But it put the fear of God in all of us.”

As Marshall hung up the phone, he imagined Cecilia Sinclair and her purple white hair and crooked, spindly fingers, sitting by the window with a rosary and praying for her husband to come home. Then he thought of Thomas Sinclair, lying still as the sound of death, with tubes up his nose and machines by his bed. He felt his forehead to see if he had a fever, then squeezed his temples with his thumbs to rid of the throbbing. Then he took a deep breath and looked around the parlor. His eyes fell to Sarah's white cashmere sash, and he stared at it for a very long time. Then instantly his tightened his jaw, for he had made a decision.

“It's time,” he voiced aloud and stood from the sofa.

The night had been bludgeoning cutting and painful for Marshall - but at that very moment it had opened his eyes to acceptance of some kind. “It's time,” was Marshall's voiced decision that it was finally time to pack Sarah's things. It was time to get rid of her creamy lipsticks and perfumes. It was time to rid of her silky nighties and floppy hats. It was time to box her dresses and white cotton slippers, and the white cashmere sash that he had given her for Christmas so many years ago.

He started on the main floor. For an hour or so, he worked silently and diligently. Jazz followed him from room to room, suspiciously supervising Marshall's moves.

Eventually, all of Sarah's things from the parlor, den and main floor bathrooms lay in piles of garbage bags at the foyer.

Next, he started in Sarah's closet. He began with the longest rows of clothes and by the handful, dropped dresses and slacks and blouses and scarves and skirts into more bags, until the hallway was piled high with Sarah's things.

When he caught a glimpse of Jazz's chocolate paws inside one of the bags, he knelt down and peaked inside inside. Jazz had curled up onto one of Sarah's sweaters and his tiny pink nose was inhaling her scent.

"Hey Jazzman!" Marshall spoke softly. "Come on out. Come on. I'll get you some tuna."

Rather than acknowledge the feast that Marshall had offered, Jazz let out a tiny and hardly audible meow.

"Lets go. Come on, my man," Marshall said more convincingly than he felt and reached into the bag, immediately yelping out in pain.

"Ouch! Dam you!" he cried out as small droplets of blood oozed from his wrist where Jazz had bit him. "Out!" Marshall yelled, louder thus time. Jazz didn't budge.

"Out!" Marshall cried again as he rustled the bag.

But Jazz wasn't going anywhere soon, and when Marshall concluded this he sat on the floor and stared at the wall. He was exhausted, and after a long while let out a sigh that echoed off the hallway walls. Then he picked himself up and started again in Sarah's closet.

There were hat boxes and shoeboxes and boxes filled with belts and others with costume jewelry. The first he opened held the blue cashmere hat with the yellow flower embroidered on its side, and Marshall's expression filled with melancholy, immediately surprised that Sarah had kept this after all of these years. It was the very hat that she had worn on their honeymoon in Providence, Paris. It had sat snug around her exquisite face, accenting her blue eyes and pouty lips as they walked blocks and blocks up and down cobblestone streets and stairways in search of the perfect place to celebrate. Sarah had been on a mission to find the quaintest piano bar possible. Finally, she had turned to Marshall with a smile - and nod of approval.

It was small, intimate pub off a side street - the type that neighborly sorts gathered around a piano for song and drink. The type that visitors immediately felt at home and welcomed. The type that strangers fell in love. And the type that beckoned music well into the night and wee hours of the morning. It was not the sort of place that Marshall would have chosen - but at one time he would have done anything, absolutely anything, for Sarah.

"The perfect place for us, yes?" she had whispered into Marshall's ear. Her sweet breath had made Marshall tingle, and he felt loved and complete - for the first time in his life.

This was the evening that Sarah had sipped on her first - and only - martini. This was the evening that they had sang Sarah's favorite song around the piano. This was also the first evening that held hands as husband and wife as they also held fast to their bright and invincible future.

Marshall wiped both of his eyes with his fingers. Then he placed the hat with the yellow flower embroidered on its side back into the box and gently closed the lid.

He didn't have to open most of the other boxes to know what they held - Sarah's neat handwriting labelled the front of each box - but he did so anyways - slowly pulling off each lid and then cautiously peering inside. If something looked looked familiar, he would pull it out and stare at it for a moment, sometimes two. Sometimes he would stare at it much longer, if it enabled him grasp onto a memory. With this sometimes came another shed of tears.

About two hours later (although it felt much longer to Marshall, it felt like eternity), he reached up to the very back, left hand corner of closet. He wouldn't have seen this last box if he was just half an inch shorter, and had spotted it out of the corner of his eye. The moment he held it in his hands he knew that this box was different from the others. He knew this because Sarah's neat printing wasn't voicing what it held.

It took him a moment to register what he had just discovered, but when he did he dropped to his knees. Within seconds he had dumped the contents of the entire box, which held dozens of letters and greeting cards. Confused, his hand timidly reached for the letter on top. It was a letter from Charlie to Sarah...

Dearest Mom;

I am writing from Afghanistan in a safe place, so please don't worry.

Still, I am struggling, I want to shout or cry aloud as I write this, but I can't. I need to stay strong for Zig. Christina has disappeared. One night a few weeks back she just up and walked out of the hospital. She simply left! What will I tell Zig if something happens to her mother?

The last time I visited Christina she was hardly able to speak. The others were forceful in her imagination and they consumed the hospital room. Once, in a brief, but clearer moment, she mentioned Zig (but she was so drugged that it came and went in an instant). All she said was that Zig needed a new winter coat, and then began raging at the invisible men that continue to torment her. It brought tears to my eyes.

The doctors explained that they had just put her on yet <u>another</u> new medication. They had tried several others, and were concerned that she had hardly responded.

Until that last hospital visit I didn't realize how difficult the sickness. I saw glimpses of it, even before we were married, but I never imagined how horrendous the disease. I remember now, it was when she was about six months pregnant that she began to spiral downward when her old medications stopped working.

I fear for Zig. The doctors are relatively confident that Christina is the third generation with the disease. They think that her mother as well as her grandmother suffered from it. That must be the family curse that she had so frequently made reference to! I can only pray for Zig that the disease doesn't haunt her!

How such a miracle can unfold from tragedy, Mom, I don't know. Zig is incredible. So sweet and kind and so very smart. I think that she looks a little bit like me! And I can't imagine loving a child as I love her.

I also need to tell you that this trip to Afghanistan will be my last overseas assignment (at least until Zig gets older). I wasn't going to take this one, but with Lynette healthy and able to watch over Zig, I saw it as my one last chance to cover an important international issue. Perhaps I'll get the bug out of my system , and wouldn't you like this:) I have been offered a full-time position in Vancouver when I return, and will fill you in with the details. It will certainly curtail my career (or perhaps my traveling bug) but I will be able to there for Zig, and more so then ever before Zig needs her father.

I hope that you will come to Vancouver when I return and spend some quality time with the two of us. It has been too long (and I think of you daily). I often hope that your life with the old guy is bearable. Are you nearing any decisions on changes that you have talked about? I hope so, but whatever your decision, dearest Mom, you know I am behind you all of the way. You must remember that you are not responsible for Dad. That insufferable, selfish bugger will always fare well on his own. When it comes to Dad, you know that I am at a loss for words. Too much water under the bridge…

I know, I know! You are thinking "Charlie at a loss for words?" I am trying to lighten things up for the moment, dear Mom, for as I write this I wonder if our world is falling apart. There seems to be a war across every ocean. Life is so tender. Love is so tender. I love you so dearly!

I must go, but before I do I will say, again, that I promise to be safe. I love you and will call as soon as I return to Canadian soil.

Love always, Charlie

Marshall stayed on the floor until almost four o'clock that morning. Letters were strewn across the closet floor and around his legs and feet in little piles. His anguish was overwhelming. The cold words in the first letter that Marshall read from

Charlie to Sarah were unbearable. His son called him an insufferable, selfish bugger, he thought again and again as he cringed. Also, Marshall had never imagined that it had gotten so bad that Sarah would think about leaving him. And the news of the birth of Charlie's daughter, in another letter, had torn Marshall into two. Dry heaves often escaped his chest as he read something new, each time struggling to find a morsel of composure before tightening his jaw and continuing.

Finally, when he found love notes from Tony to Sarah, and others from Sarah to Tony that she had never sent, the room erupted into fierce begging cries.

"No!" he shouted in defiance to the walls. "No! Please God! No! No! No!"

Chapter Nineteen

Three hours later, just after seven, Marshall awoke to his cell phone ringing.

"Is this Mr. Stein? From Rocky Mountain Estates?"

"Yes." Marshall mumbled as he lifted his head from the sofa and looked up to the grandfather clock.

"Mr. Stein, I am scared for you."

"Excuse me?"

"It's going to get worse," a woman's voice whispered. "He's not going to stop."

"Who is this?" Marshall asked gravely as he rubbed his eyes.

"Look. Please," the voice said in angst. "I feel so terrible. He's so angry! I just can't believe what he has done!"

"Are you talking about the poisoning at the Estates?" Marshall asked pointedly.

"Yes," the woman whispered.

"Look," Marshall replied evenly as he pulled himself up. "You need to help me out here. *Whom* are we talking about?"

"I knew. I knew that fall. He hated losing the land. He said that you and your partner squeezed him out of five hundred thousand dollars. He never wanted to sell. But I had no idea it would come to this!"

It had been almost four years since Marshall had begun assembling the land, but he was certain that he would have remembered a deal that would have padded his pockets with an extra half million dollars. He searched again, to remember a face, or a sideways comment, or something, like some off-color incident, that would point him to the culprit.

"Why don't you help me out here," Marshall said quickly. "Why don't you tell me…"

"He will know that it was me. I can't."

"Look," Marshall continued as anger surfaced, "what he did was criminal. He has cost Rocky Mountain Estates a vast amount of money and has ruined many families' plans to build their dream homes. Someone has to stop him!"

"I know. I know," she hushed. "I feel so terrible about this. I am having reoccurring nightmares."

"If you feel so bad," Marshall raised his voice, "then you *will* give me his name *and* report him to the police!"

There was a long pause on the other end of the phone before a hoarse whisper broke the silence, “Do you remember the big blue truck?”

“A big blue truck?” Marshall repeated quickly, but it wasn’t quick enough, for whoever was on the other end of the line instantly ended the call with this one tip.

Marshall placed a call to the Morretti residence.

“Vivian, I need to speak to Tony.”

“He’s still sleeping.” Vivian's voice sounded tired and drawn.

Marshall knew that Tony never slept past six. “You have to wake him.”

“Oh, I think it’s better if I let him sleep, with the company Christmas party tonight.”

“Vivian, this is urgent."

Within a minute, Tony's hoarse voice mumbled a hello. Marshall briefly explained what he needed and why.

“Can Cheryl get the documents ready for us this morning?”

Tony yawned. “Marshall, Cheryl’s got kids in every music and dance lesson this city has to offer. I don’t know.”

“Then someone else has to...” Marshall insisted.

Tony interrupted Marshall. “I get it Stein. If she can’t do it, I’ll have her find someone else that can help.”

The two agreed to meet at the offices at two o’clock that afternoon. Marshall drove as quickly as he was able through the snow-swept roads, arriving half an hour early. He was relieved to find Cheryl, albeit an obviously annoyed Cheryl for having her Saturday interrupted, arranging the documents that Tony had asked her to pull from the filing cabinets and spread around the large board room table.

Marshall carefully read and reread page after page of sales agreements for the next forty-five minutes. He perused the seller's names, property titles and purchase prices with a fine tooth comb. He vaguely remembered banging on the doors of the once sprawling countryside as he worked to acquire the properties, and the faces that answered the doors, but for the life of him he couldn't recall anything unusual.

At quarter past two, Tony stood at the door to the board room. He was red-eyed but perkier than expected, and the two men went over the files again for a couple of hours.

"There's nothing here," Tony said in exasperation as he closed the last file and fell back in his chair. "There's nothing here. No psycho, no ill-feeling deal and no big blue truck. And there's not one seller here that we cheated out of half a million dollars!"

Marshall had been struggling with a memory all afternoon. Dust flying from the back tires. Someone swearing in anger. A shiny chrome bumper. "I remember something…" he admittedly quietly with a perplexed look on his face.

"Basta!" Tony exclaimed in frustration. "*Something* isn't good enough." Then he left the boardroom, only to return a minute later with a bottle of scotch and two glasses.

"Drink?" he asked.

Marshall hesitated. "No. Sure. Yeah, sure, I'll have a shot."

As Tony slid a half-filled glass across the table towards Marshall, he asked him if he was going to the Christmas party.

"I suppose."

"You suppose?" Tony repeated. "I'm guessing that means yes."

Marshall felt surreal as he sat across from his friend. Tony was acting as if nothing had been said the previous evening! Tony was acting as if nothing had happened between Sarah and him!

He took a small sip of scotch and then very evenly confronted Tony. "You didn't tell me about Sarah."

Tony's face feigned innocence. “Sarah. What about Sarah?”

“You and Sarah. You met Sarah in Paris, you son-of-a-bitch.”

Tony's face turned ashen. “No,” he whispered, finishing his drink.

“No? That’s all you have to say?”

“I didn’t meet Sarah in Paris. And wherever you got your piece of information, it isn’t what it looks like.”

“No?”

“No.”

“Then what, *exactly,* was it?”

Tony's eyes dropped to the files strewn across the boardroom table. Then he took a deep breath before looking up to Marshall. "Sarah needed a friend, Marshall," he began very gravely. “But we never…never…” Tony paused as he struggled with his own memories, and as his mind worked his face slowly filled with anger. “Basta!” Tony hushed bitterly. “She was alone and beautiful and so very vulnerable. And she was exquisite. A creature that should have been smiling all the time! The further you drifted way the more she came running to me.”

Tony’s words were painful, but Marshall didn’t flinch.

“After Charlie,” Tony added with a snicker, “Sarah would have run to anybody, so I can’t take any credit. She knew about all of your affairs Marshall.”

Marshall’s eyes widened marginally with these last words. “So you were comforting my wife as I was confiding in you?”

"Whoa! Hang on a minute! I never told Sarah a damn thing! She was a smart woman. She figured it out on her own. I played dumb. I swear to God! I never even *hinted* that I knew about any, or should I say, *all* of your infidelities!" Then Tony took off his glasses and through them on the table. He rubbed his eyes and sighed in exhaustion before looking sheepishly towards Marshall. "And you have to believe me," he said with a painful look on his face, "I never slept with her."

Marshall openly scoffed. "You never slept with her?" he replied in a low, growly tone.

"I wanted to," Tony instantly and bravely admitted. "I remember the Christmas party way back when. Remember, the one you missed for a rendezvous with that young apprentice?"

Marshall grimaced. On the pretense of a pressing deal, he had spent four days in London with a voluptuous blonde, an up and coming architect that he had met at a conference. Tony and Vivian had insisted that Sarah go to the party with them.

Tony's expression had filled with melancholy, and he continued, almost as if he was talking to himself. "She was wearing this red strappy dress," Tony reminisced. "It fell to her knees, and the material wrapped itself around her legs. The color was perfect for her. It made her face looked flushed and her lips look so pinky-red. I remember thinking, Marshall could be kissing off that lipstick. But I wasn't sure if she was wearing lipstick. I'd never seen such sultry lips. I was desperate to kiss her, where you hadn't kissed her. But you had kissed her everywhere, and she was longing for you... She was the loneliest woman in this city, for God sakes. She was longing for you, so she wanted nothing to do with me."

Marshall remembered the dress. It was the very one that he had found in the storage room. The one that had been wrapped up in the plastic bag with the zipper. The one that he remembered thinking, when he had discovered it, why it had been packed away. He had bought the silky piece out of guilt, the prior spring, after a fling with a woman whose face he couldn't remember, even if he tried.

"It was the color of cranberry juice, and silky soft. I bought it for her in Europe," Marshall said quite matter-of-factly.

Tony was surprised at Marshall's words, or the way he said them, and a puzzled look fell across his face.

"So were you screwing my wife the same time you were consoling me," Marshall accused again.

"No!" Tony exclaimed. "I never touched her! It began years after you started wandering. Somewhere in between the blonde in London and the redhead in Florida. But I swear to you, I never laid a finger on her. But did I want to? You bet! But Sarah would never let it happen."

"But you were with her in Paris?"

Tony shook his head adamantly. "No! No! I wasn't, Marshall!" Then his eyes fell in defeat and he admitted in a hush, "But the day you got the call from the police in Paris, I was on my way to the airport to meet her..."

"To Paris?"

Tony's chin dropped to his chest. "Yeah," he finally replied, then looked up to Marshall in admittance. "Yeah, Marshall, I was on my way to Paris. I was like a damn puppy dog. On her heels for months. Silently begging her to give me a chance. After spending a week in one of the most enchanting cities in the world, alone I might add, she called me and asked me to join her."

. . .

"Marshall," Sarah began softly, "I thought I would come with you to Europe. On your next trip. We could window shop, and walk along the ocean, and sip on wine in quaint bistros along the way...We could sit by the fire at night and relish what we have left...Remember that quaint little inn that we stayed at in Paris, Marshall?" she added in a whisper verging on a beg. "We can do this for Charlie," she added softly. "Charlie would have wanted us to be happy."

. . .

Chapter Twenty

Marshall left Tony and Stein Morretti's offices with hundreds of words left unspoken. He was numb and mentally drained. Maybe he was in shock, he thought. Sarah would have known if he was in shock, or if he was coming down with something. The thought of Sarah knowing what, exactly, was wrong with Marshall comforted him a great deal, but still, he felt his forehead.

The moment he entered "A Gift to My Family" he scaled the stairs to the master bedroom, fell to the floor in front of the toilet and vomited. His stomach erupted again and again with the poisoned truth that filled him, until his muscles ached from its release, and the vomit was nothing but yellow bile.

Then he showered and shaved. He put on his charcoal gray suit, matching socks and soft black leather shoes. With a wretched taste still pungent in his mouth, he went downstairs to the parlor and poured himself a scotch.

Next, he called the Peter Lougheed Hospital Gift Store and ordered a large bouquet of flowers and a large box of chocolates to be sent to Thomas Sinclair's room. As he hung up the phone, his eyes fell to Sarah's piano, and then the stool where her white cashmere shawl once lay and he remembered it packed away in one of dozens of green plastic bags that now held all of the other things that reminded him of her. Then his eyes fell to the painting on the wall behind it, and he stared at it for a very long time, until a firm and decisive look filled his eyes.

He gently lifted the original Tarkay painting off it's hinge and set it on the floor. This painting must go too, he thought. He'd never really liked it much. It was too vivid and bright, and reminded him of something he couldn't quite put his finger on. He would sell it, he thought. He would take it to an art dealer and sell it along with the grand piano and all of the other things that he didn't need, or things that reminded him of other things.

Things that reminded him that Charlie had gone to Afghanistan.

Things that reminded him that Sarah had gone to Paris.

Marshall tried the combination to the safe three times before its steel door swung open. His hand reached up to the top of the cold metal wall and he felt the envelope and quickly peeled off several strips of scotch tape that had held it in place - and kept it hidden. When the small package fell into his hand he quickly ripped it open and his eyes instantly fell to a small white gold buffalo, about the size of a quarter, hanging from a black silk chain. As he held the tiny pendant in the palm of his hands, he pondered how something so small could look so powerful.

. . .

"What could it be?" he said playfully as he shook the silver package.

"It's not breakable," she whispered, curling up beside him on the bed. Her golden mane teased his arm and he inhaled, to hold her scent.

"It's not breakable?" he whispered back.

"No, I don't give presents that are breakable... life is too delicate."

. . .

Marshall thoughts at this very moment travelled miles and spanned years. They ran in circles and did somersaults and backflips. He started with one thought, then quickly moved to another, and then to another. From Tony's accusations, to Sarah's plans to divorce him, to Sarah with Tony - or almost with Tony - to Charlie his hurtful letters...

Since Charlie had become a man, father and son had had their share of differences, but Marshall had no idea that Charlie thought so little of him. It must have been Christina, he thought. Perhaps Charlie had found out that he had had his son's wife, loved his son's wife, before his son. That probably explained the magnitude of dissension, Marshall reasoned. Sarah's knowledge of his infidelities, well, that would be why the only woman that he had ever truly loved had been planning on leaving him. Undeniably, Christina was to blame for all of this. And undeniably, had Christina and her bizarre sickness not come into Marshall's life, or Charlie's life, or Sarah's life, life as a whole would have turned out better. It would have been kinder and more fulfilling and with his family by his side. Full of music and the bursts of seasons and children's laughter and song. And perhaps Thomas Sinclair wouldn't be in the Peter Lougheed hospital with tubes up his nose, fighting for his life, if he hadn't exerted so much energy on finding the bitch and the child.

Then he thought about Cecilia Sinclair again, her purple white hair and crooked fingers, and imagined her sitting by the window, waiting for her husband to come home. Just like Sarah had sat at her piano, day after day, year after year, waiting for Marshall to return in body and mind.

The white gold buffalo remained tightly clutched in the palm of Marshall's hand for almost an hour.

For Charlie had gone to Afghanistan.

And Sarah had gone to Paris.

And Charlie had wanted to see the world.

And Sarah had begun to change her world.

Finally, Marshall pulled himself off of the sofa and tripped over Jazz, who had been curled up by his feet in sleep.

"Jazzman!" Marshall muttered in surprise, and then leaned down to pet the chocolate and vanilla head.

Jazz hissed.

"Come here," Marshall said gently as he kneeled down and held out his hand.

Electric eyes opened wider as Marshall's hand reached further, and he rubbed Jazz behind the ears, then under the chin. As Jazz relented his deep blue eyes disappeared as he accepted the affection that he had been starved of for so long.

"Hey, Jazzman," Marshall muttered as his thick fingers twirled his hair. "Hey there, buddy, it's Christmas."

Jazz's eyes opened wide to Marshall's voice. Then he opened his mouth, and his pink lips moved surreally as a long, soft and almost content sound escaped his throat. Marshall sat on the floor for a several minutes as he stared into space and continued to gently pet his foe. Finally, he let out a long, windy sigh, pulled himself up and moved to the patio doors.

The winter's air grabbed him and he shivered as he stepped onto the terrace. An angry wind whistled across the landscape, lifting snow recklessly in ferocious breaths. Marshall wrapped his arms into his chest as his eyes fell to the river, and its pure blanket that had enveloped it for the eve. Sarah would have embraced the night, Marshall thought. She would have called it magical, and had he let her, her full lips would have kissed his own very tenderly.

Marshall looked down to the pendant in the palm of his hand again, and then without hesitation, flung it into the air. It soared across the pathway and towards the river, and at its height, the clouds danced past the moon's light and the white gold glowed for the briefest of seconds before falling into the cold water below.

Marshall let out a deep and shaky sound that breathed grief. He had ruined the lives of the two people that he had loved the most in his life.

But it wasn't the bitch's fault, he concluded at this very juncture.

It was his fault. The blame, in its entirety, could only be pointed to him, he thought, and he dropped his chin to his chest and closed his eyes. Then, for the first time since Marshall had locked himself behind "A Gift to My Family" he felt a morsel of relief that he was able admit that he had done wrong.

Chapter Twenty-one

Katy's landscaping job at Rocky Mountain Estates eventually led to much more than she had ever imagined. Marshall Stein had officially rolled up his sleeves "Until the problem is resolved," Tony had reported in a tired and drawn voice as his made the announcement to the staff. Nervous, overworked Randy was fired two weeks later after several outbursts and accusations about the contamination, most of them directed toward Marshall himself. That same afternoon Tony offered an ecstatic Rory Randy's position.

First thing the next morning, Katy was summoned to Stein Morretti's boardroom. Katy guessed that it was to either officially warn her that "mum" was the word - or to give her walking papers. She hadn't spoken to either man since the afternoon they had found her near the staff cabin, and was intimidated to see both Tony and Marshall sitting across from one another at the large boardroom table.

The offer to assist Marshall Stein came as a blinding surprise.

"We need someone that knows the game," Tony explained matter-of-factly. "And someone with experience dealing with the whistle blowers that will inevitably end up on our door steps any day now. I suspect you know what I'm talking about?"

"I am sure that you can appreciate we've got a lot at stake," Marshall added, "and we need an educated and diplomatic voice to help us navigate through this nasty mess. Tony has a lot on his plate and I've stepped back in on a temporary basis to give him a hand. You'd be working with me. You'd be that voice that will help us salvage what we are able to salvage."

Katy's surprise blinded her for a moment, and she hesitated. Then she instantly realized that full disclosure was an absolute must at this very juncture. "Do you know that I was fired from my last position?" she asked pointedly, lifting her chin in defiance.

Marshall didn't flinch. "Your father wrote a book that broke the news. He used highly confidential information that only you and the top executives would have had access to. You were a Director and Publicist for the company. You worked in their head office, in New York, and contended that it was a leak and you had no part in it, outside of your relation to your father."

Katy opened her eyes wide in surprise. "That's a lot of information."

"We have our sources," Tony said dryly. "And you might be surprised," he added, raising his brow, "that word on the street is that you are one of the best and that you were the fall guy."

Katy was astonished with this news. Relief instantly showed its face. "That certainly is good news to the ears," she replied evenly, thinking that this still didn't answer the reason for her father's deception.

For the next hour the three discussed the timely and sensitive tasks ahead. They began with the most precedent, which was formulating a communication strategy for the landowners as well as the conspicuous media, who had become tenacious with questions. Then they negotiated a salary.

"Just about forgot," Tony piped up as they all stood to leave. "I'll get Sharon to get you a Confidentiality Agreement to sign. And we'll also finalize a new employment contract. I'll make sure that we get everything to you by lunchtime."

"Thank you.

"But I need one more thing from you."

"What is that?"

"Any chance we can get a copy of your real resume?" he asked with a grin on his face," for our records?" he added, holding up Katy's fabricated resume.

"Of course," she grinned back. "I'll have it on your desk by morning," she replied calmly, but she didn't feel calm. She felt hopeful and suddenly warm from head to toe, as if the skies had turned to the vivid hue of blue that she so loved.

Thus, as spring turned to summer, summer to fall, and winter showed its beard, Fourdow's equipment continued to throb day and night to remove the poisons. The Estates buzzed with a new kind of energy and both hope and desperation clung to the trees as everyone waited for the prognosis. Katy fell into her new role with a natural ease. She felt exhilarated and fulfilled. She didn't feel as humbled - the humiliation that once consumed her was replaced with a confidence that she hadn't felt in a long, long time.

The days were long and exhausting as she crafted press releases and communication strategies. Other days were consumed with meetings with Marshall and city officials, environmental groups, landowners, existing homeowners and builders - some looking for answers and timelines, and others wanting out of their contracts. Marshall and Katy worked like clockwork, succinct and in tune as they did everything possible to save what they could and buy Stein Morretti time.

Admittedly, Katy found herself thinking more about Marshall than she cared to admit. She found his long, hippy-like hair and chiseled but rugged features endearing, his lean physique alluring, his strong hands and muscular arms sensual, and his brilliant mind electric. Sometimes, she found herself wondering what it would be like to be intimate with him - but would almost always quickly discard this thought. Sometimes, she hoped that she wasn't blushing when he entered the room. Sometimes, when they spoke she wondered if he could feel her attraction - although she tried very hard to hide it. Sometimes, when he stood close enough, she inhaled his manhood, earthy, raw and exposed, and she would close her eyes for a millisecond...

She had long ago accepted that her attraction to Marshall had been instant; from the moment she looked into his eyes she had felt something more than the grief that they shared. They shared something kindred and natural, and she knew that it might be explored. However, as the months took them both forward, Katy wasn't ready or able to face - or accept - that she had fallen in love. Nor did she dare imagine what this might deliver. As triumphant and thankful as she was to be given another chance in her profession, she still felt raw and exposed. She still hung onto a deeply instilled sense of pride. She still had little to her name. And she still hadn't quite found her feet. What exactly would a man like Marshall want with a woman in her position? she often thought.

As attracted as she was to Marshall, he also deeply intrigued her, and she found the secret intoxication of learning this man delightful. She witnessed firsthand how he could be cantankerous and impatient. Although she didn't always agree with his ways, she respected that he had no time for nonsense. She learned to respect his clear cut vision, and how he was fair and to the point. Daily, she embraced his knowledge and inbred business acumen and often watched him from a distance in admiration. Occasionally, she even smiled at a soft spot that Marshall would reveal, and when she did, she would wonder if Marshall himself knew that he had exposed this raw and gentle side, or if he even knew that it existed.

Over the months, Katy had also grown fond of the rough and "simple" Rory, a man much more complex than she had originally given him credit. He surprised her with his little anecdotes, and shared stories about his kids, and grinned that ruggedly crooked that was his trademark. However, even more importantly, Rory reminded her of the truth. Of a genuine smile. Of pure vanilla ice cream. Of the honesty of a sunset as one reminisced about what the day had delivered. Rory was real and tangible, and Katy loved him for this. By that winter, the two had developed an open and respectful rapport and had become trustworthy friends and colleagues as both sets of eyes continued fixed on saving the Estates.

The day the invitation to the Stein Morretti Christmas party showed up in Katy's in-basket she thought of several different excuses so that she wouldn't have to attend. She dreaded the thought of going alone, nor did she trust herself to hide how she felt about Marshall in a social setting.

It was a convincing Rory that had changed her mind. A week before the party, he poked his head into her office, "The problem's solved," he said with a grin on his face.

"What problem?" she asked suspiciously.

"Wife and I decided that I'd escort the both of you. I even have a tie. Just one. It's in my closet, somewhere deep beside my work boots and coveralls. But I'll find it for you and the wife!"

Chapter Twenty-two

The afternoon of the Christmas party, classical music played softly on Katy's computer. It had been playing since early that morning. She had opened her eyes at just after five to an ongoing commotion from the night before, and had turned on the music to drown out the shouting. She now stood in front of the open oven door and watched its elements change from red to black, then back to red, as she tried to stay warm.

Katy swore under her breath with the newest commotion, and pulled the wool blanket tighter around her shoulders. Norm had been on the rampage since the boiler had gone off the night before, and his loud and obnoxious voice had been a perpetual echo up and down the hallways and plaster walls ever since. Now he was harassing Wanda, the prostitute who lived one floor below, and Wanda was threatening to call the police.

"You better get that frigid' heat on, you asshole. And you go through my apartment one more time, you creep, I'll call the cops!" Wanda screamed from somewhere below.

"Sure you will!" Norm bellowed. "Bet they'd like to keep you warm!" he added in his early afternoon slur as he shuffled up the flight of stairs. As he made his way towards Katy's door, he began to sing. "Jingle bells. Jingle bells. Jingle all the way. Oh what fun it is to ride Wanda and her broken sleigh."

"I'm calling the cops, you smelly creep!" Wanda screamed from her doorway. An instant later the cold, old walls of the building rattled in complaint as she slammed her door shut with a vengeance.

Katy shook her head in disbelief. Norm's outbreaks and bullying had become a constant over the months. Only a few days earlier she had called the property management company for the third time in as many weeks. Norm had become unbearable, she would explain, insisting with each call that the source of the call would remain anonymous, for Norm was beginning to scare her.

Within seconds, Norm began knocking on Katy's door. She wrapped her blanket around her before unlatching the deadbolt. Combative, bloodshot eyes stared back at her.

"You're intolerable, Norm," she said dryly, with a fake smile on her face.

Norm's eyes fell beyond Katy's face, to below the shawl that was wrapped around her shoulders and the skin between her sweat top and pants. "Don't you look a sight today," he said with hungry eyes.

Katy ignored him. "Do you know when the furnace will be fixed?"

"They just got it workin'. But it needs a few hours to kick in before the temperature 'ill go up. Damn thing shoulda been replaced five years ago. I told them. I told them this was gonna happen in the middle of the friggin winter!" he spat.

"So *when* will there be hot water?" she asked pointedly. She needed to shower and dress for the party.

"'bout an hour."

Katy looked at the clock on the stove. That would give her half hour to get ready. "Shit," she muttered, half to herself, and started to close the door, but Norm had stuck a dirty-gray running shoe in the doorway.

"What else?" Katy asked as her pupils widened slightly.

Norm's bulging eyes turned to suspicious slits. "You didn't call Prosperity Management, now did ya?"

Katy knew exactly what Norm was asking. "Whom?" she asked, feigning innocence.

"Someone complained 'bout me to the management company. Thought it might'a been you."

"For goodness sakes, Norm," she retorted with an air. "Now why on earth would I be doing something like that? I need a place to live."

"Sons-of-bitches don't know what it`s like doin' this job. Dealin' with derelicts day and night, night and day. Do ya know that my phone rings at two, four, sometimes three, four, five in the morning!" he spat again, and then turned into the hallway. “Always somethin’ wrong. It’s like babysittin’ a buncha damn babies,” he grumbled. “Damn if I’ll be chatised for doin’ my job.”

“It’s chastised, Norm,” Katy said, emphasizing the first “s” that Norm had missed.

“Chatised! Chastised! Don’t give no shit ‘bout that,” he retorted as he shuffled down the hallway. “Can’t wait to find out which derelict thinks they don’t need a sitter in this hole!” he boomed, and a second later, began pounding on apartment 220. “R-o-l-i-e-e-e! Get the fuck out of bed. Rent`s three weeks late. I need a check!”

As Katy closed the door and leaned against it her eyes fell to the envelope on the table.

David Baker, L.L.B.

Baker, Chadwich & Sons

The letter had arrived from Vancouver by courier two days earlier, the day after the telephone phone call from David Baker. Katy had been shocked to hear the voice of her father’s lifetime friend on the line - and had instinctively closed her eyes. She knew that something was terribly wrong. As the eighty-year old gently gave Katy the news, she felt a numbness creeping up her back.

Si Fields had taken his life three weeks prior. He overdosed on prescription drugs and whiskey, the curly white-haired lawyer had explained. The letter from “the prematurely white pundit of the law”, as her father had often called his dearest friend, confirmed more of the truth.

. . .

Katrina, my dear, due to the many complicated circumstances around your father’s death, and his estate, I suspect that sorting things out will take a great deal of time.

I hadn’t spoken to your father in months, despite numerous attempts to connect. Admittedly, I suspected that something was not quite right. He was vague and confused the last few times that we had talked. I simply figured that he was writing another book and had a lot on his mind. (We used to call it the "Si Zone" when he was writing). Had I any idea that he was in such a bad state of mind, well, I would have taken the first ferry from the mainland. I will always blame myself for not reaching out. From what I am discovering, it breaks my heart as I write this, but Si Fields most certainly got caught in the snare of the devil.

As I explained on the telephone, I made a trip to the Island right after your father's death. Apparently, he had been living like a hermit for many months, drinking himself to death. The locals suspect that he was in late stages of dementia. He had grown forgetful as well as more belligerent. This belligerence was probably a product of his helplessness. Knowing that something wasn't right with his mind.

I know that I also explained that it appears that Si may have more debt than assets. As I write this, I am hoping that we do not have to sell the property to make amends on the outstanding bills and stock margin accounts. Perhaps his royalty checks will help us get out from under, and leave you with something? Time will tell - but I am simply forewarning you. Also, as you are the executor of his will, and the only beneficiary, I hope that you and I can meet very shortly. We need to make some sense of the finances, and I need explain to you what we need to do, step by step, as it is somewhat of a convoluted mess.

I also need to apologize profusely, again. My dear, I have known you since you were a newborn. I was dismayed that we couldn't find you in time for your father's funeral, but we searched for you frantically. Even my grandchildren were helping, but according to my oldest grandson, you have essentially fallen off the map. He even tried to find you on the social media sites but to no avail. We thought perhaps you had married and changed your last name? But then I thought again. Your father would have certainly shared this with me! It was eventually through your emails to your father that we found you. My grandson's idea.

My dear, I can only assume that Si never responded because of his sickness. You need to remember that he loved you dearly and that you were his proud constant. It was his illness that bred his silence and deception. Don't read anything more into this than need be. I am one hundred percent certain!

Please, let me know as soon as possible when you can meet me in Vancouver. Better yet, I would prefer to meet you on the Island, if you can find the time.

Dear woman, it is so terribly unfortunate that we have to meet again under such circumstances and after all of these years. You know that your father was near and dear to my heart for most of my life. I can only hope that he is in a more peaceful place.

Yours sincerely,

David Baker, L.L.B.

Senior Partner, Baker, Chadwich & Sons

Katy had already read the letter several times, but she still hadn't shed a tear. She wondered how long Si had been alone and sick with dementia, and felt guilty and helpless with this thought. She also felt confused. She wished desperately that she could have spoken with her father, at least one more time. Maybe this would have given her the answers that she needed? Perhaps Si was already ill when he cost her her job? Perhaps this explained everything?

She set the letter back down on the table beside her computer and fell into her chair. The computer screen was open to her manuscript and as she stared at it her eyes became glassy as she remembered sitting on her father's knee in front of his desk.

. . .

"I am finished my story Katrina," he said, a thick stack of papers lay beside his typewriter. "Why don't you write the last line?"

"But I don't know what to say, Papa!" she exclaimed softly as she turned to him.

Si Fields looked at her fondly. He squeezed her shoulder, then rubbed her hair and smiled. "Tell my editor that the story is complete," he replied.

She turned back toward the desk. She read the gold letters at the bottom of the old machine. Underwood Standard Typewriter No. 5. She slowly ran her fingers across the bottom keys. Then she stared at the black and red ribbon, and then the blank piece of paper above it. She bit her lip as she thought very hard what to type.

"Oh! I know!" she finally squealed softly, and began typing.

T H E E N D

"The end!" she gushed proudly, and turned into her father's arms.

"Well," her father said. "I couldn't have said it better!" he boasted. "I think that one day you might want to write?"

. . .

Except for the Epilogue, she had finished the first draft of her manuscript. For a few days, just days before receiving the call from David Baker, she had silently rejoiced that she was almost complete. Several times she had wondered if Si might have been proud of her. If he would have appreciated that except for living through what was in the book, writing it had been the hardest thing that she had ever done. Or if the mastermind story teller and best-selling author would have given his own daughter some feedback and edits?

Then, with this very thought, Katy realized for the very first time that she had written this book for her father! It was then that silent tears cascaded down her cheeks in grief - and the beginnings of acceptance.

Chapter Twenty-three

The shrill ring of her cell phone pulled Katy out of her thoughts.

It was Rory Goodman. “Yo, there.”

Katy wiped her cheeks and looked up to the clock on the stove. "Hi," she said, surprised at the time.

"Sue and I are leaving here in 'bout half an hour. We'll be there by six fifteen."

Katy solemnly prepared for the Christmas party. She showered, then put on a silky black bra and matching panties. The she began to pull on sheer black pantyhose, first over her right foot and then her left. As the soft material crept over the purple of her little toe, and then her arch, she paused for a moment as she stared. The scar would never go away, she thought. It would always be there as a reminder of where she had been. Then she pulled on a sleeveless black dress and put on sling back pumps. Next, a tiny pair of pearl earrings and perfume and then she stood and looked at her reflection, remembering the last time that she dressed up for an occasion.

. . .

"You look beautiful," Brad murmured into her neck.

She tingled at the feel of his breath. Except for Si, no one had ever called her beautiful, and she felt loved and warm. She found his reflection in the mirror. The deep set brown eyes, the locks of dark brown, almost black hair, the somewhat handsome features.

"We have a few minutes," he whispered again.

She turned to face him, and kissed his lips playfully. "No, we don't," she chuckled softly. "We're already late."

"I'm sure they wouldn't mind. I could tell them that I had to meet a client..."

. . .

It was the very evening that the warehouse had exploded, lighting up Chelsea in a burst of orange and blue flames as Katy and Brad lay sleeping in Brad's loft after a night out for dinner with friends. For a long time after the tragedy, Katy used to beg that she could wrap her arms around Brad one more time. Or, at very least lay him to rest in a peaceful graveyard with a tombstone overlooking the ocean's edge, where he could watch the sail boats from a distance and breathe in the fresh air that had been his escape. Just like she had found a resting place for her dear mother when she had passed.

However, as time had passed, and the seasons changed, Katy had begun to realize that she had to move on and accept that Brad was gone. She didn't think of him as often now, and the aching pain of missing him, although still very painful, wasn't as pungent. With this acceptance, life and hope now breathed a little more freely, and when she felt this, she inhaled it. She felt more alive. She didn't struggle to breathe. She felt vulnerable, yet stronger. Bitter, yet more forgiving. More suspecting, yet more resilient.

When she done she stood back in the mirror and looked at her reflection. Then for the first time in a long while, she found her own eyes in the mirror. As she lifted her chin she smiled. Yes, life had chiseled pieces of Katy away, she thought whimsically, but the new Katy was emerging.

. . .

The Plaza Hotel breathed pure eloquence as Katy followed Rory and Sue Spradlum across the marble floors to the Crystal Ballroom. The songs of Christmas filtered down from the cathedral ceilings, and a teasing tingle crawled down her back. Except for the letter on her desk and the emptiness that it delivered, it would have felt like Christmas for the first time in years.

As they waited for the bartender to pour their drinks, Katy looked around the room. This event wasn't just a Christmas party, she thought. The decadent room was full of politicians and city officials, environmental pundits, including the entire team from Fourdow Environmental. She looked around for Marshall, but he was nowhere in sight, and she realized for the first time that she would have to tell him soon that she needed to resign, and why she was resigning. With this thought, she suddenly felt overwhelmed with the thought of leaving. And with the thought of dealing with Si's estate, or lack thereof.

As Rory handed her a glass of Chardonnay, he turned his head to the side and asked what was wrong.

“Wrong,” she said with a small smile. “Nothing is wrong. Just didn’t get much sleep last night.”

On the way there, she had told Rory and Sue about the heat going out in the complex, and described, with a great deal of humor, her colorful neighbors and obnoxious Norm.

“What? Did Norm try and crawl into your bed last night too?” Rory asked with a chuckle as she felt a hand on her arm.

She smelled him first, that familiar hint of earthy cologne, and turned to greet him. “Marshall!” she exclaimed as her cheeks flushed. “You made it!”

“I made it alright,” Marshall replied with a grin.

“You got all dressed up for me,” she said with a tease. She’d said it because she was nervous and the moment she did, regretted opening her mouth.

Marshall’s eyes flickered in surprise for a moment. It was the tiniest movement, but Katy caught it.

“I even polished my shoes,” he added with a boyish smile.

Katy grinned. “Yes, I see you did,” she chuckled, then nervously changed the subject. “We got quite the turnout,” she added, nodding to the crowd in the room.

Marshall looked around the room, not to pursue the “turnout” but to confirm that it was safe to talk with Katy in private. Rory and Sue had moved just feet away, and had struck up a conversation with someone from Fourdow. Except for two couples that Marshall didn’t know standing at the bar behind them, they had a moment alone. He leaned towards Katy. “Any chance you know anything about a big blue truck on the Estates?” he asked.

Katy’s brows turned up in question.

“I received an odd telephone call this morning,” Marshall said grimly, and quickly recapped the telephone conversation from that morning. “Tony and I spent three hours this afternoon going through every land sales agreement. We can't remember one deal with a big blue truck. Especially a deal where we took someone for a half million dollars!"

The fleet of red Stein Morretti trucks was vivid in Katy's memory. But she couldn't remember a big blue truck. "No," she answered confidently. "Absolutely no recollection of a big blue truck. What about Rory?" she asked.

"I called him this afternoon. He doesn't recall anything."

At that moment, Tony took the podium, and in an overly boisterous and upbeat tone he welcomed everyone and announced that dinner would soon be served.

Marshall quickly looked around the room and then back to Katy. "Are you here by yourself?"

"Technically, no," Katy grinned shyly. "I wasn't sure which suitor to bring, so I decided to come with Rory and his wife Sue."

"I'm also here solo," Marshall replied with a boyish grin. He hesitated for a moment, then cocking his head to the side, quietly asked if Katy would like to join him for dinner at the same table as Tony and his wife.

The meal started with a salad, followed by Alberta Prime Rib, Yorkshire pudding and asparagus tips. Katy found herself relaxed as food, drink and lively conversation flowed around the table. She also observed with a great deal of curiosity as Marshall and Tony exchanged glances.

Over the months, she had felt a growing tension between the two men, but it seemed to escalate more so over the past couple of days. Undeniably, everyone at Stein Morretti had been tense and stressed as they worked overtime, however, Katy was certain that whatever it was that brewing between Marshall and Tony was much more than the poisoning of the Estates.

Just as coffee and dessert were being served, Tony pushed his chair back from the table and took the podium again. He began with a toast. "To the team!" he celebrated as he took a drink from his glass. "All I can say is that I extend a heartfelt thanks to every one of you!" He continued by thanking everyone, and after mentioning a long list of names, added, "Yes, even George Bushell, Susan Hemsley and Travis Graham from the City. Thanks for your patience and support! But I need to make it clear that I am still contesting our tax bill."

The room erupted in laughter.

As Tony continued, his voice shifted from boisterous to grave. "I also need to thank someone else. Someone that I have known for most all of my life."

Knowingly, heads in the room turned as Tony acknowledged Marshall.

"Needless to say, as most of you already know, Marshall Stein is a genius. I have had the privilege of working with him for many years," he added. "I don't need to tell many of you that Marshall can be difficult to work with at times. Don't I know that! But I want to thank him publicly now for coming back to fill his old shoes. Because if there is anyone in this great city that can work outside of the box to help get the Estates back on track, it is absolutely my partner *and* my lifelong friend, Marshall Stein."

The room filled with whispers and clapping.

"I don't know..." Tony continued, and then paused, obviously struggling with his emotions. He took off his glasses and laid them on the podium and cleared his throat. "It appears," he began slowly, in a slight intoxicated drawl, "that we aren't able to save all of trees at the Estates. But I promise all of you that we are doing our best - and that we are winning! By the turn of the new year we should be able to begin developing Phase Two and show this city that we are on track and that we mean business!" Tony's emotional voice lifted with each word and when he was done, the room exploded in cheers and more clapping.

"Season's Greetings to all," Tony added. "Enjoy the rest of the evening! And Cheryl...where is Cheryl?" He paused as he looked around the ballroom for his secretary. When he found her, he smiled and nodded in her direction. "Cheryl has asked me to remind everyone that Associated Taxi is on standby, compliments of Stein Morretti - for anyone that needs a ride. Please don't drink and drive."

Offering taxi services at any Stein Morretti function had been an ongoing tradition for years, so Tony's comment came as no surprise to anyone that had attended the Company's corporate functions in the past. However, what Tony said next was a surprise to many, especially Marshall.

"One more thing," Tony added, probably more loudly than he had anticipated, for the microphone whined and spit above his words. "Just about forgot," he continued as he held up his wine glass. "The hotel has been instructed to pull out the finest of scotches and aperitifs. The Plaza Hotel's selection is one of the finest in the city. It's my way of saying thanks once again to all of you for all of your help and support."

Katy watched out of the corner of her eye as Marshall followed Tony back to his chair with cool and calculating eyes.

"Now isn't that a fine treat," Marshall replied dryly as Tony sat down.

Tony's eyes found Marshall's in defiance. "It's Christmas! I'll do want I want!" he retorted like a child and then reached for a bottle of wine.

Katy was well aware, probably more so than anyone other than Marshall and Tony, that Stein Morretti was financially strapped. The lost sales, the halt in new sales and the millions of dollars in projected expenses to remediate the land was breaking the bank. As she lifted her glass to join in another toast from Tony's corner, Vivian Morretti piped up with a question. Katy calculated at that very moment that Vivian Morretti was no dummy. She knew exactly what she was doing. She had posed this very question at this very time to change the subject.

"Marshall, have you heard any news about your grandchild?"

"Not lately," Marshall said grimly.

"I'm so sorry," Vivian offered.

"It is what it is. And I just found out that the private investigator I hired is in the hospital. He had a stroke. I can't imagine anything significant will unfold for a while now."

Sometimes, when Katy still had pangs of pain over her own losses, she would think of Marshall, and remind herself to stop feeling so sorry for herself. She had heard plenty about Marshall's losses over the months, including the quest for his missing grandchild. Sometimes, when they were sitting across a table or desk, she thought of opening up dialogue, and inviting Marshall to talk about it - but she would always hesitate, and then change her mind.

"Didn't Tony tell me that you thought she might be here, in Calgary?" Vivian looked at Tony, but Tony was lost in his drink, or the room, or something beyond the table.

"She's here. At least, she *was* here," Marshall corrected. "But we lost the trail."

"The are no records? I can hardly believe that!"

Marshall shook his head. "The mother's sister took her in when Charlie went to Afghanistan. She had or has an abuse problem," he scoffed slightly. "Thomas, the PI, discovered that she was living with, or at least sleeping with some Hell's Angels members, so it isn't good."

"Oh, my!" Vivian exclaimed. "Charlie would have adored his own child! He wouldn't leave her with someone like that!"

"Apparently, the sister had been clean for a year when Charlie left," Marshall said grimly. "Charlie helped her through rehab before his assignment."

"How old is she now, Stein?" Tony asked in a bit of a slur.

"Nine," Marshall answered without looking in Tony's direction.

"Nine already!" Tony piped up.

"Still a baby!" Vivian said as she shook her head. "Hardly capable of fending for herself."

"Hey, Stein!" Tony raised his voice to get Marshall's attention. "Didn't you say the detective found another woman in Vancouver? Someone remembered something about a party?"

"It was her birthday party," Marshall replied vaguely then turned to Katy. What he said next surprised the entire table. "The band has started and it's been a while since I have danced. What do you say we put some life into this party?"

Katy tried not to show her surprise, but her eyes opened a tiny bit wider as Marshall stood and held out his hand.

"He doesn't bite!" Tony boomed. "Might seem like it sometime, with all the enemies that he has made, but he's soft like a puppy!"

Katy took Marshall's hand and they joined the half dozen or so other couples on the dance floor. She leaned into him, to take his other hand, and as they began to dance to the slow but sassy song, she inhaled his scent. It smelled familiar, she thought. It reminded her of a forest, or trees, or something clean and fresh.

"Pardon me," she said, lifting her head up to Marshall.

"Do you have children?" he asked.

His question surprised her. Their relationship had been strictly professional – this was the first personal question that Marshall had asked. "No," she replied, shaking her head. "I always thought I would have children, but it didn't happen."

"We had one," Marshall replied. "My wife and I had a son."

Katy didn't know how to reply. "I heard about your son, Marshall. I'm very sorry."

Marshall remained silent and Katy continued blindly. "Sometimes," she added, "I feel as though I have missed something spectacular, not having a child."

Dark, green brooding eyes found Katy's. "I suppose you might have," Marshall replied solemnly.

"I am also sorry about your granddaughter," Katy offered.

Marshall simply nodded and Katy sensed that he was closing up. She became more brazen. She wanted him to talk.

"You can talk to me. I don't bite either," she replied with a gentle grin.

Marshall's dark green eyes brightened momentarily as he stared into Katy's. Then he leaned towards her right ear, and he talked and he talked and he talked. He talked about losing his son and his wife, and then he talked about his grandchild.

"Yes, I have a granddaughter out there, somewhere. Sometimes, I feel as if she is so close to me that I could touch her. I was an orphan, so the word family didn't exist in my vocabulary when I was a kid," he added with a thin smile. "Except that it was something that I didn't have. I suppose I've accepted that I might never find her. Today, all that I know for certain is her first name. And that she is out there somewhere. And that sadly, it has likely been a rough and rocky road for the kid. It's a helpless feeling. It's been very frustrating…"

As a new song began, Marshall leaned into Katy. "That's it!" he exclaimed softly. "You smell like strawberries," he said softly. "I thought that I smelled strawberries!"

"Strawberries! I am wearing…"

"You're wearing Channel Number 5," he said, finding her eyes. "Don't ask me why, but that perfume has always reminded me of my favorite fruit."

He looked awkward, or boyish, Katy thought, and she blushed.

"Yes, Marshall, I am wearing Channel Number 5. But I have never been told I smell like strawberries," she chuckled. "Interesting."

"Yes, it is interesting," Marshall mused.

Katy wanted to hear the rest of Marshall's story. She also sensed that he needed to talk. "I can't imagine how helpless it must feel, not being able to find your granddaughter," she offered gently.

Marshall stopped and looked at Katy for a moment, then leaned into her and talked some more. "Sometimes, when I'm out in public, the bank, the grocery store, I'll see a child about her age, and can you believe that I sometimes think of asking her if her name is Zig? Then I shake my head in disbelief. Go get a life, Stein, I say to myself," he added with a humble shrug. "Time to get a life."

Katy's eyes opened wide with the child's name. It was an unusual name, but it was also oddly familiar. Her mind worked hard for a moment as she tried to place it. Suddenly, the child's face from the river consumed her.

"What is her name?" she asked calmly, but her adrenaline soared.

"Zigourney. Baptized Zigourney Jessica Stein but she goes under the last name Orman. And apparently they call her Zig."

Katy's mind worked frantically. What was Zig's aunt's name? she begged silently. Then, without knowing what she was doing, her feet stopped moving.

"You don't like the way I dance," Marshall teased.

"Marshall," she said, and then she paused, struggling with how much to information - or how much hope - to give this broken, but charming man. A man that had lost his entire family.

"I met a little girl on the river by my house," she began slowly. "She's nine years old. And her name is Zig. I can't remember her aunt's name - she lives with her aunt," she explained. "And her father..." Katy struggled with the memory of the conversation that she had had with the child.

. . .

"He went to work. In Abganston."

"Abganston?" Katy repeated, wrinkling her brow.

"You know, Abganston, where the President made the army go."

"Afghanistan!" Katy exclaimed. "Was your father in the army?"

"I don't think so," the child replied. "I think he wrote stories."

. . .

Marshall eyes were questioning and thirsty as Katy continued.

“What did your son do for a living?” she asked.

Something told Marshal that he had reached the pinnacle. “Charlie was a journalist,” he replied very calmly.

“Marshall!” Katy hushed as she wrapped her fingers around his arm. “I am absolutely positive that Zig said that her father was a writer. And that he had gone to Afghanistan to do a story!”

Chapter Twenty-four

The following twenty-four hours were a whirlwind of ups and downs. Katy and Marshall left the hotel without saying goodbye to anyone, creating a roomful of raised eyebrows and whispers as they scurried out of the Crystal Room and through the lobby of The Plaza Hotel. As Marshall steered his Lexus out of the parkade, Katy gave him directions. “I don’t know the address, or even the street,” she explained, “but head south out of the downtown core. Take 4th Street.”

Marshall was silent as they neared the next turn.

“We are almost there, just a few more blocks,” Katy offered. “Take a left at the next intersection and its only a few blocks from Mission Bridge.”

Marshall’s face lit up in surprise. “This is my neighborhood. She’s within blocks of my home!”

Katy and Marshall frantically canvassed the complex. They knocked on door after door, asking anyone that answered if they knew which unit Lynette and a child named Zig might live. Finally, at the very end of the south side of the complex a tall, thin boy about ten years answered the door.

“Yeah,” he replied in a nonchalant shrug. “She goes to my school. Live three doors down. That-a-way.”

The unit was dark and lightless, and except for a handmade Christmas card that was taped crookedly to the front door, it appeared void of life. After knocking several times, Katy suggested that they go to Mission Bridge.

“Why the bridge?” Marshall asked.

“That’s where I met her,” Katy explained.

Marshall parked his Lexus right in front of Katy’s apartment building. Her eyes briefly drifted from a whimsical strand of Christmas lights on a second floor balcony to the clock on the dashboard. “It’s already ten-thirty,” she said, half to herself.

“I never, in my wildest imagination, thought that I would be looking for a child in the middle of the night in the middle of winter on a river!” Marshall shook his head as he turned off the ignition.

As they reached the Elbow River's edge, Katy looked to the cement walls and then her gaze shifted to the river's icy embankment. "She was here last night, maybe today," she whispered. "Winnie the Pooh," she explained as she pointed towards the river, "has a new outfit."

Marshall's eyes fell to the stuffed animal and then looked back towards Katy. "You met her *here*?" he asked.

"Yes," Katy whispered. "I think the woman that lives here is home," she added in a hush as she nodded toward the mattress on the ground.

Marshall slowly drank in the meaning of Katy's words as he perused the vagrant's home, instantly realizing that this was where the chants were coming from. "So this is where she lives!" he whispered in disgust. "She chants on this river every night! Its about the most annoying thing that I have heard!"

Of course! Katy thought, and her eyes widened. Of course! Marshall would hear the song from his side of the river. But she realized that he didn't wait for it, or anticipate it, as she did, and she wondered why. She wanted to ask him this very question.

"She might know if Zig was here…" Katy started just as a desperate plea filled the night air.

"Maci-manitow!" the woman suddenly shrieked from the mattress. "Maci-manitow! Maci-manitow!" she cried again and again. "Devils! I beg you, leave me!" she pleaded, this time in English.

"Let's go," Marshall said, firmly taking Katy's arm. "She doesn't know night from day. Can't imagine her remembering a child. She's probably stoned and your not safe here."

They walked silently across the icy snow-covered pathways and towards Marshall's vehicle. As they neared the Lexus Katy suggested that they visit the townhouse one more time.

Marshall hesitated. “No. I’ve waited this long, I’ll wait until morning,” he replied quietly.

“I’ll come with you, in the morning,” Katy offered gently. “If you would like me to,” she added.

Marshall smiled and was just about to tell Katy that he would like it very much if she came with him in the morning, but before he could speak the chanting from the river opened the night. Eyes that were bright and almost hopeful only seconds before darkened. “That voice!” he said, shaking his head. “I have to contend with it nightly!”

“I hear it too.”

Marshall looked surprised. “*You* hear it?”

“I live right here.”

“There?” Marshall asked as his eyes followed Katy’s nod to the dilapidated apartment building and its balconies of mismatch.

“Sometimes, I wait for her song,” Katy said. “I think that she is beckoning resolve. I don’t understand what she is saying, but I know that she is looking for peace.”

“Peace?” Marshall questioned doubtfully. “No, no, I don’t think that at all.”

“What do you think she is saying?” Katy wanted to understand.

Marshall’s eyes were still on her apartment building. Katy followed his gaze to see what he saw. The building looked old and forlorn; several of the windows were cracked. Many of the balconies were strewn with old bicycles and furniture. He saw poverty, she realized, and with this conclusion she lifted her chin.

“She is angry at the world,” Marshall replied very slowly and very quietly. “She is bitter and preparing to die,” he added solemnly, and then he turned and looked into Katy’s eyes. “So this is where you live?” he asked.

"Yes."

"You live right across the river from me."

Katy didn't know how to read Marshall's reaction - or how to respond.

"Well, now that's a long way from New York," he finally stated.

"About two thousand miles, and then some," Katy offered in lightness.

Marshall cocked his head to the side. "And then some," he repeated with compassion and understanding in his eyes. "I've come a long way too," he added sheepishly. Then he took a step towards Katy and held out his hands, as if asking permission to come closer.

"Yes, come closer," Katy whispered huskily.

Marshall wrapped his arms around Katy. She nestled into his chest and they held one another tenderly, and in silence, for a long, long while. Finally, Marshall took a step back and wiped a wisp of hair away from Katy's face. Then he leaned over and softly kissed her on the lips.

"I've wanted to do that for quite a long time," he confessed.

"I've wanted you to do that for quite a long time."

Marshall opened his mouth to say something else, then it suddenly dawned on him that Katy wasn't dressed for the cold winter's eve. "I'm sorry!" he exclaimed. "You are all dressed up for a party and we are standing outside in the middle of winter! You must be very cold! Let me walk you to your door."

"I'm okay," Katy said softly. "You warmed me up with your hug."

Marshall smiled mischievously then. "So, let's go back to the question you asked me a few minutes ago - and I will let you escape from me to the warmth of your bed. Is there any chance that I can persuade you to come with me tomorrow?"

Katy smiled. “Of course.“

“Good. Good,” Marshall replied with a fresh, boyish grin, and for a brief moment he looked remarkably young and happy. “I can’t think of a better way to celebrate Christmas. The possibility of the gift of my own flesh and blood on my doorstep? And you by my side? It is because of you, Katy Fields, that we might witness a miracle in the making this Christmas. Thank you,” he said with such genuine appreciation and kindness that, if possible, it would have melted the snowflakes that began to fall from the sky. Then, with a lighter step than Marshall had known for many years, he walked Katy to her apartment doors and kissed her tenderly goodnight.

Chapter Twenty-five

Zig could hardly wait for Christmas to officially begin. She kept her opals on the clock as she prematurely and impatiently waited for midnight to arrive - for this was the hour that Auntie had promised would truly bring in the season. She also anxiously waited for her Auntie to return. The night prior, Lynette had taken Zig to a boyfriend's home - only to drag her back home late that very afternoon but to disappear again.

Zig's sole comfort with this was that Lynette had left with a promise to return with a Christmas tree - and presents to put under the tree. Zig could hardly wait and did exactly as her Aunt had asked of her. She folded her blankets on the sofa. She redecorated the living room with bits of tinsel and Christmas decorations that she had made at school, arranging the few items here and there for better effect. Then she completed a homemade card with a Santa made of cotton batting and eyes from buttons, and taped it to their front door.

"Merry Christmas!" it read in bright red and green crayon.

Lynette finally returned at about six-thirty with her stinky boyfriend, and both were as high as a kite. As she danced through the doorway with a fresh bottle of Alberta Vodka and a jug of orange juice, Zig held her breath as she waited for the tree.

"Where's the tree, Auntie?" she asked with great big eyes. As she looked from Lynette to her stinky boyfriend with dwindling hope, Lynette pulled something out of her purse.

"Darn city is out of Christmas trees," Lynette giggled. "But look what I found you! It's a baby tree!" she giggled again. "It's a mistletoe!" she added as she held it above her head. Then she danced over to her boyfriend, kissed him hungrily on the lips, and then did the same to the child. "It's a kissing tree, baby girl!"

Zig's eyes went dark as she wiped the saliva off of her lips. "I - I - thought..." she stuttered, but Lynette wasn't listening. The boyfriend was looking very impatient and saying something about being late.

"Gotta go out again for a while," Lynette said to Zig. "Before all the stores close. But I brought you something to eat baby girl. Until we get back."

Had Lynette known that a woman and man had knocked on their door several times the night prior - and again that morning and early afternoon - she would have made *other* plans. For this would have surely meant that the law was on her doorstep to take the child away. However, Lynette, unaware of the visitors, and not yet ready to settle in for the night, left Zig once again to stare at the clock and count down the seconds to Christmas.

Only minutes later, as Zig was rereading the letter from Charlie, there was a loud knock on the door. At first, she thought her Auntie had forgotten something, but when she heard a muffled, unfamiliar man's voice, and then a woman's, her eyes opened wide in fear. They had come to get her! she thought, and both the photograph of Charlie and his letter glided to the floor as she quickly hid under the kitchen table. As Zig crouched on her hands and knees, her tiny chest heaved in and out as she stay very still and listened. Until the knocking stopped and she was certain that the strangers had left. Then she crawled across the floor to pick up the photograph of Charlie, and her long slender fingers brushed his smiling lips.

"Merry Christmas, Charlie," she whispered. "I haven't forgotten about you. And I asked Santa to help me find you."

Since she had found the envelope, earlier that year, she had stared at his photograph and read Charlie's words hundreds of times, and each time she got to the words "Love Charlie," a tiny place in her heart felt warm. And on many occasions she wondered if the lady that Charlie called Sarah would know where Charlie was. Or what would happen if she called this lady, and asked her this very question. Or if maybe the woman named Sarah would call the government and the government would take her away, just like her Auntie had warned.

Then Zig wondered exactly where "away" was - and if it was possibly any better than here.

Suddenly overwhelmed with the stress of the day and the emptiness of the evening, but for the strangers that had paid them a visit, Zig bit her lower lip so hard that it drew blood. As she licked her bottom lip her dark opals spotted the mistletoe that Auntie had left on the kitchen counter, and she remembered that it was Christmas Eve and then fragments of a Christmas story that Charlie had once told her... Without processing the consequences of her Auntie getting home before she did, she pulled on her running shoes, grabbed her parka and headed out the door.

Snowflakes fell onto her hair and eyelashes as her thin legs carried her down the driveway, down the street and towards the bridge. As she passed houses and apartment blocks of all shapes and sizes, her eyes brightened. For with every step she took she heard the sounds of Christmas. They were faint, muffled songs behind strangers' doors, homes filled with Christmas trees and shiny boxes under the trees and cookies and milk set out for Santa, she was certain, and she began to sing. Chestnuts Roasting on an Open Fire. Jingle Bell Rock. Frosty the Snowman. And then, So it is Christmas.

When she neared the bridge's underground she grew silent and tippy toed across the path that she knew well, until she reached the bridge's concrete walls. Her eyes traveled to the kitchen, first to five or six dark brown apples, and she wrinkled her nose at the sight. Then she saw Sally, the scraggly red-haired rag doll, still propped up on the ledge, exactly as she had left her that summer. This gave her a great deal of satisfaction and a sweet smile touched her lips,

Then her eyes roamed further, towards the river and Winnie the Pooh and within a moment her two small, bare hands gently lifted him from the lawn chair and she sat where the bear had sat and cradled the warmth of the stuffed animal against her chest.

"It`s Christmas Eve, Pooh Bear," she murmured into his fur. The silhouette of the child and the bear, still dressed in the bright blue wool hat and orange scarf, decorated the dark river's edge with a picturesque color of hope. The bear felt comforting and warm in Zig's arms, but she found the darkness somewhat unsettling and she was cold. Several times she lifted her eyes to the sky to find the moon, and when she did she didn't feel so alone. It was so pretty and bright, she thought. Then she would wonder, as she had already done many that night, if Santa would ever show his sleigh.

When an occasional gust of wind would recklessly blow snow across the embankment and into her face she would shiver. Then she would hug Winnie the Pooh tighter and exhale into his fur, again, and again, until a warm breath of air fell back to her cheeks.

"Pooh Bear," she whispered, when her lips and her cheeks felt toasty again, "Charlie told me a story a long time ago that if I watched the moon on Christmas Eve that I would see Santa and his reindeer ride across it, in the sky. Now," she said, lifting the stuffed animal's head so that his eyes were pointed toward the moon, "you can watch with me. But we have to be very quiet," she whispered, putting her finger to her lips in a hush. "You see, we don't want to disturb the woman that lives here and we can't let Santa know that we are watching. If we do, he might not bring the presents I asked for."

"I wrote Santa a letter," she continued, "I asked him to bring Charlie home. And for a puppy, a little black one, and a Harry Potter book. And for my Aunt Lynette, a new boyfriend. And for *you*," she exclaimed, pausing and kissing the yellow fluff that was the top of Winnie the Pooh's head, "I asked for some boots and hot chocolate. You see, you sit here every day, and I know how much you like it. It's a very pretty view. But last night, when I visited you, I thought snuggly boots and hot chocolate might make you feel all warm and fuzzy inside, just like if I felt when Charlie tucked me into bed."

"I really liked it when Charlie told me stories," Zig continued in an animated, story-like tone. "He said he was the master storyteller, and that I was his Princess, and he would always make me beg for the ending. He said that the stories came from the books he read when he was a little boy."

Suddenly, a sound from behind Zig startled her. She quickly turned and her eyes instantly fell on a silhouette in a bright yellow parka. It was about thirty feet away, pushing a shopping cart brimming to the top.

Zig's heart skipped a beat. She pulled Winnie the Pooh tight into her chest. Perhaps if she sat very still she wouldn't be found, she thought, just like she did when Auntie brought a boyfriend home and she pretended she was sleeping. And that is exactly what Zig did for a minute, perhaps two. Until she heard the crunching snow, until she realized that the footsteps were nearing her - and for a brief moment she thought of getting up and running.

But it was too late. "Who are you," a hoarse woman's voice questioned.

Zig lifted her head slightly. "Hi," she muttered and then nuzzled the side of her face deep into Winnie the Pooh's fur, the whole while her eyes of the stranger.

The lady nodded and the night was eerily silent for a moment.

Finally, "Are they bothering you too?" the lady asked.

Zig's eyes filled with confusion. Then she nervously explained why she was there. "I'm watching for him in the sky," she whispered timidly as she lifted her head and pointed to the moon above.

"Him?" the lady asked.

"My father told me if I watch the moon on Christmas Eve I'd see Santa and his reindeer ride across the sky."

The lady's eyes slowly lifted to the sky and its bragging moon above. "I'll make a fire," she finally said.

Zig smiled nervously. She liked the idea of a fire. She wiggled her cold toes, then curling them up under her legs and watched with a great deal of curiosity as the lady pulled out item after item from the shopping cart. First a blanket, then a kettle, then a large jar full of rocks. A bright green bow appeared, and then a piece of fur and so on and so on. Finally, the lady lifted out a small box and then a handful of twigs and grunted something that Zig couldn't understand.

When small flames burst alive just feet from Zig, she pulled her legs from beneath her buttocks and stretched them toward the fire, uncurling her toes to the flames. "That's a very nice little fire," she said sweetly.

An indecipherable, funny noise came from the lady's throat, perhaps another grunt, but she didn't speak. Zig's eyes roamed from the weathered face to the collection of the home behind her, and she remembered the pink running shoes that she had seen beside the bed.

"Is this your house?" Zig asked as her eyes looked down to the lady's black rubber boots.

"Is this where you live?" Zig questioned again, this time with less confidence, for the stranger's silence was unsettling.

The lady's dark eyes widened as they darted across the river, and then towards the bridge, and then down to the Zig's lap. Finally, she nodded toward the bear and asked a question. "Did you give him those?"

Zig told the woman that it was Winnie the Pooh's Christmas surprise, for the scarf and hat didn't fit her anymore. Then, feeling somewhat bolder than she had moments before, she added in a very grown up voice, "I thought I'd better keep him warm. It's going to be very cold tonight."

"I thought so. I thought it was a child that left them," the woman muttered as she stared at Zig.

Zig held fast to the lady's stare. She wondered then if the lady was going to tell her that she should be wearing socks. Instead, her next words surprised her.

"You are hungry like me," the lady said.

Yes! I am hungry! Very hungry! Zig thought, but her Auntie's warning to never admit such a thing - or why - was etched clearly in her memory. Zig hesitated. "Maybe a little," she finally admitted, again dropping her chin back into the warmth of the yellow bear on her lap.

Zig watched out of the corner of her eye as the lady walked across the snow toward the concrete ledge. As her hands reached up toward the spoiled apples, Zig instantly hoped that this wouldn't be what the lady would give her. A moment later the lady stood in front of Zig with three tiny, sparkling Christmas boxes in the palms of her hands.

"Chocolate," she said, when Zig hesitated.

Zig felt a tingle of excitement dance in her stomach as she took the one wrapped in purple foil.

"Take them all. They will keep you warm. For a while."

"They look like itsy-bitsy Christmas presents," Zig gushed, and a smile lit up her face as she placed the red one on the softness of Winnie the Pooh's stomach and the silver one in the side pocket of her parka. Then she unwrapped the purple foil and put the chocolate in her mouth. "Mmm," she cooed, "my favorite. Melts in your mouth like magic."

For the next few minutes, the woman and child silently stared at the fire by their feet. Zig felt *almost* safe - and not *so* alone - and licked her lips several times to taste every drop of chocolate that she was able. As she reached for the red foiled chocolate in Winnie the Pooh's lap, the wind picked up in an angry gust. The lady stood up and moved slowly to her shopping cart. A moment later she awkwardly wrapped a blanket around Zig's shoulders.

Zig embraced its warmth, even though it smelled like her Auntie's boyfriends. "It's cozy," she replied timidly.

The lady crouched down in the snow to a half kneeling position. She had asked Zig a question, but Zig didn't understand.

"Are you on the street?" she asked again as her's bore into Zig's opals.

"On the street?" Zig repeated, for she had no idea what the lady was asking.

"Are you a runaway?"

"A runaway?" Zig repeated in fear. "Oh, no!" she said as her eyes opened wide and she remembered her promise to her Auntie.

Then the lady asked where she lived and Zig grew suspicious. She waited for another nasty cough to leave the lady's body before she answered vaguely. She lifted her hand and pointed to the southeast.

"Over there," she said. "I live across the river." Zig had quickly processed "Over there" could have meant anywhere, and she felt quite proud of herself for she knew that her Auntie would have approved of her answer.

"Do you live in a house?" the lady asked as her eyes shifted to the other side of the river.

Zig's eyes followed the lady's gaze and the pretty Christmas lights that lit up the landscape. Then she told the lady that she lived in an apartment, but that very soon, her Auntie had promised they would move and she would get her very own bedroom.

“I have to sleep on the couch,” she added, as if that explained everything, and wrinkled her nose in disapproval.

Without warning, the lady began coughing again and Zig’s eyes filled with concern. She thought of suggesting that cough syrup might help her cold, just as her Auntie sometimes suggested, but the coughing stopped almost as quickly as it had started and the lady spoke again.

“You should be at home,” the lady hushed as she stared at the fire. “It’s Christmas Eve.”

Just as Zig began to tell the lady that she was certain to see Santa in the sky, another cold gust of wind flew across the embankment, and the peaceful night broke out into a flurry of snow, and then with this, a rage.

“Leave her alone!” the lady shouted in deep, throaty growls as her eyes closed to slits. Then she spat into the snow. “You’re filth! Nothing but filth!”

Zig’s eyes grew wide as she searched the riverbank.

“Filth!” The lady spat again and waved her arms in the air. “Maci-manitow! Maci-manitow! Devil!”

Zig nestled her chin back into the warmth of Winnie the Pooh and she watched the lady out of the corner of her eye.

“Filth!” the lady growled again and moved toward the river’s edge. “Maci-manitow!” she said again. Then black nails lifted to her chest and she clutched a pendant around her neck and the cold air filled with song. Zig didn’t recognize the words, for they were sung in Cree, but she listened and watched very intently as the lady’s silhouette danced playfully and her body rocked gently with each word.

Please be merciful.

Please be merciful to me.

I want to embrace the truth.

The white buffalo has come to me.

I can see it through the fog.

I am on the river's edge, reaching for its strength.

I am on the river's edge, reaching for its powers.

I beg you now, to let me live in peace.

And without the evil storm, for it still follows me.

I want to live in peace.

Please give me hope.

Except for the wind's faint breaths now and again, the river's edge fell silent again. Zig's face had broken out into a precious smile, and when she spoke, her words came out like honey.

"That was a very pretty song," she finally whispered so very sweetly.

The lady's eyes fell down to Zig momentarily. Then again, as she had done many times that evening, her eyes spanned the landscape. From north to south, and then south to north. Then across the river, then to bridge and its concrete wall. "Hmf," she finally grunted, an expression that simply meant that she was content that they were alone again, at least for the time being. Then she rubbed her dry lips with the back of her hand and knelt down to the fire.

Zig opened her mouth to ask if she would sing the song again, but the lady spoke first.

"Where is your family tonight?"

"My family?" Zig repeated the two words as if she hadn't heard them before. She shrugged her thin shoulders and furrowed her brow. "I don't know," she admitted in a whisper, "My Auntie takes care of me."

For an instant, the two shared a moment of understanding as their eyes locked and unspoken compassion filled the night as winter's flurry spoke the cold. As snow scattered here and there and speckles of white flakes frolicked around their feet and torsos and already cold faces, the passage of time became a moment never lost. A moment that marked a change in destiny for both of them.

The lady asked another question. "Where is your mother?"

Zig hesitated. "I don't know where my mother is," she answered sadly. "She left when I was a baby. But my father, his name is Charlie," she added proudly, "is a *very* important writer. He went to Abganstan. I live with my Auntie Lynette. She takes care of me until Charlie comes home."

The small fire had dwindled and a cloud had moved over the moon and the night was black and Zig didn't see the lady's eyes grow wide in fear, as if she had seen a ghost. Several seconds of silent passed until the night broke into a rage.

"Maci-maintop!"

"Maci-manitow!"

"Maci-manitow!"

The lady repeated this one word again and again as she crossed herself with the hope of god. Zig sat very still, almost holding her breath. Then, when the prayer was done and the night silenced yet again, the lady pulled herself up and took a few steps towards Zig. Then leaning over, she gently touched Zig's face and then caressed her forehead.

Zig sensed that something had just happened. She had no idea what this might be, but she knew that it was something important.

"You have your father's eyes," the lady finally murmured as she knelt in front of Zig.

Zig's opals opened wide in surprise. Then she opened her mouth, to ask the lady how she knew such a thing. However, at that very instant something in the distance caught their attention. The silhouettes of two individuals were walking toward them. On the bridge, red and blue flashing lights lit up the sky.

"They've come to get me!" Zig cried out in alarm.

The lady's eyes darted back and forth, from the child to the two shadows nearing, to the police car on the bridge. It wasn't the same squad that sometimes came and told her to move and she looked back toward the child. Gently, she squeezed Zig's shoulder. "Wait," she whispered. "This time is different."

"Zig," a woman's voice beckoned.

Zig's eyes opened wider with the call of her name. It was the lady from Apartment 222! And she had brought another man and a policeman! They had found her out! she thought and jumped off the chair.

"No! No! No!" she shrieked as Winnie the Pooh tumbled into the snow. "No! No! No!" she begged as she tripped over the blanket. "No! No! No! she cried as she picked herself up and began running her first marathon along the river's edge.

Zig could feel the lady from Apartment 222 behind her.

"It's me. It's Katy." Katy cried out, "From apartment 222. We won't hurt you, Zig. We are here to help you."

Raw fear pushed Zig's thin, long legs and she darted like a small rabbit across the snow as Katy shouted repeatedly. "It`s me Zig. It`s okay. Please stop."

Zig's legs carried her faster than they had ever moved in her entire lifetime as she struggled to get as far away from Katy possible. But Katy was faster, and as she neared her, Zig gasped as she felt her footsteps behind her, and then her arm around her waist.

"It's okay, Zig. It's okay. I promise you, it's okay."

But Zig's adrenaline had soared, and her arms and legs flailed this way and that as she desperately tried to escape from Katy's hold. "No! No! No!" she begged again and again into the night.

"No! No! No!"

Finally, exhausted and out of breath, Zig had no choice but to succumb and she stopped fighting for release. She felt Katy's breath on her face, and then her lips in her hair.

"It`s okay. Zig," Katy whispered as she kissed her hair and then her forehead. "It's okay. We aren't here to hurt you. You are going to be okay. I promise."

Zig eyes were still wild. Still full of fear. "They found me out," she whispered shakily.

"Zig," Katy whispered, "no one has found you out. But someone very special has found you," she said. "Look," she added, nodding toward the man that she had come with, who was now standing only feet away. "This is Marshall. Marshall knows Charlie. He also knows your Aunt Lynette. And he wants to talk to you."

Zig's eyes brightened slightly with the mention of Charlie, but she was still wildly confused and intensely scared. Reluctantly, she looked up to the man.

"Hello, Zig," the man said very gently, and Zig wondered why he was crying.

Within minutes, Zig was sitting in the back seat of a big black truck beside Katy, who was wrapping a soft blanket around Zig's shoulders and across her legs to keep her warm. The man who had cried was outside talking to the policeman. Zig watched from the window for a moment.

"Where are you taking me?" she asked Katy. "I want to see my Auntie."

"You will see your Auntie, sweetheart," Katy replied calmly.

Then, "How does that man know Charlie?" Zig questioned very quietly, as if she was scared to hear the answer.

"Marshall is going to take you home. And then he can explain."

Zig's looked through the windshield to find the man called Marshall. Huge, fluffy snowflakes had began to fall from the sky again, and she watched as they fell into the man's hair and onto his nice face as he talked and nodded to the policeman. She watched him as he shook the policeman's hand and smiled. And she watched him as he got back into the truck. A faint scent of clean winter filled the cabin as he turned to face the two of them.

"Is everything okay?" Katy asked.

"Yes. He's going to follow me," Marshall said.

"Follow you to Auntie's?" Zig asked with both fear and hope in her voice.

Marshall turned and looked directly at Zig. And then he smiled. "You need to trust me, Zig. I am Charlie's father. My name is Marshall Stein and I am taking you home and somewhere safe," he added gently.

Zig liked the man's voice. It sounded strong and kind, but her eyes were wide as she clasped her hands together nervously and then bit her lip. This man knows Charlie! she thought and looked out the window and up to the moon. Then her next words came out very quietly.

"Do you think that I have Charlie's eyes," she asked.

Marshall took a deep breath and looked lovingly at Katy with new tears in his eyes. Then he turned to Zig. "Zig, yes! You most certainly have Charlie's eyes," he replied gently. Then, "Can we take you to a warm home and I can tell you more? Is that okay with you?"

A shaky sigh escaped Zig's lips as she slowly nodded her head. Then her eyes fell from Marshall's kind face to the river below. The lady who had told her that she had Charlie's eyes was sitting in the lawn chair. Winnie the Pooh was in her lap. Two other policeman stood by her side.

Chapter Twenty-six

The following summer delivered all the gifts that Sarah would have marveled at, as if she had never seen them before, Marshall thought on occasion. The season's allure appeared almost overnight as the trees budded and blossomed and the dancing colors of the sun shone bright in all of its moods. The river, high from heavy rains that spring, held a newfound magic as it flowed north to south between the rainbow of splendor. It looked more spectacular than ever, Marshall often thought, and embraced it.

However, now, when Marshall thought of Sarah, or Charlie, or the darkness that had been his life for so long after their deaths, his thoughts weren't as pungent with grief and guilt as they had once been. It was as if he was remembering scenes from a movie that took him from Calgary to Vancouver, from Paris to Afghanistan, and from the flowing water at his doorstep to the bridge's darkness. Memories of Sarah sitting at her piano, with her soft face, her pouty lips, lips that never really pouted. Charlie, the day he was born. Charlie at two, at six, at eighteen. Charlie and Sarah's tombstones, side by side in a graveyard, that sat high on a hill, overlooking the mountains, valleys and sunsets.

Sarah had purchased the three plots the year Charlie was born. "So we are always a family," she had said. "So that after we enjoy our sunset years, we can curl up beside one another and hold hands, and watch a new marvel, a new sunrise, every day," she had murmured in that voice that Marshall had so adored.

Sometimes, Marshall would find himself humming a tune, when he felt happy or free, or when he noticed the changes in "A Gift to My Family" with a profound appreciation. It was a song that Sarah and he had sung around a piano in Paris the day they got married, years before life had disrupted their youth and upset their dreams - years before Marshall's infidelities. Time had crystallized this moment, and it was one that Marshall needed to hang onto for salvation - to ensure that Sarah had found a safe place - and a haven. He was even able to remember the name of the song. It was Sarah's favorite. It was MacArther Park.

Marshall had moved to a different place, and with acceptance and forgiveness, life had again opened its doors in offering.

DNA tests had confirmed the truth. Marshall had locked the report in the safe behind the Tarkay painting, the same safe that once held one of two white gold buffalos. Sometimes he would think of the pendant, now lost somewhere at the bottom of the river, but this thought was rare. Sometimes, he remembered the other white gold buffalo that once hung on the ivory white neck and the remarkably beautiful face. However, now, when he had these thoughts it wasn't with the raw passion or guilt that he had hung on to - and lived with - for so many years. He'd rarely think of Christina's enchanting ways, or her idiosyncrasies, or how exotic she had looked when she flung her long hair over her supple bare breasts, or how he had craved her, even if he had just had her.

Marshall also no longer placed blame on Christina. Instead, now when he thought of Christina he would immediately think of the package of life that had been delivered to his doorstep and he would immediately go in search of Zig, always instantly comforted at the sight of her dark opal eyes and her tiny grin. And he would marvel at how so many tragic and uncanny turn of events could to lead to such a miracle.

He hadn't yet decided when he would tell the child who her mother was, or that he was her father - or if he would ever tell her.

"She is yours Spunk," Christina had whispered hoarsely as his eyes fixated on the white gold buffalo that hung below her tormented face.

She is yours Spunk.

She is yours Spunk.

Christina had whispered these words just as Katy had begun to chase Zig down the river's edge.

It had taken Marshall only a split second to fully comprehend their meaning, and as he accepted the shocking and profound truth, he stopped in his tracks.

"No! No! No!" he had silently begged, echoing the words of his child's as she had tried to escape.

Instantly, his eyes had fallen to Christina's neck and then the white gold buffalo. As the moon's light cast a golden hue on the pendant, Marshall was certain that he was hallucinating.

. . .

"It's for life," she had said softly. "It'll bring you a good life. And here," she said, leaning her chest toward him. "I have one too. They are symbolic of our love for one another."

. . .

After Zig was safely under Marshall's wings, it was only once the scientific proof was in his hands that he calculated that he had impregnated Christina on their last weekend in New York. Almost exactly nine months to the day Christina had walked out of the hotel room to meet Charlie was the child's birthday. With this confirmation, Marshall vowed that this secret would remain just that for the time being; Zig's life had been much too hard and convoluted for something this big to be unveiled. At least for now, Marshall had justified. At least for now.

Although safe and knowingly loved, Zig struggled in the early months. Sometimes, when she was at school she would fill with that sickly feeling that the house would be empty or that Marshall wouldn't come home until late into the night. She was also both cautious and clingy towards Marshall, subconsciously questioning how long he would be around. And she had been hungry for so long that she had a difficult time understanding that the Stein household would never run out nourishment. Several times Marshall found chicken bones or pieces of apples and other food hidden under her pillow.

The child psychologist that they visited weekly had warned Marshall that Zig's scars could be deep - and that her recovery might take a great deal of time and patience.

"You need to show her consistency, Marshall. She needs to learn how to trust you," she reminded him privately at the end of every session.

Marshall listened carefully, and focused diligently on nurturing his daughter and day-by-day he was able to give her much more of his time than he had ever been able to give Charlie. He went above and beyond the call of duty to ensure that Zig believed that he would always be there for her, and that she was loved, and the payoff came gradually.

As weeks grew into months, Zig responded to Marshall's commitment. Her face and arms filled out, and a natural pink hue filled her cheeks. Her long mane of honeysuckle hair, which she was taught to wash and brush daily, hung like silk around her tiny face of splendor. By that summer, it was obvious to Marshall and his small world of support that Zig had learned to trust him, relied on him a great deal and had grown very fond of him.

During this time, Marshall also grew - as both a man and a father. Sometimes, he found himself having to shift in his way of thinking for a moment, to be more patient, to listen, and to physically show his affection, which he wasn't used to doing. He also made a conscious effort not to swear when Zig was within hearing distance, or to show his cantankerous side. As time moved forward and Marshall continued to focus it became easier for him to do all of these things. By summer's climax, Marshall felt at peace with himself - and for the first time in his life. He embraced knowingly that Zig and he were simply meant to be, and almost naturally, the Stein household evolved into a healthy and loving environment.

He enrolled Zig in the best private school that money could buy and drove her to school every morning before going into Stein Morretti's offices. Returning home every afternoon before the school bus dropped Zig off, he would wave and smile with such a production that even the bus driver would break out in a grin. Nightly, he read to Zig and helped her with her homework. He also stayed by her side during swimming lessons and piano lessons; for the child had taken a shine to the water and Sarah's masterpiece.

And often, the two of them would look through family photographs, a frequent request from Zig. At her begging, they would pull out the photo albums that Sarah had made over the years, and curl up in the parlor - with Jazz always at their feet. Zig had instantly fallen in love with Jazz, just as the feline had taken to her.

There were several photos of Charlie - from infancy through to his later years - and Zig would fixate on each of them. Often she would ask where a photo was taken or how old Charlie had been when it was taken. When Marshall couldn't remember, he would make something up, never once hesitating with these little white lies - for Marshall knew that Zig needed *some* answers. When they came across other family photos, Marshall would subconsciously point out that he was in the picture. "That's me!" he would say proudly, and with a boyish grin. "Now I was quite a handsome young man, don't you think?" and Zig would giggle and curl up in Marshall's lap.

Without processing why he would do this, Marshall was subconsciously reinforcing to his child that he had been younger at one time - and that he was a big part of her life, and a much more significant part of her life than Zig would likely ever know.

Katy Fields had also become an integral addition to "A Gift to My Family." After she and Marshall discovered Zig, she had remained close by Marshall's side to help with the transition. During these weeks the mental and physical attraction that they had shared quickly evolved into something deeper and more meaningful. They had an uncanny understanding of the other, and the grief and guilt that Marshall had been burdened with, as well as the loss and humility that Katy had lived were both replaced with a breast of hope and happiness that only love can deliver. Simply, their love for one another enabled them to embrace each day and look towards the future, instead of reliving the past.

Katy had tried to resign from Stein Morretti even before its inevitable bankruptcy was a certainty. A month after the Christmas party, she took a week off, at Marshall's insistence, and flew to the Island to meet with David Baker to deal with her father's estate - or what was left of it. When she returned, it was with a tighter jaw and a letter of resignation in her hands.

"He deserves some right doing," she had told Marshall after sharing Si's tragic last months. David Baker's suspicion that Si had had dementia had been bang on - and he had quietly suffered with it for at least five years. However, with the disease, Si had become a recluse, and belligerent when he set foot into town. Now, after his death some of the locals were whispering terrible things about her father. How he had become a raging a drunk. How they were hardly surprised that he committed suicide; everyone knew that his entire estate was depleted. And how he squandered his money away on prostitutes, orgies and oceans of liquor. Katy felt obligated to set the record straight and maintain her father's reputation...

As Katy and David Baker began to dig deeper, they suspected the perhaps Si hand't squandered away his fortune standalone and that criminal activity was involved. By early that spring, Katy had taken Marshall's advice and took a three-month leave of absence. Again, Marshall wouldn't accept her resignation.

Katy temporarily moved to the Island and began the daunting and complicated task of going through Si's records in search of answers. Sometimes, her days were emotional, and she stole moments to reflect - and moments to forgive - as she sifted through the mess that Si had left behind. During these daunting times Katy's breaths of fresh air were the frequent telephone conversations with Marshall and her twice a month visits to "A Gift to My Family." She would pack a small bag, catch the ferry and then the plane - and each time with butterflies in her stomach. For Katy felt loved - and she allowed herself to love.

And always, the long-haired, salt and peppered Marshall and Zig, with hair the color of sunshine honeysuckle and a smile that lit up any room, would be waiting for her at the airport, grinning and waving in such a production that it was as if they hadn't seen her in years. As fond as Katy had become of Marshall, she had also grown very attached to Zig - and her love was reciprocated. Just as the child had learned to trust and rely on Marshall, she also felt the same coming from the woman that she had originally known as "the lady from apartment 222".

Sometimes, the three of them would talk and carry on in such a natural way, that Marshall and Katy would stop and look at one another - and then at Zig - and their knowing glances silently whispered that this time, this precious time, was simply meant to be.

Marshall was able to open up to Katy, and sometimes, he talked so openly that he could hardly believe it himself. Sometimes, but not often, he talked about Sarah and shared his guilt about not being a better and more understanding husband as well as a father to his only son. Just as often, he shared the ongoing challenges at the Estates, and sometimes the ongoing search for "the big blue truck", and the tragedy of Tony...

When Marshall spoke about Tony it was with such remorse that Katy would feel his pain, and she would very gently put her hands on his face and whisper that it just wasn't his fault. That it was okay. When she did this, Marshall would always whisper back that Tony had been his only friend, his lifelong friend, and that he had failed Tony.

Tony's admittance of his wannabe relationship with Sarah had instantly ended three decades of friendship between the two men. And the tainted lands of Rocky Mountain Estates, the standstill of the development and the ensuing costs to remediate the land had put both Stein Morretti and Tony in financial despair. Just so, for the two years that Tony had operated standalone, he had overspent in the millions. The collective problems forced both the Company and Tony personally into Chapter Eleven.

Marshall was contracted by the trustees to salvage what he could, and Tony disappeared behind his million-dollar estate before the bank repossessed it. Vivian filed for divorce and Tony drank himself to death, overdosing on thirty-year-old scotch. It was Tony's oldest daughter that found his cold body two weeks later... Tony had died very broke and very alone - and after everything he had done for Marshall, Marshall was unable to accept this.

However, Katy's gentle words, and the way that she would tenderly caress Marshall's face when he spoke about Tony helped alleviate some of his pain - for he felt Katy's undefined and unselfish love in every touch and with every word. What Marshall was able to conclude during these moments was that he had become more mature with life's tragedies, and more giving and accepting. He learned, albeit a tough life lesson, that Marshall Stein, a man who had lived through tragedy and loss, guilt and despair, had found his feet, right side up - and he would never do anything again to lose his grounding or the new life. Marshall had a second chance - and quite simply, he was would do everything possible to ensure that he embraced it.

On a weekend visit in July, Marshall and Katy were sitting on the terrace sipping on a glass of wine before dinner. The once deserted structure that hung over the dewy river was now fragrant with a variety of planters bursting with flowers of all colors. As the barbecue sizzled, piano music filtered through the patio doors, and Katy raised her brows. Zig was very gifted, she was going to say, but Marshall spoke first.

"Did you bring something for me to read?" he asked as he topped off her wine glass with a crisp bottle of Chardonnay.

Katy smiled mischievously at her lover and editor. "I've made the changes you suggested. It`s finished. But I have added something new."

"And what might that be?"

Marshall's offer to edit her manuscript had come as a pleasant surprise. He was articulate, precise and extremely well read, and the two were literally on the same page when it came to editing suggestions and changes. Katy's novel was now almost in final form, except for her "something new", which had become somewhat of a regular saying for the novice writer.

"It's in my briefcase. But its better. I'll give it to you later," she said, then added, "Unless you make any changes, I think it is now officially done. And these are now words from my heart.""

Marshall had pushed Katy to write.

"Write from the heart – be honest and true," he had often repeated. "Write the truth about losing Brad. How did you *feel*? Write about losing your father. How did you *feel* when he passed away? How humbled and humiliated did you *feel* when you lost your job - your career?" he would ask. Marshall would encourage Katy with such confidence - for he had asked himself these very questions over the months as he healed and as he tried to become a better man and a better father.

"Tell your reader how you *felt* when you took the landscaping job at the Estates," he prodded. "Be real and open, and you may have a bestseller."

Marshall's prodding had enhanced Katy's writing. It had been difficult for her to tell her story in true form, for that would be exposing herself. However, with Marshall's insistence that she needed to dig deeper and get as up close and personal as her soul would allow, she blossomed as a writer.

"Even if the truth causes you pain," Marshall would sometimes prod her gently.

Marshall's words collectively gave Katy both the motivation and the stamina to continue and she spent endless nights on the Island doing just what Marshall had suggested. Writing became easier - and less painful - and she progressively felt happier, and more free and more able to love again. Katy too had found her feet.

As the summer night's air teased a breeze, Katy went indoors to finish the salad. Just as she was adding her homemade raspberry vinaigrette to the fresh vegetables they bought at the farmers market that very morning, she felt Marshall's hand on her arm.

"You okay?" he asked gently.

"Okay?" she repeated.

"You… you seem not quite *here*."

"Not here?" she repeated in surprise. Then instantly, she realized that this gentle bear of a man was feeling insecure. Perhaps she *was* acting distant? She'd had so much on her mind about Si, and it was such an intricately woven problem, that sometimes it was consuming. And she had decided on the plane the previous morning that she couldn't continue to pester Marshall with all the trivia. She wouldn't talk so much. Marshall had to be getting tired of hearing about the issues around Si and his estate.

"I'm sorry," she apologized, and moved to hold him. She put her hands around his neck and gently kissed his lips. "I realized that I talk too much. I don't want you to get tired of me."

Instantly, Marshall's face relaxed and his eyes looked lovingly into hers. "You'll never bore me. And you don't talk too much. I am surprised at how much I miss your voice. I never thought I would enjoy another voice as much as…"

He didn't finish his sentence, because he didn't want to think about Sarah. He very much wanted to embrace the now and hold and take care of this woman in front of him. He loved everything about her. Her gentle face. Her deep brazen eyes. Her ferocious pride.

Tiny beads of sweat had formed on Katy's hairline from the summer's heat. Marshall lifted his hand and swept her hair away from her forehead. Katy tilted her head backward slightly as she embraced his touch and murmured softly, "I love it when you touch me."

"You'll have to make do with loving my ribs for now," Marshall chuckled as he kissed her on the lips. "In the meantime, give me an update about your father? I really do want to hear."

Katy hesitated. "David and I are meeting on the Island next week," she finally replied. "We discovered a number of documents in Si's hidden safe. He's going to help me decipher what is important. Also, apparently," she added, "he found a forensic student at University of British Columbia. Some computer genius that is going to rip apart Si's hard drives. He had seven computers! Can you believe it?"

"Why would he need seven computers?"

Katy shook her head. "I have no idea. But believe it or not, his stock trading accounts now tally over eighty!" Katy raised her brow as she continued. "It looks like he had eighty-three online trading accounts in Canada and the States - he even had a handful overseas. And there might be more," she added, shaking her head again. "Apparently, Si was day trading like a maniac for a couple of years. It's how he lost his money."

Marshall whistled softly.

"It just doesn't make any sense," Katy added with a perplexed look on her face. "What I don't get is that Si fired all of his brokers. Every decision he made over the last few years he made on his own. And Marshall, he was trading like a wild man on cocaine."

Marshall frowned. "I haven't day traded. From what I understand there are pretty intricate charts and technical data to process."

"That's what is so very odd about all of this. Si was *not* a financial wizard. He was too creative. He never had the time - nor made the time - to pay attention to anything technical. He *always* relied on his brokers to tell him what to do. It looks like he lost over fifteen million dollars through his online accounts. But the paper trail is very intricate. David's staff have been going through every one of his accounts with a fine tooth comb to make some sense of it all. And hopefully this forensic student can uncover more and help us get to the bottom of what David keeps referring to as 'the snare of the devil'. Si couldn't have possible done this alone!"

"Sounds like the snare of the devil alright," Marshall replied grimly as he carefully prepared his next question. He had been wanting to ask it again - he had asked it several times over the months. However, over the months he had learned a great deal about this woman, including her ferocious pride - and he was uncomfortable broaching the subject again. Regardless, he needed to know that she was financially okay and he just had to ask. "Are you okay for cash? Do you need some cash for legal fees or travel?"

Katy lifted her head and smiled. Then she shook her head. "No, Marshall, I appreciate your offer - again - and again, thanks but it is not necessary. There's enough left to take care of that, until Si's property sells. Besides, his royalty checks are helping for the time being. His estate is even getting regular royalty checks from Purple Waters," she frowned, adding, "and the checks aren't small."

Katy had only recently discovered that the very book that had caused the dissension between father and daughter, the very book that had cost her job and her reputation, was pulling in thousands of dollars a month in royalty checks. The moment David Baker had shared this information with her Katy had voiced her disapproval and concern.

"I'm not entitled to any of that money," she said quickly.

"Of course you are entitled to it."

"Its devil's money," she retorted. "I don't *want* it!" she added sincerely. "Maybe we can donate the money to charity?"

The white-haired pundit was shaking his head. "Not until Si's estate is cleared and all of his debts have been paid," David Baker replied matter-of-factly.

Katy quietly shared this conversation with Marshall - and the amount of the checks - and Marshall opened his eyes in surprise. "Well," he finally replied. "that's a lot of money for a woman who has come a long way. But that is about the most admirable thing that I have heard anyone say in a long, long time."

"I am not trying to be a hero - or admirable Marshall," Katy responded with genuine sincerity in her eyes. "I simply don't want anything to do with that money. It would be better spent with a charity that needs to put food on the table - or perhaps I can find an environmental think tank that is looking for funds? I need to think about where it should go, someplace meaningful and somewhere where it will be wisely spent."

As Marshall listened his face turned from surprise to profound pride for the woman that he loved. He opened his mouth, to tell her, again, just how much he loved her, but Katy spoke first.

"She is very talented," she said like a proud mother as the parlor opened in new song.

"The parlor is Zig's escape," Marshall mused. "And to think that I was going to sell the piano!"

Marshall often thought it odd that Zig chose the same haven that Sarah had chosen. He had even convinced himself that Sarah would have liked the piano to go to the child - even though the child was tangible proof of Marshall's infidelities. Sometimes, Marshall still wondered why Sarah had kept her knowledge of Zig a secret from him. However, when he questioned this he always came to the same conclusion. He would never know for *certain*, but suspected that Sarah somehow sensed the truth...

After dinner they all went for a walk. The river's embankment was thick with wild flowers and new buds, and it breathed a spectacular freshness as the river danced and sparkled freely past the foliage.

At one point, Marshall swore under his breath for wearing the wrong shoes and glanced in embarrassment toward Zig. However, Zig hadn't heard him. Her eyes were fixated on the bridge.

"Do you think I have Charlie's eyes?" she asked.

Zig asked this question often.

"She told me that I had my father's eyes," Zig added innocently.

Marshall's eyes were both thankful and suspicious. The chanting had stopped, and he was relieved that he was no longer haunted by the song. He clutched Zig's hand tightly, too tightly, and Zig flinched.

"Marshall," she exclaimed. "You're too strong!"

"Oh, I'm sorry!" he replied, caressing Zig's hand.

Then he told Zig that yes, yes she did have her father's eyes. "I told you that you have your father's eyes. And I should know, shouldn't I?"

Thick dark lashes above opals flirted a smile. "Aunt Lynette said I didn't look like anyone in the family. And she said that the family was cursed," Zig added in a very grown up and matter-of-fact voice.

His child had already voiced this many times. Marshall responded with the same words as always. "Zig. Your Aunt Lynette shouldn't have talked like that," he replied gravely. "No one is cursed."

Zig thought for a moment. "Do you think that we can we go and see her one day?" she asked. "Maybe take her something to eat?"

These words surprised Marshall and he and Katy shared a concerned glance. It was the first time in months that the child had suggested that they visit Lynette.

"I don't know if we can find your Aunt Lynette. I think that she moved out of the city," he answered. "But we will try," he suggested, to appease the child.

Everyone suspected that Lynette Orman was long gone. The morning after Katy and Marshall had found Zig at the river, two policemen paid a visit to the one-bedroom townhouse. Except for the furniture, Zig's few clothes, the kitchen remnants and a few other odds and sods, it was deserted.

"Maybe she caught a ride with one of her boyfriends," Zig mused aloud. "Or maybe," her eyes darkened for a moment, "maybe she thought that they came and got me and she got scared and ran away."

"That's possible," Marshall answered knowingly. Everyone had concluded that this was in fact the case.

Over the months Zig also frequently asked about the lady under the bridge, and she did so again just seconds later.

"I wonder if the lady under the bridge might like to see us?"

With the broaching of this topic, Marshall's expression hardened briefly before he responded as gently as he was able. "Zig, I want you to promise me that you will stop talking about that vagrant."

"What's a vagrant Marshall?" Zig would sometimes ask. She asked this very question again.

"Someone who is homeless."

"But Marshall, she isn't homeless. Her home is there!"

As always, Marshall feared the worst when Zig spoke about Christina. "You haven't gone near that bridge, now have you Zig?"

"No, Marshall. We made a deal."

They had made a deal. Fearing for his child's safety and knowing well how Zig used to roam the streets, Marshall had set some very stringent rules. Without question, without *any* question, Zig was not allowed to go out alone. And without question, without *any* question, the bridge was absolutely off-limits.

Katy had been listening silently to the father and daughter dialogue. Marshall turned to her, and embracing her fresh, open expression, a boyish grin fell across his face for a moment. Then he turned back to his daughter. "Zig, a deal is a deal and I am very proud that you remembered. And," he added, "just because you have such a good memory and have followed through on your word, I have an idea. Do you think that maybe we should visit Katy on the ocean?"

Zig's eyes widened."Can we? Can we come to visit you?" she asked as she looked up to Katy.

Katy's eyes grew moist at the sight. So much can change in a year, she thought. So much can take us from doom to a better place. "I can't think of anything I would like more! Of course!" she said excitedly. "You'll get to see one of the prettiest places in the world. There are whales and perhaps we'll even see some dolphins."

"Whales!" Zig exclaimed. "When? When can we go?"

"When?" Katy asked, turning to Marshall.

"Very soon?" he suggested, poising it as a question. Katy simply smiled in agreement and their small world filled with genuine confirmation of their love for one another as they shared a moment of silent understanding.

"Why don't we fly back with you on Sunday?" Marshall asked. "Or is that too soon? I mean, you might be busy?"

"I can't think of anything I would like more," Katy answered as her cheeks flushed.

"Yeah!" Zig exclaimed, jumping up and down. "I can't wait! I just can't wait!" she gushed excitedly.

"Two more sleeps Zig and then we will go," Marshall explained as he took his child's hand. Suddenly, a mischievous grin spread across his face. "But first, you have to learn how to swim," he added as he playfully scooped Zig up in his arms.

"I am learning how to swim!" the child replied in a giggle.

"Yes you are! And you are doing very well with your lessons. So well, in fact," Marshall added in tease, "that I think that I should throw you in the river!"

It had become a game between father and daughter that never had an ending.

"I dare you!" Zig cried out as her eyes opened wide.

Marshall clutched Zig tightly in his arms, and slowly turned around and around as he pretended to prepare to throw her in the water. When he stopped for a moment, a little breathless, his eyes fell on Katy. Her beauty was still blushing, he thought. What a remarkable gift, this proud and strong and special woman - he couldn't imagine ever letting her go.

Zig was still giggling at the anticipation of the game.

"Katy!" she cried out playfully, "you have to help me! P-l-e-a-s-e!" she begged as her hair swayed like threads of yellow silk around Marshall's hands and arms.

Oh Zig! Marshall thought. You have such life in your eyes! Just like your mother once had! And there was nothing, there was absolutely nothing that would allow this little girl's spark to die. Marshall had vowed this many times over the months...

Marshall had hired Thomas Sinclair one more time to ensure that Zig would always be safe from the curse. Only two weeks out of the hospital, Thomas sat under the concrete wall with two tattered suitcases by his feet that he had dragged out of his attic. He was cold and damp, even though Cecilia had insisted that he wear long johns and heavy winter boots, and that layer his clothes - and he did so until he felt unusually heavy. But Thomas was another two thousand dollars richer - and he liked the feeling of the envelope in his coat pocket as he waited for Christina Shore and her shopping cart to return.

Eventually, his eyes spotted her silhouette, and he stood up and waited. When she neared, he awkwardly handed her an envelope much like the one in his pocket. "The neighbors of this, umm..." he began, and then hesitated.

Earlier that evening Marshall had given Thomas explicit instructions, rehearsing with him exactly *what* to say, not once, not twice, but three times. However, Thomas found this "speech" much more difficult than he had imagined. "This... umm, this fine community," he finally continued, "would like to give you this. Consider it a gift," he added, exactly as Marshall had requested. "But... umm..." Thomas cleared his throat, "they - the neighbors - they insist that you are gone by morning. And please - you are not to return to this city."

The envelope held exactly five hundred dollars and a bus ticket to Vancouver. "They - the - the - the neighbors," Thomas stuttered, "told me to tell you to go to Vancouver. It is warmer there," he added, with little conviction. "And I brought you some luggage, so you can take your - your - your - things."

Christina's defeated eyes flirted left and then right. Then she slowly nodded as hoarse, barely audible words came out. "Okay," she nodded. "Winters can be cold and bitter here. Vancouver is warmer," she added as took the envelope from Thomas' hand. Then she lifted one hand to hold the small white gold pendant around her neck.

Thomas didn't know what to say. His eyes fell to the pendant, then he looked apprehensively towards the bridge's wall and to mattress on the ground and the frayed blankets that had been her bed for such a long, long time. The money that Marshall had given Thomas to give to this woman would hardly cover the two nights of accommodations at The Bayshore Hotel, he thought. Five hundred dollars might feed her with alcohol or drugs, perhaps in excess, until she overdosed. But it was hardly enough to make her a real bed. And with this guilty thought, his eyes dropped to the snow, then to the black rubber boots on the ground only feet from where he stood, and then finally up, into her dark and deathly eyes. Her pupils bore into his and Thomas almost gasped as he saw the misery and torment that they held.

"Tell Spunk to take care of her," she whispered hoarsely.

"Pardon me?"

"Tell Marshall to take care of the child," she repeated. Then she stuffed the envelope in her yellow parka and knelt down on her knees and began to build a fire.

Confused, Thomas was speechless for a moment. "Yes," he finally mumbled. "Yes, I certainly will."

Thomas turned. As quickly as he was able he began to make his way to the bridge above. Suddenly, the night felt eerily empty and he was consumed with a heaviness of betrayal or disappointment in himself. As he climbed the icy pathways that would take him away from this dark place, he held his chest. "God forbid," he mumbled under his breath. Then stopped and crossed his chest with the sign of God.

"God forbid," he said again, and then turned around. Slowly, he began the descent back to the bridge's underground.

As he neared Christina he reached into his tweed jacket and pulled out the white envelope that held the thick wad of fifty and one hundred dollar bills, two thousand dollars to be exact. Then he leaned down and reached to her in the dark.

Christina looked up, hesitating. Then black nails hungrily wrapped themselves around the package.

Thomas opened his mouth to speak. "I..." he began, knowing that he needed to say something kind and reassuring. When he couldn't find the right words, he shook his head in silence. Uncomfortable and disappointed in himself, he turned to leave.

"Here," the hoarse voice offered.

Thomas slowly turned around.

"This is for you."

Black nails were spread out to the sky, as if reaching for the moon. In the palm of Christina's hands lay the white gold buffalo that had hung from her neck only moments before.

"It's for life," she said. "It'll bring you a good life."

Thomas openly choked up. "I - I - I can't," he finally muttered.

"It is yours," she said. "I want you to have it. It is time."

Thomas timidly reached out his hand, instantly welcoming the polished metal against his palm. "Thank you," he whispered, looking nowhere in particular. Then, with his head down, for he couldn't allow himself to see the misery or agony in this woman's eyes one more time, he turned to leave. "Thank you," he hushed awkwardly.

As he trekked through the snow towards the world above, he put both of his hands in his jacket pockets and closed them very tightly. As his fingers caressed the pendant, he wondered how he would explain to the wife why he came home with a pendant of a buffalo, opposed to the two thousand dollars that he had set out to earn that very evening.

Suddenly, song filled the air, and Thomas instantly realized that it was coming from where he had just stood. He stopped and closed his eyes. After a minute, perhaps two, he crossed his chest as a single teardrop rolled down his cheek. How remarkably profound, he thought. Almost like prayer. And although he wasn't quite sure what he had just heard, he knew that he had just experienced something quite beautiful.

As if a miracle, Thomas thought and he thanked God for giving him yet another day to live.

The End.

About the Author

Pamela Tchida's first self-published novel 'Something Beautiful Happened' is a product of years of writing - she has been writing fiction and poetry since she was a child.

Pamela spent the first part of her career as a stockbroker, and for the past two decades she has pursued her social entrepreneurial spirit. Working in Canada and the U.S. she has focused on the environmental sector, corporate social responsibility, real estate development, affordable housing and the non profit arena. She is also an advocate of volunteering, and over the years has given her time to a number of community-minded initiatives.

Pamela is currently working on two additional fictions, 'Snare of the Devil' - the sequel to 'Something Beautiful Happened', and an untitled romantic suspense that takes two individuals on a journey over many decades and across several continents.

Pamela is the proud mother of her beautiful and gifted daughter Jayda. She is also "mum'" to Rain, her gentle Siberian Husky who has laid patiently beside her writing desk over the years - and who every so often opens up in song.

Pamela currently resides in Calgary, Alberta.

Printed in the United States of America

First Printing July 2013

Second Printing August 2013

Third Printing November 2013

ISBN-13: 978-1484050903

ISBN-10: 1484050908

Contact the author/publisher at:

Email pamelatchida@gmail.com
Tel 403-651-2012
Blog somethingbeautifulhappened.com

Made in the USA
Middletown, DE
22 March 2017